His Hotness

by

Pamela Hearon

His Hotness

Cover Art by *Angela Anderson*

The Wild Rose Press
PO Box 706
Adams Basin, NY 14410-0706
Visit us at www.thewildrosepress.com

Publishing History
First Champagne Rose Edition, 2010
Print ISBN 1-60154-678-5

Published in the United States of America

Jade struggled in that half-awake, half-asleep state.

She'd slept well, but some gnawing memory was going to surface as soon as she allowed full consciousness to kick in, a memory sure to be unpleasant.

Oh yeah, there it was. Keeping her eyes shut didn't fool her consciousness. It screamed at her. The hottest guy you meet in months... years even... and you get sick and throw up all over yourself! Kiss that baby good-bye. On second thought, eat a breath mint and wave bye to that one from a distance.

"Quit worrying. I'll be there soon." A deep voice penetrated through the one she was trying to block out.

Her eyes shot open as she sprang up into a sitting position. Sunshine streamed through her window. She sat in her own bed in her own boxers and t-shirt... and her bra? And Kai Malone stood at the foot of the bed, watching her.

He dropped his phone into his pocket and flashed a broad smile that made her heart do a quick step. "Morning, Shank. I trust you're feeling better." He still wore yesterday's clothes, a bit wrinkled. A thick layer of dark stubble shadowed his face. Rugged. Very sexy.

She sorted through vague memories of being at the Urgent Care last night. Her fingers flew to her hair. Ick! It felt as stiff as the rest of her body. She lay back against the headboard, propping herself against the pillow to take inventory. Stiffness, but no pain. No nausea. "All in all, pretty good," she wrinkled her nose, "considering you tried to kill me."

Praise for HIS HOTNESS...

"HIS HOTNESS is fantastic and funny with characters I couldn't help adoring. I enjoyed every word."

~*Sandra Jones, author of WISH FOR THE MOON (The Wild Rose Press)*

"Sexy, smart, and fabulous! Everything I loved about chick-lit, but with a grown-up, modern twist. HIS HOTNESS is a fun, flirty, page-turning adventure."

~*Kimberly Lang, author of THE MILLIONAIRE'S MISBEHAVING MISTRESS (Harlequin Presents)*

Dedication

To my wonderful husband Dick,
the standard for all my heroes.

Chapter One

"What you need, Chickie-boom, is a good old-fashioned, head-banging, sheet-fisting, toe-curling orgasm." Gram snatched up the journal with the worn, floral cover and waved it toward the nightstand. "And by old-fashioned, I mean one involving a man, not one that requires a battery-pack and a warranty."

Jade closed her laptop on the Regency she was editing. "What I need is a job with a great publisher, so I can quit sponging off my precious-but-nosey grandmother." With her toe, she nudged her closet door closed before Gram could see the empty spaces that once housed her vast collection of Pradas and Guccis. She slid the check from the consignment shop into her desk drawer and raised a questioning eyebrow toward Gram. "How did you know where I keep my, um, toys?"

Gram shrugged. "Lucky guess. And it's the same place I keep mine." Dropping the book into Jade's lap, she leaned her hip into the desk and crossed her arms. "All kidding aside, don't let the rejection from Batemans make you lose hope. I have a lot of contacts. Want me to make some calls?"

"No." Jade shook her head. They'd been over this before. "You do too much for me now, Gram." She waved her hand at the apartment. "I've got to do this on my own. There's still Samuels Publishing and all those New York houses." She clenched her teeth to keep from grimacing at the last thought.

"Egad!" Gram pinched the bridge of her nose and spoke in her fake blueblood accent. "Fur coats

1

and scratchy wool. Enough to soon push a California girl past the edge of reason, I fear." She dropped the accent and pointed to the book in Jade's lap. "As will going too long without a date. Who's your last entry?"

Jade didn't have to look. She'd only made one entry in the Hotness journal since her break-up with Adam Brock nine months ago. "Fernando."

"The golf pro?" Gram gave an appreciative whistle. "What's his score?"

"Ninety-seven. A chive on his tooth during my first lesson cost him three points."

"Well, it's time to give the lad another chance." Gram headed for the door. "I'm setting you up another lesson for this afternoon. Swing your clubs right and it's sex tonight."

Jade rolled her eyes, positive her grandmother qualified for the weirdest one in the world. "Gram, I'm too busy."

"Yep." Gram didn't even slow her stride. "That's precisely why you need the exercise. Shut the business down by four 'cause Fernando the Hotness Hopeful will be waiting."

The screen door slammed behind her.

Jade leaned on her desk and eyed the bottom drawer of the nightstand.

Buying batteries, even in bulk, *was* getting pretty expensive.

****

"My best counsel? Keep your mouth shut until this is a done deal." Zeb Hale looked at his watch.

Kai Malone didn't need to look. It was 8:57 when the obsessive-compulsive lawyer stood up to leave. Same as always. "What about the employees?" Kai asked, still not satisfied. Once he'd stood up, Zeb would turn around three times before he answered. Kai filled in the time with some specifics. "They're worried sick. Jake Prater's wife Meg has cancer.

Five kids. I don't like keeping anyone in the dark."

"Don't think of it as keeping them in the dark, then. Think of it as investing in their future." Zeb loaded the contract forms into his briefcase, one at a time, took them all out and repeated the process twice more. "One wrong word about any of this, and the whole thing could blow up around your ears. Sit tight and stay tight-lipped about Techtron. This sale's going to happen soon. Don't blow it." Zeb gathered the briefcase, holding it like a shield in front of his torso as he circled the table three times before making his exit.

Kai drummed his fingers on the table, waiting for the inevitable comment about to make its way from his best friend, brother-in-law, and business partner's mouth.

Mark didn't disappoint. "Actually, if anything's gonna get blown," he blew a puff of powdered sugar from the doughnut he was eating, "I hope it's me."

"You're nothing if not predictable." Kai rolled the espresso around his tongue, tasting it for the first time that morning. Zeb Hale and his monotonous drone had a way of making even the most exotic blend taste flat. "Now. What *are* we going to do?"

Mark shrugged. "I don't know what *you're* gonna do. I'm going home and make a baby with your hot sister."

"TMI, partner," Kai growled. "I mean, how are we going to keep this thing quiet for another week? Everybody knows something's in the works."

Mark chewed the next bite deliberately, thumping his chin with his middle finger. "We'll make this one of the blood-brother pacts we used to make as kids. We simply avoid talking about the business as much as possible. And if one of us breaks the pact by telling something we shouldn't—"

"I know, I know." Kai sliced the side of his hand

across his other palm. "The other one gets to cut him deep."

"And maybe going incognito will keep the gold diggers from sniffing you out for awhile." Mark leaned forward, making annoying sniffing sounds until Kai rolled his chair out of range. Mark grinned. "Yessir, that Shelia Stanley sure had balls."

Kai shifted in his seat, unwilling to let Mark bait him this morning. Okay, so his radar had been off with a few women. He'd learned his lesson about opportunists. Even sexy ones. He was older and wiser now and much too busy to even consider getting involved with anyone.

Dark circles under Mark's eyes stood out. If something didn't break soon, both of them were going to collapse from exhaustion. "Go on home now," Kai ordered. "The night shift makes you look like crap."

Mark didn't need much prodding. "Yeah? I don't know why. When I'm home, Jilli keeps me up all night anyway." He cackled when Kai shot him an evil glare. "Do me a favor, partner. The next time you meet a woman, make sure she's wearing a thong and not a jock strap." Grabbing a doughnut with one hand and his crotch with the other, he swaggered out the door.

Kai set to work returning calls and dictating letters. Just maybe, he'd get a couple of relaxing hours on the golf course this afternoon.

****

Jade winced as the club scraped the top of the ball and rolled in a sweeping arc, stopping short of the hole by about three feet, and way too far to the right. Damn frustrating game, always pitting you against yourself. Basketball, softball, surfing, volleyball. No other sport had ever been this hard to master. But Gram kept insisting the path to financial successful had golf carts on it, and Gram

4

was rarely wrong about anything. Jade drew a long breath. Just a few more minutes till her lesson and she could stop this boring putting practice nonsense.

Plop. The hot guy practicing on the other side of the putting green dropped another one from twelve or thirteen feet. He hadn't missed yet. Of course, guys like him never missed at anything. The world was their putting green.

He was a hundred-pointer on her scale if she rated on looks alone. Bronzed face with deep-set eyes framed by heavy, black brows. Dark wavy hair on top, cropped close on the sides. His aquiline nose and dimpled chin reminded Jade of that handsome Comanche chief from the western she'd edited a few weeks ago. Or a bird of prey that could have you in his clutches before you even realized the chase was on.

The fantasy of being in his clutches ran a pleasant shiver up her spine. She'd found that giving in to fantasy helped ease her sexual frustration some and kept her from doing some really stupid things she'd regret later.

Hawk, she dubbed him.

Maybe if she mimicked what Hawk did. She watched him unobtrusively, pretending to focus on her grip.

Feet about a foot apart. She closed her stance a bit.

He bent slightly and visually traced the path from ball to hole several times. She bent a bit and eyed the path from the ball to the hole and beyond, secretly scrutinizing Hawk's long khaki pant legs, slim waist, and buttery yellow polo that stretched across his wide shoulders. Tanned muscular arms pulled the club back and smoothly forward, making contact with the ball's sweet spot, following through as the ball beat a perfect line to the hole. *Plop.* Another perfect putt.

Hawk didn't smile or seem pleased in the least with his putt. Probably a perfectionist like Adam. That dropped him to a ninety-nine. Perfectionists could be so hard to deal with. Always thinking they know what's best for everybody else. Always needing things done their way because it's the right way.

He retrieved his ball from the hole, and when he raised up, his eyes met hers. The blue penetrating from those depths caught her by surprise. A blue-eyed hawk? Extraordinary. The thought of other things that might make him extraordinary made her face and neck hot.

Before he could read the thoughts that were surely radiating from her, she dropped her gaze and focused on the excruciatingly ordinary white ball.

She pulled her club back. Why didn't he smile? He'd be melt-me-with-one-look handsome if he smiled. Heck, he was gorgeous even without smiling. She let the weight of the putter's head pull itself into the ball. *Find the sweet spot, baby. That's the way. C'mon, Hawk, find my sweet spot.*

What? Jade raised up, startled by the depth her fantasy had plunged in so short a time. Man! She was becoming a sexual cliché personified. Worse, she was becoming Gram.

The club clipped the top of the ball, moving it all of a foot and a half, eight feet short of the hole.

"You raised up."

She wheeled around to find Fernando scratching his head. How long had he been there? "Maybe I need longer clubs. Then I could stand up straight so I'd never raise up."

"You always raise up." He smiled.

What a relief. No marring chive this time.

Fernando shook his finger at her with a chuckle. Low and throaty, the sound oozed with sensuality. "Longer clubs would just make you hit behind." He climbed a point to ninety-eight.

Jade adjusted her sunglasses, trying to get her mind off his voice and onto his words. Long club, hit behind. *Nope, better just start walking to the driving range.* She slung the bag over her shoulder.

They had the practice area to themselves. Hmm. Alone. Maybe he'd stand behind her like in the movies and wrap his arms around her, pressing against her, telling her to lean forward a bit and not raise up.

Jade sighed. No dice. Fernando planted himself at the back of the rubber tee pad.

"Now, let me see you hit a few." He sounded like an instructor, all business. "Keep your head down, swing through smoothly, and don't raise up."

"Aye-aye, cap'n." Jade saluted. She placed the ball, adjusted her grip, moved her feet shoulder-length apart, planted her feet firmly, gave just a little extra butt wiggle, and drew back slowly.

As she started the downswing, something moved in the corner of her eye. She jerked her head up, raising her torso, just as the club and ball made contact.

Whack! The ball flew off the toe of the club at breakneck speed, not out in front to her left, where it should be, but straight out from the way she was facing. A shank.

To her horror, Hawk had been the movement in her peripheral vision. Approaching the next practice tee over, he'd moved directly into the ball's path.

She opened her mouth as Hawk grabbed his crotch and sank to the ground with a moan.

"Fore?" she called lamely.

Chapter Two

Jade sprinted over to the crumpled figure. "Oh, oh, I'm so sorry! I looked up and shanked it. Here, let me help." She grabbed his arm, which didn't budge. Instead, her fists stretched the sleeve of his polo shirt, leaving behind a mass of wrinkles.

"No! Uh, no. No thanks. I'll be fine." Hawk gasped the words out in clumps, shooing her away with head movements, never moving his hands from their protective spot.

"Can you get up?" Jade slid her hand under his arm, feeling his muscles tighten at her touch.

"Not yet." His response came as a grunt through clenched teeth as his tanned face deepened to crimson.

"Need help?" Fernando strolled over, grinning. He actually seemed to be enjoying the scene.

Why did men always find it so amusing when somebody got hit in the balls? The sophomoric reaction irked Jade. "I think he needs to sit or lie still for a minute. I shanked that ball right into his..." He'd moved his hands, and she had an almost-socially acceptable reason to be staring at his quite-large-and-hopefully-not-swollen-from-her-assault groin. "...um, into him."

Fernando's chuckle rumbled into a full-blown laugh. "You sure did."

"Give me a hand," Hawk growled. His deep voice vibrated through her like someone had thrummed the lowest string on a bass violin.

Jade locked her other hand around the gigantic bicep, and he rewarded her with a gaze that shouted

"Haven't you done enough?"

Fernando shot her a warning look and shook his head. The two men grasped hands and Hawk wobbled to a semi-erect position. Jade hoped semi-erect might be an option for him again sometime in the future.

"Next time Jade's taking a lesson, I'll warn everyone to wear a cup." Fernando gave the hunched figure a clap on the back. Evidently the good-old-boy upbringing wasn't limited to the United States.

Jade gave him an icy stare, hoping to silence the next lame joke he'd opened his mouth to say.

Hawk didn't acknowledge the comment. He was already hitching slowly toward the clubhouse. "Need a beer."

Jade watched his pitiful limp as he crossed the cart path toward the clubhouse. She shook her head in self-loathing. "I'm really sorry," she called.

"Not your fault." Hawk gave a dismissive wave. "Shouldn't walk behind somebody during their backswing."

Jade watched his painful journey, wondering if he'd be able to open the massive oak doors of the clubhouse. When the time came, he made the deed look effortless.

"He's right. He should have been paying more attention." Fernando's voice turned soft and sympathetic.

Oh, so now Fernando was ready to show sympathy. For her. Not for the poor guy who'd been writhing in pain. Lack of sensitivity, definitely a turn-off. Jade mentally deducted thirteen points from his Hotness score. "That doesn't make me feel any better. He's hurt." She dropped her driver into the bag.

"C'mon." Fernando went to her bag and retrieved the hateful club. "You must hit it again."

Jade wanted to protest, but he was right, of

course. Fall off a horse, get on the horse again. Take a tumble from a bicycle, climb right back onto that seat. Castrate a perfectly formed male human with a golf club, strive to do it again.

No. She was gaining control in all facets of her life today. This would never happen again at her hands. Her resolve solidified as she gripped the gleaming graphite shaft. She would no longer be intimidated by this inanimate tool of torture. She would control it. Today. Now. Or she would quit this frustrating, asinine, dangerous game once and for all, no matter what Gram paid for these lessons.

Fernando placed the ball on the tee mat, then backed up, apparently thought better of his position and moved around to her right.

She drew back, feet planted, shoulders squared, torso twisted comfortably. Poor Hawk. He'd been folded into thirds by the time she got to him. Quite a feat for a man of his size. Ah yes, size. From what she could tell when he moved his hands away, his crotch provided a rather difficult target to miss. Hopefully a drink had numbed the pain by now.

Her club head reached the top of its swing. "Relax your right arm." Fernando's instructions were barely audible, his voice smooth and calming like a masseuse at a spa.

Jade relaxed and let the club head do its work. The weight swung down and through and up again into a perfect three-sixty. The "ping" floated up to her ears and she watched in astonishment as the ball sailed straight toward the 190-yard marker.

"My God! That was gorgeous!" Fernando applauded. "Try it again."

Jade rolled another ball from the wire basket and placed it on the tee. She checked her grip, stance, and shoulders, then swung. She imagined Hawk's muscled arm around her shoulder as he limped across the cart path, leaning on her for support, bodies connected like the club head to the ball. Another "ping". The tiny white sphere passed its predecessor on the fly and landed a good thirty yards beyond.

Fernando passed his hands over his eyes. "Sonofabitch! What's happening here?"

Jade smiled and shrugged in response but began setting up the next scenario in her head. Maybe it would involve Hawk without his shirt. She placed the ball on the tee and eyed the two buckets of practice balls. Eighty balls total. A sexy scenario with each.

This game might be fun after all.

****

"I'm not sure what you did or how you did it, but that was amazing." Fernando pulled Jade to him and planted a light kiss on her cheek.

For the past forty-five minutes, Jade had even amazed herself. Every practice ball down the middle, hovering around the two-hundred-yard mark. All connected to an image of Hawk. "I think hitting Ha-," she caught herself, "...him got my mind off hitting the ball. I wasn't trying so hard."

"Well, it worked. Keep it up and you won't need me."

"Don't worry. I'm sure by tomorrow I'll be back to my shanking self."

As if on cue, Elena Dellisio, the Women's Trainer at the club, appeared in the doorway and started her model's runway walk toward them, legs crossing with each step, hips swinging provocatively. The lime halter she wore was cut so low she couldn't possibly raise a club without popping free. *Hmmm. The collared-shirt rule for the course must not apply to 38DDs,* Jade decided. With perfect dramatic timing, the breeze caught Elena's ebony hair and blew a bit across her face. She turned her face up toward the breeze, closing her eyes, raising her chest even higher.

Jade could hear the click of the imaginary shutter in Fernando's mind. The look on the poor guy's face was unadulterated lust. He even licked his lips.

"Are you ready to play with me?" Elena certainly knew how to coo effectively although she had a brain the size of a walnut and more manmade parts than R2D2. She swayed over to the pro, plastered herself against him and ran a finger across his lips before kissing him lightly.

"Oh baby, I'm always ready to play with you." Fernando nibbled her ear.

That ghastly comment cost him another ten points on the Hotness scale. Jade wanted to gag but chose a light cough instead. That managed to get their attention.

"Oh, sorry, Jade." His apology didn't sound very sincere. Five more points off. "See you next week."

"I might have to cancel next week," she decided on-the-spot. "Can I just give you a call later on?"

"Sure. Let me know." Fernando whispered something in Elena's ear, which brought a giggle.

That was too much. The Licentious Latin dropped completely off the scale. Jade wanted out of this scene fast, feeling like a voyeur. She practically jogged to the car and deposited her bag into the trunk.

Several people had left the clubhouse during her lesson, but she didn't think Hawk had been one of them. He would have been hard to miss. That meant he might still be hurting. Might be unable to walk. Might be considering a lawsuit. She couldn't leave without checking on him.

The club's foyer was empty and the pro-shop closed for the night. Voices drifted from the men's locker room accompanied by enticing scents of cologne mingled with deodorant. Jade edged in that direction, stopping to listen, and sniff, and dream for a moment. None of the voices sounded like a match to what she remembered as Hawk's.

The sign at the back of the hall indicated the most likely place an injured male would go to find refuge: the bar. She stopped at the door, letting her eyes adjust to the dim light. She rubbed her arms briskly to keep the circulation moving. "Geez, this place is freezing," she muttered, a little surprised she couldn't see her breath.

It wasn't difficult to make out Hawk's giant form at the far end of the bar. His hand combed through his hair, leaving it bushy and wild, but it made him even more appealing somehow. The other hand wound around what appeared to be a pint of Guinness from the shape of the glass.

Jade ambled toward him, then stopped, remembering the way he growled at Fernando. Maybe he wouldn't want to be bothered. He might have been rubbing his head because he couldn't rub where it really hurt.

Something, maybe her movement, caught his attention. He jerked his head up and gave her an intense gaze, deep-set eyes mere slits in his dark face. "Shank!" he called and raised his glass toward her in a toast.

Jade shivered and her nipples tighten. Probably from the cold.

Chapter Three

Kai allowed himself a quick visual scan as the woman glided across the room toward him. Definitely a looker, even if she had almost made a eunuch out of him. She had the stride of a natural athlete. White shorts accented long, tan, sinewy legs. Slim hips with a nice curve. A small waist tapered up to gently rounded breasts then on to...to...to very erect nipples. He willed his eyes to continue up, but they seemed to have a mind of their own. Mercifully, when she lowered herself onto the stool at the corner of the bar, her face dropped to where the nipples had been—almost. So he finally made eye contact. With the dim light, maybe his gawking hadn't been noticed.

"It's freezing in here." She gave a shrug.

Okay, so she noticed. He would cover with something quick and original. "Sorry. Didn't mean to make you uncomfortable." *Wow, that oughta just blow her panties right off.* He drowned his humiliation with a huge gulp from his glass.

"No problem. This is California, remember?" She leaned close and flashed him a smile that revealed a dimple on one side. "A lot of women pay big bucks on surgery to get looked at like that."

Now that was quick and original. Probably thinks I'm a total tool. Uncomfortable at that thought, Kai shifted in his seat. Searing pain shot from his testicles into his stomach and he drew a quick breath.

Shank's big green eyes—with interesting gold flecks—grew even wider. The dimple disappeared into a somber expression as she scrutinized him. "I'm really sorry. I hope I didn't hurt you too badly."

Actually, the pain had been excruciating for a few minutes but ebbed away and was almost gone now as long as he didn't press the wrong spot. The cold room and even colder beer had helped. "Bernie," Kai indicated the bartender with a tilt of his glass, "made the room into an ice pack for me. I'm much better now."

Her shoulders sagged with relief. "Good. I was afraid your wife was gonna put out a contract for me or something." She tucked a stray strand of honey colored hair behind an ear.

"Nah, you can relax. I'm not married. And my ex-wife would probably pay you to do it again." That one was pretty clever. He waited for her reaction.

The dimple reappeared and with it, the pivotal point in the conversation. Kai had trained himself to recognize it, whether the situation was business or women. A drumming of fingertips on the bar would probably be followed by another quick apology, and she would slide off the stool to exit. That would mean she was in a relationship or simply not interested. Scooting farther back on the stool and settling into it more comfortably meant she wanted to stay and flirt a bit.

Kai hoped for the latter and sipped his beer, watching with anticipation. She glanced at her watch and slid the strand of hair behind her ear again. Her hands went to the stool. Which way was she going? Sliding off or scooting farther back? Forward or back? His heart speeded up a notch.

She pushed off the stool an inch or so, thigh muscles tightening as she shifted her weight to her legs. Then she settled fully onto the seat.

Kai relaxed as he exhaled slowly. "Can I buy you a drink?"

"Is the Guinness really cold?"

He nodded in slow satisfaction and motioned to Bernie.

"Then I'll have a half-pint." She extended her hand to him. "I'm Jade Bartholomew, by the way."

Her grip was gentle but firm, and he could feel some calluses on her palm. Probably lifted weights. He didn't think she'd played golf long enough to toughen her hands that much. More exotic ideas that would account for the roughness began popping into his mind, but he forced them away. "I'm Kai Malone."

Over the next hour, they chatted about all sorts of things. She explained how her parents wanted to name her in memory of her Grandpa Jed who died the year she was born. They couldn't find a feminine form of Jed, so they went with Jade instead. Her dad always told her it was a toss-up between Jade and Jedi.

His name didn't surprise her, which was a surprise to him. She confessed she'd known a boy in seventh grade named Kai and even knew to spell it K-a-i instead of K-y-e like most people. She shared that she had an online editing and critiquing business but seemed a bit evasive about it. Probably hoped to break into screenwriting like most people involved in writing around L.A.

"What do you do?" Her question was inevitable.

Kai imagined Mark holding a knife against his more-tender-than-usual balls. It took effort not to grit his teeth when he answered. "I sell software." It was the truth, just not the whole truth. The image dissolved. *Blood-brother pact still intact.*

Kai mentioned Hazel in passing. Never hurt to let an interested party know they divorced four years ago and his ex lived in New York. He didn't mention how about a year ago his ex had taken to calling twice a week or so, declaring her love for him and her desire to get back together. His rejection, or any rejection, didn't deter Hazel. She regarded it as a challenge and went after the object of her present desire with more vehemence. She always expected to get what she wanted. And usually did.

Somewhere in the conversation, after his going to Stanford on a golf scholarship and Jade's spending most of her free-time on a beach volleyball team, hence the calluses, her stomach emitted a gargantuan rumble.

"My God, it's after 8:00. Want to go grab a bite somewhere?" The words flew out of his mouth before he had time to fret over phrasing or think up possible come-backs to refusals.

"Okay."

That was too easy. No coy hesitation. No fake phone call to break fictitious other plans. This gal appeared to be the *real deal*. "You like sushi?"

"Love it."

"I know a great little place. It's close, very casual."

She slid from the bar stool without saying anything about brushing her hair or putting on lipstick. Ready to go. Just like that. "Perfect."

This girl seemed too good to be true. Kai had an overwhelming urge to wrap her in his arms and passionately explore the inside of her mouth with his tongue. Instead, he covered her hand with his and gave it a squeeze. "*You* seem perfect."

His reward for the comment was the reappearance of the cute dimple and two very erect nipples. "It really is freezing in here." Her laugh had a low, sensuous quality to it.

When they got to the parking lot, she suggested they both go in her car. She didn't have to tell him savvy woman didn't get in the cars of men they'd just met. But she surprised him by wanting him to ride with her. "I don't know Palos Verdes very well, and I'm afraid I'd lose you if I tried to follow," she offered as explanation.

Kai started to suggest they could exchange phone numbers, but this was better. They'd be together on the ride, and he wouldn't have to explain how a software salesman was able to afford a new BMW 740IL.

The drive to the restaurant took less than ten minutes. Kai wouldn't have cared if it took two hours, except that his 6'5" frame was wedged into a Solstice. Luckily, the top was off, giving him some headroom.

Being a regular at Sushi Skyway, the tacky hole-in-the-wall, had advantages. Even though the place appeared stuffed as tight as a can of sardines, Ito greeted them at the door and led them to a table, grabbing a Kirin and two glasses on the way. The level of noise actually provided a modicum of privacy. It was difficult to hear the person at your table, impossible to hear anyone at the next. Jade nodded at the suggestion to split the large beer.

"Do you need a menu?" Kai pointed at the white pad on the next table.

Jade shook her head. "I like it all. Just no scallops. I'm allergic to them."

"They have a platter with a caterpillar roll, a fried dragon roll, and whatever the Chef's Special Roll of the night is. It comes with eight individual pieces of anything. Sound okay?"

"Think that's enough?" She leaned across the table on her elbows, making sure he heard her.

He leaned forward too until their noses almost touched. "If not, we'll order more." The bamboo blind did little to block out the light of the setting sun. The rays brought out the light blonde streaks in her hair, adding a soft glow around her face. The sight somehow made his beer taste even better.

She gave a nod of satisfaction and plopped back into her seat just as Saki came over to take their order. "Konnichiwa, Kai."

"*Konnichiwa, Saki. Gokigen ikadesuka?*" Kai concentrated to get the words right.

"*Genkidesu. Anatawa ikagadesuka?*"

"*Genkidesu. Arigatou.* Jade, I'd like you to meet Saki. Saki, Jade."

"Wow! You speak Japanese?" Her green eyes sparkled with fascination.

From tool to demi-god in two hours. Not bad. "I'm trying to learn. Saki gives me a little practice when I come in." He hurried on. Didn't want her curiosity piqued too much. "Let's see, we'll have an order of edamame to start, then the three roll platter. For the *nigiri,* we'll have *sake, ama-ebi, hamachi, akami,* and *omakasede onegaishimasu.* Was that right?"

Saki repeated back. "Salmon, sweet shrimp, yellowtail, tuna, and the rest, chef's choice.

"That's it." Kai remembered Jade's allergy. "Oh, but no," he groped for the word, "*hokkigai.*" Negatives and contractions still gave him problems. He'd have to work on them.

"No *hokkigai.*" Saki repeated it back, making a note. "And I'll bring another beer with your meal."

Jade looked around the place as she sipped her beer. She tilted her head toward the table of six scrunched into a corner booth for four. "Poor ignorant souls, doing sake bombs. Reminds me of Paradise Sushi in Hermosa. That's where I usually go."

"So you live in Hermosa Beach?" That area wasn't as familiar to him as Manhattan Beach, the next community north. "I used to have friends in Manhattan. They lived on the Strand."

"Yeah, me too."

Her answer stunned him. Beachfront property on The Strand in Manhattan and Hermosa Beaches sold in the millions. She couldn't be making enough money to afford that lifestyle by critiquing manuscripts. If she was, software was the wrong business for him to be in.

As if reading his thoughts, she added, "I have a third-floor apartment with a private outside entrance. The owner lives in the house below." She paused. "We're real close, and the rent is," a longer pause, like she was searching for the word, "very affordable." She blushed and suddenly seemed much too interested in the beer. "This is good. I usually drink Sapporo."

Kai's sharpened gold-digger instincts came to full alert. What was she not telling about her landlord? Was he a sugar daddy? She hardly seemed the type. He pushed a little more but kept his voice light. "Sapporo's good. So this landlord must really like you."

Jade gave him a sweet smile. "Yeah. She loves me."

A she. Kai's guard dropped a notch. Probably a lonely old woman who enjoyed having a young person around. "Elderly?"

"Seventy-eight."

Still no explanation of how she could afford the rent in such a place, even if it was *affordable*. But the night was still young. There would be time for more probing later. He tried not to let his mind slide into the pun. With perfect timing, Saki arrived with the edamame and another icy beer.

Jade had just enough time to fill him in on the details of her best friend's upcoming wedding when two of the rolls arrived. The Chef's Special was amazing. A tender center of chopped fish mixed with wasabi and avocado, layered on top with yellowtail, shrimp, and roe. The fish had no smell, always a sure sign it was fresh. And the ginger smelled crisp and clean, not "soapy" as Mark always insisted.

"This is fabulous." Jade rolled her eyes dreamily.

"And the caterpillar's almost too cute to eat." That said, she eased a piece into her dipping bowl and topped it with a slice of pickled ginger.

"But we gotta do it." Kai nodded toward Saki, approaching with another tray.

A blush started up Jade's neck, just a slight redness underneath the golden glow. Maybe embarrassed they'd ordered too much? His phone rang and he started to get up, struggling between the bench and the close tables.

Jade motioned to him to stay there. "I don't mind if you don't."

He nodded his thanks. He should have checked the caller I.D. before he answered. "Hello?"

"Hello, Darling."

Hazel.

How many times was it going to take? "I can't talk now. I'm busy." He glanced up. Jade's face was red. She must've heard the endearment.

"But, sweetheart, I wanted to tell you my news."

"This really isn't a good time." He smiled and Jade smiled back. He hadn't noticed before how full her lips were, just made for kissing. "I'm right in the middle of dinner." Jade scratched the top of her head in an impatient manner. "And it's very difficult to hear you." No response. Kai glanced at the phone and saw it registering a dropped call. He clipped the phone back onto his belt. "I'm really sorry," he apologized as he grasped another piece of sushi with his chopsticks, avoiding eye contact until he could swallow his anger with Hazel.

"'S okay."

Her voice sounded thick and a bit whiney. Aggravated no doubt. Who could blame her though? Having dinner with a guy and he gets a call from another woman.

"Kai?"

"Yeah?" She was probably going to tell him she

needed to leave.

"I think I need to leave."

God, she sounded like she was on the verge of tears.

Letting out a long sigh, Kai finally looked up.

Jade's face was blood-red. Her eyes were puffy, and her lips weren't just full any more, they were swollen out past her nose. "I think I'm having a reaction. Must have been scallops."

Kai jumped to his feet, tipping the table and its contents. Raw fish, soy sauce, and beer combined in a heap in Jade's lap.

Saki and Ito both ran over with towels, but Jade shooed away their efforts. "Get to hospital. No time for ambulance." The words came out in a gasp.

They made their way toward the door with Saki and Ito in pursuit. People attempting to get out of the way pushed others into their path. Kai tried to stay calm. Would the hospital need to know what caused it? "There weren't any scallops. What else might bring on a reaction?"

Saki's eyes grew wide. "There were scallops in the special roll, Kai. You didn't say 'no scallops', you said 'no surf clam', *hokkigai*. Scallops is *hotatagai*."

"Oh shit!" Kai snatched the keys from Jade's hand and helped her into the passenger seat and seat belt, then raced to get the car started. He peeled out of the parking lot, spraying gravel on all the surrounding cars.

Jade's head lolled from side to side and her eyes rolled back as they sped down the street, making corners on two wheels. An Urgent Care was only seven or eight blocks away. The wheezing sounds coming from her lungs urged him to step on the gas. They made it in record time.

Jade could barely stand. Kai scooped her up— she seemed so light to be so tall—and made it through the door before a nurse met him with a stretcher. He willed his voice to stay calm and a quick glance in a security mirror convinced him of the necessity. Hair sticking out, eyes wide with terror—he looked like an escapee from a mental ward. He lowered his voice and quietly explained the situation as they hurried into an examination room.

Jade gasps were loud as she fought for air, but she was still conscious.

"Anaphylaxis. EPI. Stat!" The doctor on duty barked orders for an injection of epinephrine. "Don't worry. We'll take good care of her." She directed the last comment to Kai whose knees suddenly went weak as he watched them cover Jade's face with an oxygen mask.

A hand caught him under the arm. "Sit down out here a minute. I'll need to get some information from you." The nurse who met them at the door showed him to a chair. He sank gratefully into it.

She left for a minute, then came back holding a clipboard and a cup of water which she offered him. She gave him a couple of minutes to sip the drink and get his wits about him before moving on. "What's her name?"

"Jade, J-A-D-E Bartholomew."

"Address?"

"Um, I don't know."

"Do you know her birth date?" The nurse's eyes swept over him. He combed his fingers through his hair, hoping for a more credible look, then shook his head.

"Age?" Her words became more clipped.

"Twenty-six, I think. We just met a couple of hours ago."

The nurse emitted a sigh that dripped with disgust. "I see." Obviously she thought Jade was a pick-up. "Never mind. I'll ask her." She turned to go back into Jade's room.

"Wait! Here." Kai fumbled around in his pockets

until he located one of his business cards. "Send me the bill."

Nasty Nurse rolled her eyes. "We're an Urgent Care, not a hospital. Payment's required at the time of service."

"Then here." He produced his American Express. She snatched the card and hurried back into the room.

Forty-five minutes later, he heard Jade's voice, low and weak, but audible. He sucked in a deep breath of relief and, finding his strength again, went back in the tiny examination room. The sterile, antiseptic smell had been replaced by a sour stench.

Jade smiled at him when he entered. Her lips and eyes had lost some, but not all, of their puffiness. The dimple couldn't make its appearance yet. From appearances and smell, she'd vomited, and a nurse was wiping what she could off of the shirt, which also contained the stains from their meal. Nasty had Jade's driver's license and insurance card and was writing the information on the admissions sheet.

"She might be nauseous still, but most of that's probably passed." The doctor spoke. Kai half way listened; he was more interested in watching Jade. She seemed to be getting better, looking normal. This whole screw-up was his fault. She could've died! "...good night's sleep. The Benedryl will make sure that happens. It usually wipes people out," the doctor continued. "She'll be fine tomorrow." She gave him a brisk pat on the arm, and he managed a brief nod.

"I think you're gonna live, young lady, but we'd like to keep you a couple of more hours just to be sure." The nurse had cleaned Jade up as much as possible. "We can give you a prescription for epinephrine injections you give yourself in case of emergency, if you'd like."

"That won't be necessary. It won't happen again." Jade glanced at Kai.

The other nurse must've picked up on the unspoken message and knew he was responsible. She glared at Kai with a look that shriveled him to the core.

"When can I leave?"

"As soon as you feel strong enough. I'd advise you to stay awhile, though."

"But, I can go whenever I want?"

"What's the rush, Jade?" Kai had no desire for a repeat of tonight's drama. A couple of hours didn't seem too long to wait.

"I've got to get out of these stinky clothes." She wrinkled her nose. "I feel fine. Really. Just a little woozy. C'mon, let's go." It sounded like an order. She swung her feet and legs off the bed.

"Are you sure you're ready?" Her face still had some red bumps and splotches. Was a relapse possible?

"I want to go home." Her voice broke, and Kai sensed she was on the verge of tears. He couldn't stand it if she started crying. He already felt so awful.

"Okay, come on. I'll get you home." Kai put an arm around her shoulder, and she wrapped her arm around his waist. They made their way slowly to the car, which was still where he left it near the door.

He buckled her in and watched as she laid her head back and got comfortable. The night breeze would probably make her feel better.

He started around the car when his phone rang. He snapped it open. "Damn it, Hazel…"

"Whoa, bud. It's not Hazel."

His jaw unclenched at the sound of his partner's voice. "Sorry, Mark. What's up?"

"Two things. Just talked with Prater. Meg had an appointment today, and it's not looking good."

"Shit." Kai pinched the bridge of his nose between his thumb and finger.

"My reaction, too." Mark sounded grim. "There are some experimental treatments in Europe, but insurance won't pay."

"Then we'll pay out-of-pocket."

"I knew you'd say that. I told him to research it, and we'd fund whatever he found."

Over the years, he and Mark hadn't seen eye-to-eye on everything, but they'd never disagreed on matter of integrity. Never once had he regretted going into business with his best friend.

"Now, the second thing." Mark cleared his throat. "Mr. Yamisuto is on the line. Says he needs to talk with both of us. Won't take over ten minutes. That okay?"

Kai gave Jade a good once-over. She seemed to be doing fine. Breathing okay. Swelling almost all gone. "Jade, are you okay with me taking a call? I'll be about ten minutes." Jade nodded, eyes closed. "Yeah, Mark. It's okay." He leaned against the car and studied the stars while Mark arranged the speaker-phone

Mr. Yamisuto greeted Kai in English and Kai returned his greeting. He'd had too much Japanese this night.

The Japanese firm's representative had some questions about the pending buy-out. Mostly, he wanted to arrange a conference call for the next morning at eleven o'clock. It would be nighttime in Japan then, but he would be meeting with the firm's board until the wee hours, so time would be no problem.

True to his word, the phone call lasted precisely ten minutes. Kai got into the car. "Now, Jade, you need to tell me where you live." No answer. He turned to find her seat reclined as far back as it would go, and Jade snoozing away. "Jade." He patted her leg. "Jade." He spoke louder with some gentle taps on the cheek. "Jade." He held her jaws between his finger and thumb and shook. Nothing. No response but a light snore.

"Damn it." He hit the steering wheel in frustration. "Now what do I do?"

A glance at the building reminded him the Urgent Care had all the information he needed. He got out of the car and hurried back in. Neither the nurses nor the doctor were anywhere to be seen. A man was working the window now, busy typing. Probably Jade's admission being entered in the computer.

"Hi. I just brought a young lady in who had a food allergy. I'm supposed to take her home, but I don't know where she lives."

The man didn't look up, just kept typing on his computer. "Sorry. Not allowed to give out personal information on clients."

"But," Kai protested, "I brought her in."

The guy glanced up briefly and shrugged. "Sorry, it's the law."

"Where's the nurse that was here?" Kai tried to keep the growl out of his voice.

"Shift changed ten minutes ago. They're all gone."

"Of all the freakin', stupid-ass laws!" Kai's face heated more with every word.

"Look, buddy," the man gave him a threatening look, "I don't make the laws, I just follow them. Now get out before I call security."

Kai stormed out of the building and back to the car. Jade didn't even flinch when he slammed the door. Her breathing was deep and long and even. Evidently, the Benedryl was doing its work just like the doctor said. She appeared to be out for the duration.

The nurse had gotten information from her

driver's license. That was it. It would have her address.

Kai snatched up the small purse and pilfered through it. The license wasn't there. Not in her wallet. Not in the side zipper. Had the nurse kept it by mistake? If so, no way would the Urgent Care Nazi let him have it.

Should he take her to his house? A possibility. But then she'd know he wasn't a software salesman. That would call for an explanation that might force him to break the blood brother pact. He never really believed Mark would cut him deep, but neither of them ever broke the pact.

Jade looked so relaxed and beautiful in the seat beside him. He ran his fingertips across the moonlight shining on her hair. Their time together had certainly been interesting. He'd sure like a chance to know her better.

While considering his options, he spotted her cell phone. Somebody in her contacts list could tell him where she lived.

He flipped the phone open and punched *send* at the first name—Adam Brock.

Chapter Four

Jade struggled in that half-awake, half-asleep state. She'd slept well, but some gnawing memory was going to surface as soon as she allowed full consciousness to kick in, a memory sure to be unpleasant.

Oh yeah, there it was. Keeping her eyes shut didn't fool her consciousness. It screamed at her. *The hottest guy you meet in months, years even, and you get sick and throw up all over yourself! Kiss that baby good-bye. On second thought, eat a breath mint and wave bye to that one from a distance.*

"Quit worrying. I'll be there soon." A deep voice penetrated through the one she was trying to block out.

Her eyes shot opened as she sprang up into a sitting position. Sunshine streamed through her window. She sat in her own bed in her own boxers and t-shirt...and her bra? And Kai Malone stood at the foot of the bed, watching her.

He dropped his phone into his pocket and flashed a broad smile that made her heart do a quick step. "Morning, Shank. I trust you're feeling better." He still wore yesterday's clothes, a bit wrinkled. A thick layer of dark stubble shadowed his face. Rugged. Very sexy.

She sorted through vague memories of being at the Urgent Care last night. Her fingers flew to her hair. Ick! It felt as stiff as the rest of her body. She lay back against the headboard, propping herself against the pillow to take inventory. Stiffness, but no pain. No nausea. "All in all, pretty good, considering you tried to kill me." She wrinkled her nose.

"I'm really, really sorry about what happened." Kai wiped his hand down his face. "I never should've tried to order."

She held up her hand to silence him. "Never mind. Let's just call it even." The bra hook poked into her back. "Did you, um, get me ready for bed?"

He shrugged and gave her a sheepish grin. "I couldn't leave those clothes on you." He mimicked her nose wrinkle. "You threw up on them. And before that, I spilled sushi and beer on them."

"Yeah, I remember." *Move on to something less humiliating.* "You left my bra on." *That's less humiliating?*

He shrugged again.

"Obviously, you spent the night."

He nodded toward the living room. "On your couch. My car's still at the club." He paused while he studied something outside the window. "I wanted to make sure you were okay."

There was no way he would ever know it, but that comment earned him big points on the Hotness scale. Tall, dark, handsome, easy to talk to, a gentleman, and caring. A purebred hundred pointer. Jade wasn't at all sure she could wait until Beth's 5:15 flight arrived from New York to talk to her. "What time is it?" Maybe she'd slept most of the day away.

"A little after 9:00."

Jade sighed. "Well, I'll get dressed and take you to your car." She raised up and made to throw the covers back, but he moved quickly to the side of the bed and flipped them back on her.

He gently pushed her back into the pillow. "You need to rest today. Doctor's orders. Gram's going to take me back to the club."

Jade shot up straight. "Gram?"

"Yes, Gram." His eyes squinted when he smiled, but it didn't hide the mischievous gleam.

"How did Gram get into this?" The words sounded more like an accusation than a question, even to her ears.

"I knew I had to leave this morning, and I didn't know if you'd be awake yet. Somebody would need to check on you." He pushed her back into the pillow again. "You said your elderly landlady loved you, so I figured she was my best choice. And I was right."

"But..." she protested.

"No buts. You should've just told me your landlady was your grandmother."

He made it sound like a normal occurrence in LA. "Right," she answered. "How fast could you have run with sore testicles?"

He threw his head back and laughed, showing off those perfect teeth. God, was he gorgeous when he laughed, or grinned, or looked serious, or looked concerned. But especially when he laughed. "Anyway, we decided over breakfast that—"

She sprang up again. "Over breakfast?"

Kai sat on the edge of the bed, meeting her gaze, his strong jaw set in a defiant manner. "Over breakfast. I went downstairs to ask her to check on you later. We introduced ourselves. I found out who she was. I told her you'd gotten sick and I was afraid to leave you. She came up and checked on you, but you were still out. Then they invited me to join them for breakfast. Hey, Marvin makes a mean eggs benedict."

"There's a Marvin?" She groaned and lay back of her own volition this time.

"It appears Gram is," he cleared his throat, "um, entertaining this morning. She's very cool for seventy-eight."

Okay, this would cost him some points. Meeting Gram before being prepared was a category of point deduction she'd never even considered needing before. And having breakfast with Gram and a 'gentleman caller'? Definitely over some limit of protocol. Maybe eleven or twelve points' worth. She glanced around the room so they wouldn't have to make eye contact until the awkward moment passed. Her driver's license and insurance card lay on the bedside table. Strange. She remembered having them out at the Urgent Care, then putting them somewhere. It was all a blur.

"Those fell out of your pocket when I pulled your shorts off," Kai explained. "Wish I'd known where they were. It sure would have saved some trouble."

Her face heated at the idea of Kai removing her shorts. She hoped she hadn't moaned or done something stupid. But he'd used the word trouble. What possible trouble could two little cards have caused? She narrowed her eyes at Kai, defying him to complicate this story any further.

He stood up and took a step back. Getting out of range maybe?

"What trouble?" she asked coolly.

"I didn't know where you lived, and they wouldn't tell me at the Urgent Care." He ran his fingers through his hair a couple of times. "Cited patient confidentiality."

"Go on."

"You were completely out of it. Couldn't get you to budge. So as I was looking for your license, I found your phone."

His voice took on a defensive tone that raised the hairs on her neck. "My phone? Who did you call?"

"Adam."

"Adam?" she shrieked. This information brought her to her knees on the bed. Her heart pounded in her chest, tearing the air out of her lungs. "Why would you call Adam?" she sputtered.

"He's the first one in your contacts list." Kai

shrugged and spread his fingers in a gesture that suggested pure logic.

Jade slapped the back of her hand into the opposite palm. "Because he's an A. Beth is a B!"

Kai quirked an eyebrow at her. "And I'll bet Cindy's a C and Dad's a D."

Jade collapsed backward on the bed and stared at the ceiling. This man was insufferable. All the contacts in her phone and he chose the one she should've deleted nine months ago. She drummed her fists and heels into the mattress in a quick staccato. "Ooooh!"

"He seemed very nice," Kai offered. "Very concerned." A couple of honks came from outside below the window. "That's Gram, so I've got to go. Can I give you a call later?"

Jade didn't answer, too frustrated and angry to speak just yet. If this was a ploy to get her awake and heart-pumping before he left, it had worked.

Kai's chuckle didn't help. "I'll take that as a yes since it wasn't a no." His voice moved farther away. "By the way, Adam said to tell you he'd see you real soon."

The door slammed and she blew her breath out in a long puff. *That conversation must have been an interesting one. "Hi. I'm with Jade and she's passed out on me and I don't know where she lives."* She could imagine Adam's shocked reaction and then his smug satisfaction when he realized she hadn't deleted him—that, in fact, he was still number one in her contacts list.

She mentally deducted points on Kai's ledger that she hadn't even started yet...and maybe wouldn't. The door opened. Had Kai forgotten something?

Gram poked her head in the door. "You awake, Chickie-boom?"

"Unfortunately, yes." Jade sat up on the edge of

the bed. Paisley rushed in the open door and leaped onto her lap, bumping her chin. "I thought you were taking Kai back to his car."

"Marvin took him." Gram came in, looking like a model out of a fashion catalogue in a lime tunic and white capris. Her gold flip-flops were trimmed with lime and white beading.

"Who's Marvin?" The aroma of the coffee in the cup Gram held got stronger as she drew closer. Jade's mouth watered. Man, was she hungry. She cringed, remembering. Her stomach was empty because she threw up.

"A perfect wonder of a man. Met him at the gym." Gram cupped Jade's chin and gave her a kiss on the forehead. "Feelin' better?"

Jade nodded, scratching behind Paisley's ears.

"Brought you some coffee."

Paisley moved to the pillow and began his morning bath ritual. Jade wrapped her hands around the cup Gram held out to her. She appreciated its warmth and grasping something solid anchored her. "Thanks." She kissed the air in Gram's direction.

"C'mon out to the deck. I've got you some breakfast if you want it." Gram steadied the coffee and pulled Jade to a standing position.

Jade dropped her phone into her pocket and shot Gram a sidelong look. "Marvin's eggs benedict?"

"Whoooo-eeee!" Gram winked and shook her head as she led the way down the steps to the patio table. "The things that man can do with butter."

Jade didn't think her stomach could take the images suggested by the sparkle in her grandmother's eyes. She shooed Gram into the house, feigning death by starvation if she didn't get food soon.

The morning was perfect with a sky so clear she could see Catalina in the distance. The light breeze brought the tangy smell of the Pacific to her nose and it blended with the aroma of the coffee. She didn't just feel better, she felt great. How could that be possible considering how her last twenty-four hours had gone?

A lady in a suit, probably a realtor, was replacing the "For Sale" sign on the house next door with one that announced "Sold". New neighbors soon. The Langstons had been loud and obnoxious. She wasn't sorry when they told her of their impending move to Malibu. Good riddance. The new neighbors would have to be an improvement.

"New blood'll be coming in." Gram motioned with the plate before she set it down. Cantaloupe and honeydew were artfully displayed in a fan shape on the side.

"Marvin's doings?" Jade cocked an eyebrow.

"One of many." Gram poured herself some coffee and settled into the seat next to Jade. "Now tell me about 'His Hotness'."

Jade nibbled on the cantaloupe, testing the effect food would have on her stomach this morning. "He hasn't made it to the book yet. I'm not sure he will." She added a bit of salt to the melon then dusted it heavily with black pepper.

Gram sipped her coffee and followed the passage of a well-built shirtless jogger along The Strand. "He will." She sounded sure of herself. "So how'd you meet? He wouldn't say. Just said it was a little embarrassing." She directed the stage whisper with a hand to the side of her mouth.

Jade kept a straight face as she swallowed a bite of the eggs. The sauce was scrumptious, tangy with a slight sting in the aftertaste. Kai was right. Marvin made a mean eggs benedict. "I shanked a drive into his balls," she answered finally.

Grams eyes grew wide and she sputtered a bit on her drink. "Well, did you offer to kiss 'em and make 'em better?"

"No, and by the way, Fernando's a jerk." Jade scarfed down another bite then continued her tale in clipped tones. "We went for sushi. I got sick on scallops. He spilled dinner in my lap. Went to Urgent Care. Threw up. Got a shot. Fell asleep. Woke up to find he'd had breakfast with my grandmother and her sleep-over guest and phoned my ex." She let out a long, sigh before the next bite.

Gram's eyebrows drew in and she cocked her head in question. "Who'd he call?"

"Adam." So, Kai really hadn't shared too much of the sordid story. Jade finished the last couple of bites of egg and topped them with a bite of honeydew. The sweet melon cut through the heaviness.

"Why'd he call the Brat?"

Jade snickered at Gram's use of the nickname she'd given Adam. Gram never much liked him and didn't try to cover it, even to his face. She'd even been known to lecture him about his careless use of the money he inherited when his parents died. Apparently, his absence hadn't made Gram's heart grow fonder.

"Adam was the first name in my phone, and I guess Kai panicked when he realized he didn't know where I lived."

"So he called Adam." Gram clapped her hands in applause. "That's great."

"That's awful," Jade pouted. "Now Adam knows he's still in my phone. Probably thinks I'm brooding over him. Probably thinks this guy picked me up in a bar or that I can't get a date so I'm picking up guys now and passing out on them."

"Nah, Chickie-boom." She patted Jade's arm. "He probably thinks you dismissed him so readily, you forgot to delete him." She shook her head and the movement set her gold coin earrings to tinkling.

"And imagine Kai's voice, full of concern and fear for you."

Jade did imagine the deep voice, a growl at times, sensuous. Very masculine. Very hot. She pulled her phone out and proceeded to delete Adam Brock from her life for good.

"Mmmmm." Gram sipped her coffee. "Yep. I definitely think Mr. Kai should go in the book."

Jade finally relinquished a smile. "Well, he's not out of the picture. He asked if he could call me," she snorted, "but I was so frustrated I didn't answer."

"No problem, Chickie. I tried giving him your number, but he said he already had it." Gram's cheek dimpled. "Don't fret. He'll call."

There had been a certain something between them, Jade decided. They'd seen each other at their worst, yet the interest was still there. She leaned her head onto the back of the chair, letting the lapping waves and the warm sunshine on her face lull her into relaxation mode.

"He told us he was trying to impress you with his Japanese and told the waiter no clams instead of no scallops."

"Yeah." So he was trying to impress her. Cool.

"He's a keeper."

Jade's eyes were closed, but she heard the punctuation of Gram's fingernails clicking on the tabletop. "Because he tried to kill me?"

"Because he admitted his mistake. Lots of guys won't. Brat never could."

Mention of Adam reminded Jade of Kai's last words. "Adam told Kai to tell me he'd be seeing me real soon."

"Mmmmph." Gram wasn't going to acknowledge that with a comeback.

They sat quietly for a while. Gram poured more coffee and they sipped, enjoying the view like they did most every morning.

Jade's phone vibrated against the tabletop, breaking the silence. She didn't recognize the number. "Hello?"

"Hello, this is John Levitt with Samuels Publishing. Could I speak with Jade Bartholomew, please?" The voice was smooth and even with perfect diction, and the eggs benedict flipped over in her stomach.

Jade cleared her throat and took a deep breath. "This is she." Her heartbeat pounded louder than the surf in her ears. *Please, please, please let the news be good.*

"Miss Bartholomew, we've been reviewing your resume, and I must admit I'm impressed. I was hoping you'd be able to come in for an interview."

"Oh, yes. Yes, I can do that. When?" Ack! Did that sound desperate? Well, she *was* desperate.

"Would the 21st work for you? 11:00?"

"Yes, that would be fine. Perfect. Thank you." *Breathe. Don't hyperventilate.*

"You have the address of our office. Do you need directions?"

"No. I know exactly where it is."

"Fine, then. I'll look forward to talking with you on the 21st."

"Yes. I'll be there. And thank you again." She closed the phone and laid it gingerly on the table before she let out a squeal. "Gram, I got the interview with Samuels!"

"Good for you, Chickie!" Gram gave her a high five. "Kai and the job, too? This is your lucky day."

"Whoa, lady." Jade laughed. "You're jumping way too far ahead on both. We don't want to jinx it...them." But oh! This really did feel good. She leaned back and sipped her coffee, trying to recapture the tranquility of a few moments earlier. But it was no use. USC's band was tromping through her stomach. "Aiee! And Beth's at a conference, so I won't be able to talk to her until tonight."

"Ooooo, ooooo, that reminds me." Gram drummed the table for effect. "I've got an idea for her bachelorette party."

Jade rolled her eyes. Not another idea. Since the Café Provence burned last week, finding another place to book the party had been a pain in the ass. Gram had been bombarding her with ideas, all revolving around sex of some sort. "No fair taking advantage of my good mood. We're not going to hire Chippendales. Forget it."

"No, no, no. Something better."

She seemed really excited about this idea, which meant Jade would really hate it. "No sex toys. No hopping vaginas. No vibrators. No lingerie shows."

Gram flipped her off. "Would you be still and listen? Marvin has his own chef, Carlton, and Carlton's wife is a...a dance instructor."

Sounded okay so far. There was sure to be a catch. "Go on. I'm listening."

"You have it here," Gram indicated the deck, "and make this place into a little French café. Yellow tablecloths, blue napkins."

Jade envisioned the deck the way Gram described it. Cute, and they had lots of stuff from Provence to set around.

"Simone, that's his wife, gives you all a dance lesson."

"What kind of dance lesson?" Too many options in this category made Jade suspicious.

"Whatever kind she teaches. Rumba? Tango? Belly?" Gram stood up and started wiggling her way around the deck with an invisible partner. "Come on, Chickie-boom. Let's do our girl dance." She pulled Jade to her feet, and Jade was just giddy enough about the job interview to go along with it.

"Ready? One, two, three, four."

They launched into the routine Gram taught her when she was five. Part Charleston, part hoochie-coochie, a lot of shimmy, and a bit of tap. Gram had learned it her first week in Hollywood when she tried out for a chorus line. She didn't get the job, but she never forgot the routine. It had been a while since their last go at it. Jade was amazed to hear herself breathing harder than Gram.

"Right hip, shimmy, left hip, shimmy," Gram directed, "and stomp."

They finished to a round of applause from several people on The Strand who'd stopped to watch.

"Either of you girls free tonight?" It was a beefy kid of about eighteen who spoke.

"Not free, sweetie, but damn cheap," Gram answered and the group applauded again.

Assuring everyone the show was over Gram settled back into her chair and picked up where she left off. "After the dance lesson, Carlton gives you a cooking lesson. Something easy and light. Dessert maybe. Carlton makes dinner while you serve cocktails and appetizers out here." She gave a sweeping gesture around the deck. "Then, you're served the dinner and afterward the desserts you made yourselves."

Jade had to admit she was pretty taken with the idea. "No belly dancing and that would be perfect. But can we get this arranged? We're talking less than a month."

Gram struck a majestic pose, chin high, one hand over her heart, the other pointing gracefully skyward. "Chickie-boom, you just leave everything to me. And no belly dancing. Promise." She winked.

Gram was up to something, but it sounded like fun, and the sun was shining on Jade's world again.

Maybe it was time for some dreams to come true.

Chapter Five

"So he undressed you and didn't do anything? Sounds like a weirdo to me." Pryce crumpled his empty beer can and shot it at the trashcan several feet away. The can made a perfect arc and dropped in. "Whoosh! Goodman hasn't lost his touch."

"I could have told you that." Beth ran her toe down the length of his thigh.

Pryce grabbed the foot firmly and started massaging, pressing with his thumbs in circular motions beneath the toes and down toward the arch. Beth's head fell back in a languid pose, and she groaned in pleasure.

"Yes sir, if I'd undressed you the night we met, I would've—"

"Enough already." Jade covered her ears. "Have some pity on a poor celibate." Watching Beth and Pryce together was almost like renting an erotic movie. Not that they ever did anything gross or x-rated. There was just a sensuousness they elicited from each other simply by being in the same proximity, and the last nine months *sans* sex made her more aware of anything sensuous. Like seeing couples touch, or drinking wine. Or getting sand in her eyes. God, she was pitiful.

Beth rolled her head to the side and opened one eye Jade's direction. "Well, I think he sounds divine. What's his score?"

"You still keeping up with that journal thing?" Pryce continued working his magical chiropractor's hands, moving to the other foot Beth proffered. "When you going to bury it with the rest of your high school memories?"

Jade started toward the stairs to her apartment for another round of beer but stopped long enough to tousle Pryce's bright red hair. How could a redhead with freckles be this handsome? Usually they were cute, but Pryce went way beyond cute. He was take-me-to-bed-before-I-throw-myself-on-my-vibrator fabulous. And he still had a sweet boyishness about him, just like when he and Beth met his junior year in college, their freshman. "Not until I find a Pryce Goodman," she answered.

He stopped massaging long enough to catch Jade's hand on his head and pull her back for a quick peck on her forehead. "And if there's only one of me in existence?"

"You're planning on kids aren't you? Maybe I'll wait."

He released her with a shudder. "Eeeww. Now you're talking like Gram."

Her phone was ringing when she got upstairs. She wasn't expecting anyone to call now that Beth was home. "Hello?"

"Shank? Hi, it's Kai."

Her stomach did a somersault. She'd expected him to call sometime, but not today. "Hey, Kai." No time to think of something cute or provocative.

"I wanted to see how you were feeling. Any lingering problems from last night?"

By that, if he meant did it make her out-of-her-mind horny to imagine him removing her clothes, then she'd have to say there were definite problems, but if he was inquiring about her health... "No, um-hum." She cleared her throat and her mind. "I'm fine, really."

"Good. Glad to hear that."

Gram and Beth's chiding of her sullen behavior toward him won out. "And I'm sorry about acting so childish this morning. You got me home safely, so no matter how you did it, I appreciate it."

"Enough to have dinner with me?" She could hear the smile in his voice.

"Why? So you can finish me off?" She cringed hoping he took that as a death joke and not with the sexual innuendo. She had to quit being so flippant, or he was going to think she didn't take anything seriously.

"Well, there are a few things I'd like to finish." He chuckled and the sound tingled down her spine. "Like dinner, so what do you say? Are you busy tonight?"

Their introduction definitely deserved a new start, but would he mind meeting her friends? Only one way to find out. "My friends Beth and Pryce are here. I think I mentioned their wedding last night. Anyway, we're going to order pizza. Want to join us?"

"Oh, I wouldn't want to intrude. You guys probably have wedding plans to talk about."

It didn't really sound like a refusal. She decided to offer again. "I think they'd enjoy meeting you. I told them about last night." In fact, Beth had stopped at her own place only long enough to drop off luggage and change clothes once she heard the teaser to last night's adventure. Pryce wasn't thrilled, but Beth's promise of pizza, beer, and hot sex later had brought him around.

"So they wanna meet the goofball, eh?"

"Well, let's just say they've heard about the goofball and the golf ball."

"Sooo, this could be my chance to redeem myself."

"Absolutely, and if you'd bring a medium pepperoni and a medium spinach and mushroom they might recommend you for sainthood."

"Now that's an offer I can't refuse. I'll be there in half an hour."

Jade's stomach tightened then did a flip-flop.

Tonight needed to go well. Another disaster would probably mean no more chances with this Hotness. She hurried to tell Beth and Pryce about the additional guest.

"What's this guy's name? I don't think you ever said." Pryce had moved behind Beth and was massaging her shoulders and neck.

"Hotness," Beth interjected before Jade could answer. "His Hotness. And he gets her so hot just talking on the phone, she forgot our beer."

Jade's face grew warm. Beth knew her too well.

Pryce stopped massaging and peeled off his shirt. "I want to go on a quick run before I eat anyway. I'll be back." He vaulted over the railing of the deck and was gone.

"Now." Beth rubbed her hands together as if plotting something sinister. "Let's go check out this journal entry."

They took the steps in double-time, giggling like high school girls.

Beth belly-flopped onto the bed while Jade settled into the chair with the book, flipping the pages to the one she wanted. "Uh-hum." She cleared her throat dramatically. "Kai Malone," she read. "Very hot. Looks are reminiscent of a hawk or a brooding Comanche chief. Took being hit in the balls like a man. Pleasant and interesting to talk to. Invited me to dinner. 100 points."

"Good start. Go on." Beth examined a section of hair for split ends, which were always nonexistent. She had the most gorgeous, healthy, jet-black hair on the planet.

"Tried to kill me with scallops, minus twelve," Jade continued.

"Accidentally," Beth reminded her. "Twelve seems a little high."

"We're talking near-death." Jade rolled her eyes. Beth always went too soft on them. "Called ex-boyfriend, minus fifteen."

"I'll sign-off on that one. But, it's pretty funny."

Jade gave a haughty sniff. "All he had to do was scroll down one and he'd have had you." She read the next entry. "Breakfast with Gram. Minus three. And Marvin. Minus five. For a whopping," she faked a drum roll with her tongue, "sixty-five."

"Well, I'd say by this time tomorrow, he'll be back up in the nineties," Beth sat up and quirked a perfectly-arched eyebrow, "if I can get Pryce out of here at a decent hour."

"Nope," Jade assured her. "Even in my tightly-strung condition, one-night-stands aren't appealing, and we haven't even had an official date yet. We'll just see what develops." She tossed the journal back onto the desk.

They stayed upstairs a little while, discussing the definitive suit to wear to the interview. Jade was careful not to mention the things she took to the consignment shop, giving Beth only the few choices that remained in her closet. This time, she remembered the beer before they headed back downstairs.

Jade heard the voices first and stopped on the steps. Kai's deep chuckle floated their way. Pryce was knee-deep in one of his stories. "And if the poor guy's score ever drops below a sixty, his page is ripped out. Symbolic of a crash-and-burn sequence."

Jade shook her head with a sigh. "Does he always have to tell everything?"

Beth shrugged. "Gotta love him, though." She tugged Jade's sleeve, pulling her forward. "C'mon. Sixty-five needs to get his score up."

"Among other things," Jade whispered.

Pryce and Kai seemed to have caught on quickly—a good sign. Having approval from Beth and Pryce ranked high on her list. She should have listened to them and Gram when they tried to warn her about Adam.

Kai's face broke into a knee-weakening smile when Jade crossed the deck. His eyes nearly squinted closed, making his white teeth the only light spot in his dark face. He crossed over to her and took her hand. "You sure you're okay?" The gentleness in his voice caused her words to catch. She nodded mutely. "Good." He gave her hand a quick squeeze. "I brought pizza, so you can call me Saint Kai."

Jade introduced Beth and Kai, and when he glanced away to respond to Pryce, Beth shot her a wide-eyed nod of approval.

Pryce opened the pizza boxes and the smell of pepperoni pulled Jade toward the table.

"So you guys introduced yourselves?" She grabbed a plate and a slice from each box.

"Yeah, and his name sounds really familiar to me..."

"Don't take a bite of the pepperoni yet," Kai interjected quickly. "You'll burn your mouth. Uh, Pryce, you probably recognize my name because of my short-lived golf career."

"Yeah, that's right." Pryce snapped his fingers in recognition. "You went pro for awhile, didn't you?" He held his bottle aloft. "Here's to those of us who have to make our living away from the golf course." They all answered his salute and took a swig of beer in response to the toast.

The pizza and beer disappeared quickly as conversation became more animated. Jade and Kai related their first meeting again in tag-team fashion. He had a fun sense of humor and an easy laugh. She enjoyed his laugh. It rumbled up out of him, gaining volume as it rose.

Kai explained about his call to Adam. "I just panicked when I realized I had no idea where she lived." His sheepish tone made Jade soften toward him, even on that matter.

"Hey, don't apologize. I think it was quick thinking on your part." Pryce nodded his approval. "In fact, the only thing I'd have done differently was, when you undressed her, I would've—"

Jade and Beth shrieked their protest. Kai and Pryce laughed and clinked their bottles together at the reaction.

"By the way, speaking of Adam." Pryce addressed Beth but cut his eyes toward Jade. "Caitlyn Treece is bringing the dickhead to the wedding."

"What?" Beth shrieked again.

Jade choked on the mouthful of beer and fought to keep it from spewing.

"Yeah, she called while you were in New York. We gave her the option of bringing a guest, and he's coming as her guest."

"I thought he was in Costa Rica." Jade tried to sound nonchalant but couldn't keep the angry tinge out of her voice.

"Didn't like it. He's back."

"Here?" Jade fought the frustration that rose with every nod of Pryce's head.

"He said he'd see you soon," Kai reminded her.

She groaned inwardly. She'd assumed that statement had just been a nicety. Well, Adam Brock's presence was not going to ruin her best friend's wedding for her. She would just ignore him or be barely civil if the situation called for interaction. She could handle this.

Jade deftly changed the subject. "Gram had a great idea for your bachelorette party." She went on explaining the whole layout to Beth's eager attention. Gram's idea was a hit with the guest-of-honor.

As she and Beth talked over the details, Kai and Pryce turned to their own conversation of golf and

Pebble Beach and the new course under construction.

Time passed quickly. Much too soon it seemed, Beth gave Jade a sly wink and yawned loudly declaring her intention to sleep right there if Pryce didn't get her home soon.

The redhead's actions became frenzied as he hustled to clean up the mess of boxes and bottles. They all laughed at the horrified look on his face that dissolved into relief when Kai assured him he'd take care of everything.

Kai was a man of his word. As soon as they left, he gathered up the bottles. Jade followed suit by piling everything left into the empty boxes and leading the way to the trash dumpster.

Back on the deck, Jade motioned to the stairs. "Want to come up for a while?"

Kai shook his head and leaned against the wall between the house and the sidewalk. "I'd like to, but I've got a long day tomorrow. I'd better get on home."

Damn! If this man doesn't touch me soon, I'm going to consider having one of those "Easy" buttons attached to my shoulder. Jade sighed, hoping her disappointment didn't show too much.

He reached out and took her hand, letting out a sigh of his own. Jade realized his sigh had meaning. She stiffened, waiting for whatever it was he wanted to say. Probably nothing she wanted to hear.

"I have to go to Japan for three or four weeks."

That wasn't the terrible news she'd expected. She relaxed and stepped closer into him. "Business?"

He nodded.

She inched closer. "That must be some company. Sending its salesmen to Japan."

Kai leaned his head back and his luscious eyes broke contact for a minute. "Yeah, um, well I'm the only, uh, salesman going. I know a lot about the technical aspects of the software." He paused for a second, like he was going to add something, but then he gave a little shake of his head.

No doubt, someone as charming as Kai Malone would be an asset to any company. Gram had said he could probably sell an ice machine to an Eskimo. Jade was about to prod him further to talk about his job when his arms went around her waist and clasped behind her. The firmness of his arms drew all her attention. She was caught in his steel grip, and it was like being tethered to a mountain of rock. Mmmm. She could climb that mountain in record time, and when she reached his peak…

"I leave the day after tomorrow."

"Oh." She stuck out her lower lip in a pretend pout and ran her hands along his arms, silently urging him not to loosen his grip. If he did, she might just slide to the ground.

"So, I know it's kind of presumptuous of me, but I'd love to see you again before I go. A real date. Dinner."

She smoothed her hands across his broad, rugged shoulders… *My God, he could have modeled for Michelangelo*…and looped her arms around his neck, her breasts barely brushing the stone wall of his chest. Her softness, his hardness. Opposites attracted. Her body was moving into sensation overload, but she managed a couple of coherent words. "Tomorrow night?"

His eyes squinted into that grin that made her want to melt right there in his arms. "That okay with you?"

"I'd love it." She leaned fully against him, feeling the length of his erection, and held back the little gasp that seemed inappropriate right then. There would be time tomorrow night. "Could we stay close by? Maybe walking distance?" *Close to my apartment and my bedroom?* "You said it was going to be a long day."

"Whatever you want." He whispered it as his lips moved toward hers.

Jade closed her eyes in anticipation of that first touch of the lips, which she always found extremely erotic. This time it was soft, gentle. Their mouths fit together perfectly. *Whatever I want indeed.* She pulled his head closer, opening her mouth a bit in encouragement. His response came with the tip of his tongue brushing her lips then a slow exploration of the inside of her mouth.

Movements never became hurried. His palms moved along her back in sensuous circles as his head changed positions to take her mouth from every angle.

She responded, fingers brushing through his hair, fingernails lightly caressing the back of his neck. Time stopped as if in acknowledgement that this kiss could go on forever if they so chose.

She'd always been a sucker for good kissers. It didn't take long before she admitted to herself Mr. Malone's Hotness score had already soared well over a hundred.

Yessiree, this man was a born salesman.

Chapter Six

Jade woke with the feel of Kai's lips on hers. Soft. Gentle. Furry? She opened her eyes to find Paisley asleep in the crook of her arm, paw stretched just far enough to rest on her mouth. She kissed the little pink pads and tucked the paw into her side.

Last night, Kai's kisses had her so keyed up she thought she wouldn't be able to sleep. On the contrary, she'd konked out on the couch as soon as he left, clothed and somewhat satisfied. Ten or fifteen minutes of steamy, leisurely kissing had been almost as good as sex. Almost. Or had nine months dulled her memory of what good sex was? Maybe. But tonight would hopefully bring it all back.

Her heart started to beat faster. Going back to sleep now would be impossible. Even at—6:02? She hadn't gotten up this early since the hot air balloon ride with Adam when he'd told her he'd been "transferred" to Costa Rica. She should've known he was lying. He'd go to any lengths to get his way. At first, he tried to act upset. But the longer he talked, the more evident it became he was excited, sure of himself, sure he could convince her to love the idea. He'd even made all the arrangements without consulting her, including one-way tickets.

She pulled Paisley onto her chest and rubbed his nose with hers. If Pryce hadn't stumbled on the truth about the move when he talked to that other guy from the company, she might be lying here this morning, never even knowing what Kai's kisses were like. Mmm. What a pity that would have been.

The muscles she'd tensed with the memories of

Adam needed some strenuous physical exertion. Various scenes of how to relieve those muscles played across her mind. She and Kai running naked along the beach, falling to the sand, bodies entwined, him on top, her on top, moaning at the sensation of his hungry mouth on her nipples...

Wait a minute. She didn't moan, at least not out loud. Those sounds of moaning and loud grunting and rhythmic pounding were coming from below her and her living room was positioned directly above...No! She covered her ears and hustled to find her running shoes. Gram and Marvin were doing it right below. She had to get out of there fast!

Usually a jogger, she ran at breakneck speed down The Strand passing walkers, joggers, even a couple of slow cyclists. She allowed the morning mist to clear the creepy images of Gram and Marvin from her mind.

Three miles later, Starbucks marked her turn-around, and she ducked in for a grande latte.

****

"Soooo?" Mark strolled into Kai's office holding his crotch.

Normally this was his time with Mark to shoot the breeze for a while. But with leaving for Japan early tomorrow and meetings all morning today, Kai had no time for chit chat. "So what?" Where was that damn contract he'd set down not two seconds ago? Ah, there it was! He tossed it on the "to-do-immediately" pile.

"Jock strap or thong?" Mark began an in-depth pantomime of his interpretation of a thong caught in one's butt-cheeks.

Kai held the laugh as long as he could, but eventually gave in. He didn't mind a couple of minutes of Jade-centered conversation. "Thong. Visually confirmed."

"You hooked up, Big Kai?

"No. She threw up, remember? I had to change her clothes." Kai's memory quickly pushed past the puke and moved on to the sight of Jade's amazing legs as he'd pulled off her shorts.

"But what about last night?" Mark's hand was circling in the air like he could reel the information in like a fish.

Kai shrugged. "I met her friends. We ate pizza, drank beer." And then her kisses had him so rock-hard he thought he'd explode.

"You didn't tell her anything about Techtron, did you?" Mark snipped the air, using his fingers as scissors. "If you did, I'd have to cut you deep."

"Don't worry. The blood-brother pact is still secure."

"Yeah well, just keep your guard up about who you are and what you do. And what you're worth."

Kai snorted and ran his hand through his hair. "Jade's different. She won't be impressed. Her grandmother's obviously wealthy."

"Lora was wealthy. May was wealthy." Mark gave an itemized statement of women with money Kai had dated. "Hazel was rolling in it."

Kai hoped Mark's calling of her name didn't conjure up a call from Hazel. She'd been quiet for a day and a half now. "Okay, okay. I get the point. But this duplicity with Jade feels like bullshit."

Mark sighed, his favorite signal of exasperation. "Only if you don't like her. If you think she's a good thing, it may be your best move toward a strong relationship."

Jade was definitely a good thing. Like a breath of fresh air in his cigar-smoke-filled day. "Got it. Now go home and—"

"I know, I know. Go home and make a baby with my wife." Mark held his hands up in surrender.

"Hey," Kai's laugh rumbled out of his stomach, "it's a tough job, but somebody's got to do it."

Mark grabbed his crotch again and sprinted out the door.

Kai shook his head as he watched him leave. His brother-in-law was certainly one-of-a-kind. *Thank God.*

He let his thoughts turn briefly back to Jade. He was really looking forward to seeing her again. With any luck, there would be lots of dates with Ms. Bartholomew.

****

During the walk home, Jade sipped her coffee and prayed Marvin wasn't taking the drug that gave men erections lasting four hours.

Her prayers were answered. Everything was quiet when she got back. Relaxed and clear-headed, she settled down at the laptop. If she put in a ten-hour day, it would almost make up for the lost time yesterday.

Sometimes the editing became so consuming she forgot to eat. She shouldn't let that happen today, didn't want to be starved tonight. She set her alarm for noon.

She wrapped up the regency around 9:45 thankful to be done with it. The characters of the elderly duke and duchess kept reminding her of Marvin and Gram. Then she started on a chick-lit which was the perfect pre-date reading material—a fun romp with some steamy sex scenes. She even groaned when the alarm went off and forced her to break for a while.

By six, she was ready to call it a day. Thirty minutes of pilates unkinked knotted muscles, and the shower invigorated her from zombie mode back to human.

The chick-lit helped her zero in on an outfit to wear. The short pink skirt of tiered ruffles sat low on her hips, and the pink camisole with built-in bra gave some support plus a bit of cleavage. It made her breasts look perky. She made the right choice keeping this outfit as one of the few left in her closet.

Mom would be thrilled to hear she wore the Emilio Puccis she'd bought her. Mom had presented her with the outrageously expensive, strappy little pink sandals and instructed her not to be intimidated by the three-inch heels. They'd sat in their box until tonight, waiting for the right time to shine.

The ensemble seemed perfect for a date with Kai. Usually not too girlie, tonight she wanted to be flirty and fun and give him an evening to remember during those weeks in Japan. She'd even curled her hair.

A heavy knock on the door cut her thoughts short.

His whistle when she answered convinced her she'd chosen correctly. "You look fabulous." He kissed her forehead and ran his palms along the exposed skin of her shoulders and down her arms. "And you have the most amazing shoulders."

Well, that was different. No one had ever commented on her shoulders before. His hands were warm against her, so the little shiver running through her had to be pure excitement. She felt ultra-feminine lifting her chin to offer her mouth, even in three-inch heels. He met her kiss with the eagerness she'd hoped for, an unspoken promise of what was in store.

She leaned against Kai's arm as they climbed the hill to Mangia Bene. The Puccis might be cute, but they were damn hard to walk in uphill. His bulging bicep provided the support she needed and made her eager to learn about his other bulges.

The Italian restaurant was one of Jade's favorites. Beth and Pryce's engagement party had been there. Good memories and good food.

Kai's turquoise polo brought out the intriguing

color of his eyes. She hadn't really thought much about them since the blue-eyed hawk captivated her on the putting green, focusing more on the cute way he squinted when he laughed or smiled. But tonight, she got lost in them. Deep blue, like the ocean, fringed with long, black lashes. She imagined them gazing down at her on a moonlit beach.

"So tell me about your family." He pulled her out of her reverie. With a bottle of cabernet to sip, the wait for a table wouldn't seem too long.

"Well, my mom and dad practice law together. They met at Harvard."

"Bartholomew, Bartholomew, & Lence, no doubt." Kai's raised eyebrows showed his surprise.

Jade nodded. So he'd heard of them. Most people in the area had unless they'd been on a different planet last year during the sensational Fetterman murder trial. "That's them. Grandpa Pete, Gram's husband, started the firm in the forties. He died three years ago."

"How'd he and Gram meet?" Kai seemed genuinely interested, not just making conversation. He tucked a loose strand of hair behind her ear, and his touch sent another one of those pleasant shivers down her spine.

"Gram came to L.A. from Erin, Tennessee right after the war. Wanted to be a star, but took a job as a legal secretary in order to eat. The young partner fell head-over-heels for her. They got married, had my dad, and here I am."

"*The Beverly Hillbillies*' Reality Show, eh?"

"Oh, wow. I used to watch that on Nick at Night."

"Yeah? Me too. I loved those old fifties and sixties sit-com reruns." He paused then gave a little snort. "Watching those was about the only thing my ex and I had in common."

Jade bristled ever-so-slightly at the mention of

his ex. She hoped he wasn't one of those guys who cut down his ex constantly. Or made her the center of conversation. She waited to see if he said any more. He didn't. Relieved, she picked up the topic again. "My favorite was *Andy Griffith*."

"Mine, too. Especially the ones with Barney in them."

Exchanging tales of Barney Fife kept them laughing until their table was ready. After they ordered, he asked about her mom's side of the family.

"Mimi, that's what I call my Grandmother Marie, was from Provence. She met Papa Jed. He's the one I'm named for. They met during the war and returned to the States afterward. Now, Mimi and Gram and Mom and Dad own a cottage together in Villefranche-sur-Mer on the Cote d'Azure. I spent most summers in France when I was growing up. Mom and Dad and Mimes are there now."

Kai leaned across the table and ran a finger across her lips. "I realized last night you were fluent in French."

"*Oui, monsieur.*" She gave him what she hoped was a coquettish smile and brushed her tongue where his finger had been.

She was rewarded by his groan and a shake of his head. "What is taking the damn food so long?"

"*Alors, monsieur*, we just ordered!"

"Well, maybe we should get it to go." He winked, and those ocean blue eyes swept her away.

"*Ooo-la-la.*"

He told her about his mom and dad, who lived in Pasadena where he grew up. His dad was an astronomer at the Jet Propulsion Laboratory, and his mom was principal of his high school. He was the oldest of five children with four younger sisters.

His youngest sister, Cassie, called during dinner, obviously needing boyfriend advice. He took the call. His manner with her was protective and sweet, and it made him all the more endearing.

His best friend Mark started the software company he worked for, but he seemed reluctant to say much else.

"I think Mark was probably very smart to have hired you," Jade told him. "I'll bet you're the best salesman in the company." He blushed at the compliment. So he was modest, too. *Refreshing,* she thought.

Despite the earlier discussion, they ate their meal at a slow pace, exchanging bites like a couple who'd been together for ages. Jade had never had so much fun on a first date. And he seemed totally relaxed and into her. That phrasing in her thoughts caused her nipples to protrude through the fabric of the camisole.

"Are you cold?" Kai asked.

Their eyes met and she gave him a look that told him she knew where his had been. His face burned a slow red. They laughed together at this turn-of-the-tables while he paid the check.

"How about a stroll on the beach?"

He surely read her mind. A beautiful sliver moon begged to be observed from a stretch of soft sand while wrapped in somebody's arms.

They came out of their shoes at The Strand and ran all the way to the edge of the water. Waves lapped around their ankles as Kai pulled her into a kiss that started out slow, but soon took her breath. She didn't have any more points to add to his Hotness score. Instead, she just relaxed and let his kisses consume her. They traveled around her ear, down her neck, and back up to find her mouth again. She leaned into him and pulled her mouth free to brush her tongue along his neck under his ear. He clenched her tighter and she could feel his hardness growing with every gasp for air.

She glanced around. Why not here? The beach was deserted except for them. The night dark with little moonlight. It would fulfill one of her fantasies. She pulled free, smiling coyly at his look of surprise. Taking his hand, she led him a little farther down the beach to an area even more secluded.

Jade sat down on the sand and pulled him down beside her. Their impassioned kisses helped them quickly figure out where they'd left off. His hand moved to a strap of her top and she slid her arm loose, letting the front fall away to bare her breast.

"You are so beautiful." His whisper fluttered warm against her neck, and she arched and leaned back into the sand, soft and cool. The ocean scent mixed with Kai's cologne, an exotic blend with a primordial edge. He brushed her nipple with his thumb as he stretched out beside her, propping himself on an elbow.

She slid the other strap down her arm then reached out to pull his shirt from the waistband of his trousers. A wave tickled at her toes as his mouth slid down her neck to enclose an achingly erect nipple. She gasped at the sensation and ran her hands under his shirt to feel the ripple of the muscles in her abs. Eyes closed she concentrated on the sensation of touch.

His hand moved along the outside of her thigh and under her skirt to make contact with the strap of her thong. He gave a little tug, and she raised her rear to assist.

Her mouth opened and she gave a little involuntary cry of release, but suddenly, her mouth was full of water. Ack! Sea water! Salty, foamy, gritty sea water.

The shock brought them both to a sitting position, coughing and sputtering, trying to clear their mouths and lungs of the vile liquid.

"Are you okay?" Kai gasped. He was holding her

arm as if he feared another wave might sweep her away.

"I'm fine." She coughed hard and saltwater ran out of her nose. She looked for something to wipe it on, and Kai produced a sopping handkerchief. The sight of the wilted fabric and the clothes now clinging to every part of their bodies sent them into a fit of laughter.

They laughed so hard they rolled in the sand, which made things ever so much worse. They looked as though they'd been washed up from the sea.

Jade finally caught her breath. "Let's rinse off and go back to my place." She took Kai's hand and pulled him into the water, dreading the reaction the additional "cold shower" would have on her plans.

Something floating a few yards out caught her eye. Something small and shimmery and pink. "My Puccis!" she cried.

Kai looked around, bewildered. "You have a dog?"

"Not poochies. Puccis! My shoes!" She dove in and swam toward the tiny object bobbing on the surface of the dark expanse.

The shoe firmly in her hand, she paused to get her bearings. The other one couldn't be too far away. She spotted it on the crest of a wave farther out.

"Don't even think about it." Kai's growl came from directly behind her. "Get back to shore," he ordered. He dove under the waves in the direction of the shoe still on the lam.

Jade swam back to the beach, panting to catch her breath, and watched Kai's body glide effortlessly through the water. As he captured the runaway and made his way back to her, she remembered that last growl. Her heart sank. He'd sounded mad.

He emerged from the water, wet fabric emphasizing each ripple and bulge, a fountain sculpture brought to life. When Jade tasted saltwater, she realized she'd actually licked her lips in appreciation. This was one tasty catch she didn't want to get away.

She pulled herself up straight and thrust out her perky little breasts, nipples all hard and tight against the damp camisole. They'd served her well so far with Kai. *Don't fail me now, girls.*

She took the dripping shoe from his hand and tried for a light giggle, but saltwater dribbled down her throat and she choked. "You mad?" she croaked, sounding like the Sea Hag from Popeye.

Kai's hands were on his hips, making his broad frame even more foreboding. "Yeah." That growl again.

"Oh." Jade sagged her shoulders, putting the perky little breasts 'at ease'.

"But not at you." Kai's hands swept through his hair from the nape up. It stood out all over his head so now the sculpture looked deranged. "I lost my freakin' phone." His hand touched the empty holder on his belt. "Normally, that wouldn't be much of a problem, but I've got to have a phone in Tokyo. I had it all programmed and ready to go."

Jade's fingers curled around the strap of her shoes, anticipating the outcome of this latest development. "What time's your flight?"

"Eight-fifteen. And for an international flight, I need to be there two hours early." He wiped his hand down his face. "Damn! I'll have to take care of it tonight." The frustration in his tone matched the sinking in Jade's stomach.

"Do you know someplace you can get one tonight?" She hoped he'd say no. If he didn't know a place, there was no reason to call things off so quickly.

"Yeah, fortunately."

Jade mentally slapped herself out of the self-pity. Kai needed a phone. If he was truly interested in her, he'd need a phone to call her during his trip. And what was another three weeks? Just more time to let sexual tension build. Hopefully their foreplay hadn't started some countdown sequence to detonation in her clit.

She released the tension in her jaw and forced a smile. "C'mon. Let's get those phone arrangements made." She scooped his shoes out of the sand and looped her arm through his. "Saving my shoes ranks you as my knight in shining armor, you know."

"Sainthood one night, knighthood the next." He loosened his arm from her grip and settled it around her shoulder as they walked. "I might get that 'Hotness' title after another one."

She jabbed her elbow into his ribs, eliciting an 'oof'. "Pryce talks too much. And while what you say may be true, *monsieur*, rest assured it would take a really looonnggggg night."

His deep laugh rumbled against her side. She shivered as a stream of water droplets broke loose from her hair and cascaded down her back. Kai pulled her closer, rubbing her arm with his massive hand. She snuggled against him with a sigh.

Back in her apartment, she offered her phone, but Kai turned it down. "I've got On-Star in the car. I'll get it all taken care of from there." He pulled her close. "Wish I could have taken care of you instead."

The wet clothing warmed as their bodies pressed together, making it even more difficult to think about moving apart. His kisses were long and deep and slow, time after time. If they were anything like his love making, and she suspected they were precisely indicative of it, three weeks would be an agonizing length of time. But she could bear it. Good things were worth waiting for, especially when there wasn't anything to do but wait. She pulled away reluctantly and motioned toward the door with her head. "It's now or never."

On his way out, he paused. "Can I call you?"

"I'll be disappointed if you don't." She blew him a kiss.

His face crinkled into a smile that closed his eyes then she heard his heavy tread on the steps.

Au revoir, Monsieur Kai. Hello, Mr. Vibrator.

****

Kai had Tim on the car phone before he got to the first stop sign. "Tim? Kai. I need your help."

"Yeah? What's up?" No matter what Kai needed, Tim could provide it.

"The Pacific just ate my cell phone, and I'm headed to Japan tomorrow morning early."

"I can do that." Tim seemed unfazed by the request or the time element involved. "Wanna tell me how that happened?"

Kai chuckled. "It's a long story. I'll tell you when I get there."

"So, do you have numbers to program in?"

Kai considered the quickest options for that. "Yeah, but I can download them from my computer."

"No problem then. I'll have the phone ready by the time you get here, provided you won't be here for half an hour or so."

Techtron employees had to be the best in the world to work with. Always ready no matter what he and Mark threw at them. "Thanks, Tim. See you in forty-five minutes."

Kai settled back and tried to relax, but something niggled at the back of his brain. He was forgetting something, but for the life of him, he couldn't imagine what it was.

Oh well, if it was anything too important, somebody at Techtron would be able to take care of it.

Chapter Seven

For the fourth time that day, Kai dialed Stubo's number. He'd have to consider giving the guy a raise.

Between jet lag, overflowing cups of sake, and negotiations as slow as Jack Nicklaus's putts, Kai's head felt the size of a watermelon and about to explode. His concentration during the last ten-hour marathon meeting had been off, and while he tried to blame it on various other things, the truth was he couldn't get the woman off his mind.

"Never should've let this happen," he muttered as he listened for the anticipated ring. "Getting involved with somebody with everything else going on in my life right now."

The rings started. That should have relaxed him some. Instead, each one wound him tighter. "Damn it, Stubo, answer the freakin' phone."

"'Lo?" The voice on the other end was barely audible.

"Stube? Kai."

"Yeah, I figured. It's three in the morning. Who else would be calling me?"

"Any luck?"

"No. Dead ends all the way around. The golf pro's away until Wednesday, and they wouldn't give out his personal number or any names or numbers of members."

"I doubt she's a member anyway. I think her grandmother is, but not Jade personally." Kai washed down the Tylenol he'd been holding with a swig of bottled water. He'd held them so long some of the red had faded onto his hand.

"Either way, I got nothing there. I Googled her name, but nothing came up. No land line evidently or phone line's in somebody else's name. Professionally, probably goes by 'Ms. Crit' or something. Tried checking websites, but there are thousands of online critiquing services—62,000 plus to be exact. I've no way of knowing which one is hers."

"Can't you just contact them all?" This suggestion was met with silence. "What about her parents' law firm?"

"Receptionist wouldn't give me anything. I even explained the entire situation. My guess is your friend had a bad break-up somewhere along the line. Must've had some harassment afterward."

Kai ran his free hand through his hair. "Any luck on the friends?" How could getting one little phone number be this freakin' difficult?

"Bridal registries need at least one last name. Same for chiropractors. Beth and Pryce or Pryce alone aren't getting me anywhere."

"She lives in an apartment above her grandmother's house on The Strand in Manhattan Beach."

"Geez, Kai. I don't like hearing you like this. You're losing it, man. Or else you got it worse for her than I've ever seen you."

"I'll worry about me. You get her number."

"I'm running out of ideas, big guy. It'd sure help if you could just remember her address."

"I told you it's 3820 or 4220...it's something 20." How many 20's could there be on The Strand Manhattan Beach? "Look, if you start at Mangia Bene restaurant, you can walk straight down to The Strand, turn left, and go about two blocks. The house is a three-story stucco. White, or beige, or light green. Something light. She lives in the top floor apartment with a private entrance on the south side. Outside stairs going up to it."

"Kai, get a grip. I'll bet you've just described half the houses in that area."

"It's the best I can do." Kai checked his watch. Another meeting in a little over an hour.

"You're wanting me to go door-to-door to find this woman?"

"For what I'm paying you, you ought to crawl door-to-door if you have to." Okay, he'd definitely give Stubo a raise.

"Well, all I got to say is, this Jade Bartholomew must be one fine piece of a—"

Kai didn't give Stubo a chance to finish his remark. He snapped his phone closed and tossed it on the bedside table. "I have no idea. But my gut says you're right." He stretched out across the bed and massaged his throbbing temples.

A private investigator could get an answer pronto. That thought brought a bitter taste to his mouth, remembering how violated he'd felt when Hazel hired one during the early days of their divorce. She'd gone way too far trying to dig up a reason for more alimony and found nothing. He clambered off the bed, intent on finding some relief from this headache.

The sunken Jacuzzi seemed like just the ticket. He turned the water on and breathed the steam as the tub filled. He didn't like strong-arm tactics, didn't want to be the stereotypical business mogul who made the world adapt to his demands. Hazel couldn't understand that. She wanted attention and fame. He, on the other hand, preferred to remain just a regular guy. But Hazel could never settle for regular in anything.

Wouldn't she love this fiasco—especially if she knew the part she'd played in it? If he hadn't seized on the opportunity to stop her calling, he wouldn't have closed his old phone account, wouldn't have gotten a new number with his new phone. If he hadn't closed out the old account, the phone company wouldn't have reassigned his number to somebody else. And if they hadn't reassigned his number, he could've accessed his account online, looked in the history, and be talking to Jade right now. Instead, the freakin', Homeland Security Act and privacy laws were keeping that from happening. He'd run into the damn privacy laws at the Urgent Care with Jade, too.

Frustrated, he rubbed his head vigorously with both hands. It didn't ease the pain, but it didn't make it any worse either.

Maybe Fate was trying to tell him something. They'd only had three dates. Well, actually only one *official* date. Maybe he was making too big a deal out of this. Maybe Jade hadn't even noticed he hadn't called. Maybe she didn't even care.

"Damn it! Why didn't I enter her number in my computer the day I got it? Then I could get my mind on Japan instead of California." He eased himself into the bubbly froth to let it work its wonders and let his mind drift to the last night with Jade on the beach.

His memory skimmed along those fabulous legs to the flat, tanned stomach that peeked out between her skirt and top. He could still feel the silkiness of her thighs as his hands had moved along them. He hadn't seen her naked, but after the wave's assault her clothing had clung to her body and left little to his imagination. The image was tattooed on his brain, and he had come back to it time after time. She was magnificent. If he were ever lucky enough to have her in his bed, he would explore every inch of her, slowly making his way from one end to the other.

The pain in his head eased some, thanks to

Jade. She was quite a woman. Beautiful and funny and witty and smart and unpretentious about it all. She hardly seemed the type to care about money, was more interested in a guy's Hotness quotient. He chuckled and his neck muscles loosened as he did. According to Pryce, her Hotness scale was all about the guy's character with physical attraction thrown in. Couldn't blame her for that. Something had to draw people together that first time.

One thing was for sure; he wasn't about to listen to Fate. If he and Jade shouldn't date for some reason, he wanted to hear it from Jade herself.

He didn't like to push his weight around, but he would if he had to.

He'd find a way to contact her.

Chapter Eight

Jade checked the clock. 8:20. The long jog and shower had relaxed the rest of her body, but her stomach was still a tight knot. Would eating help or make it worse? She pulled out the toaster. Maybe just one piece to give the juices something to quiet them. She didn't want her stomach letting out one of its notoriously loud growls in the middle of the interview.

Gram's "shave-and-a-haircut" knock sounded on the door. "C'mon in," Jade called, eyeing the bread wrapper. Two pieces, both heels. Hmph. Sort of reminded her of Adam. And maybe Kai Malone.

Gram strolled in holding out a tall glass filled with a gorgeous sherbet-colored concoction. "Smoothie, Chickie-boom?"

"Perfect." Jade held up the near-empty bread wrapper. "You must be psychic."

"Not exactly." Gram winked. "I borrowed bread from you last night and only left the heels."

Jade's hand shook as she took the glass. She had to steady it with the other one. She kept telling herself in five hours this interview would be over.

"Calm down, Chickie." Gram covered Jade's hands with her own. "You're ready for this, and you're gonna do great. Breathe now." Gram took a deep breath and let it out slowly.

Jade obeyed, mimicking the action. As the breath slid out, her stomach let go of some of the tension. The knot wasn't nearly so big now. She nodded to Gram and took a small sip, hoping to avoid a brain freeze. The blended fruit was frosty and thick and refreshing going down. She tried to discern the flavors playing across her tongue. Strawberry, banana, mango with maybe a touch of balsamic vinegar? "Mmm, this is fabulous."

Gram shrugged. "Another of Marvin's specialties. He adds some protein powder, too. Wants to keep his energy up."

Jade waited to let the gulp in her mouth ease down slowly. It was too big, but passed with just a slight tinge of pain at the back of her palate. Marvin again. So he was still around. Horny Marvin. Marvin with the Eveready battery penis. The Eveready battery jack rabbit penis. Gram got great sex, and she got a silent phone. It wouldn't even help to set it on vibrate since no one was calling. *Oooooo. Stop it. Stop this instant! Don't do this. Don't take the frustration out on Gram. None of this was her fault.* Jade forced herself to smile and gave Gram a kiss on the top of her head. "Thanks for the smoothie." Okay, the time had come to give Gram the information she was dying to ask for. "So does Marvin have a grandson he'd like to introduce me to?"

"Still haven't heard from Kai, eh?"

Jade shook her head and took another big gulp in anticipation. That way the angry hiss building inside her could be accounted for by the painful cold in her mouth and not the gut-wrenching rejection. "I tried to call him. I used the number in my phone memory, but it turned out to be an On-Star number, so he must've called me that one time from his car."

More than once, she'd pondered the fact she met Kai the day before she got the call for the interview. Both had been the stuff of dreams. If Kai wasn't interested in her, what did that portend for today's interview?

Well, she would not get upset over a guy she barely knew. He was fun, and nice, and easy to talk to, and had seemed genuinely interested in her. She took another drink, then regretted it, rubbing the back of her head to stop the growing pain there. But he'd left her, excited and hot and wanting him so badly she could scream. He'd left, saying he'd call, but he hadn't bothered to call. And it had been six days, so it probably wasn't going to happen. That was that.

She hadn't had the heart to open the Hotness journal, trying to give him the benefit of the doubt the first three days, making up all kinds of excuses for him. Jet lag. Sixteen hours time difference according to the internet site she checked. Business trip. But the last three days were a different matter.

She'd checked her phone, hoping for a text message or a voicemail she'd missed, mentally deducting a point each time. Twenty-seven so far and still growing.

Today, she had to be at her best and couldn't let preoccupations break her concentration.

But he could've left without saying he was going to call instead of making a big deal out of it. She wasn't some high school girl who was going to be all gah-gah over a guy. She was Ms. Independent. She didn't need Kai Malone. Or any man, for that matter.

The last gulp finished the smoothie. Her stomach was full but knotted again. She took another deep breath.

"Something's wrong, Chickie. He wasn't the kind of guy who'd leave a woman hanging like that. I know men, and he's not the play-it-cool type. Maybe he didn't get a phone."

Jade shrugged and turned to the sink so she wouldn't have to make eye contact. Gram could read her too well. She'd hoped for that very thing, but it seemed unlikely a company would send an employee off to Japan without a means to contact them.

Besides, every hotel room had a phone. Cell phones weren't the only means of communication. She was just being foolish to let herself believe anything except she'd been given the brush-off. But it was the first time it ever happened to her that she was aware of. Damn, it sucked.

She ran the glass under warm water to rinse it, then added a couple of drops of dishwashing liquid and started scrubbing, letting out her frustration.

"Here, gimme that." Gram took the glass from her and rinsed it. "I like for the monogramming to stay on these." She nudged Jade in the side with her elbow.

"I think your radar may be off on this one, Gram. He's probably a jerk in hunk clothing."

"Nope, you're confusing him with the Brat. This guy's the real McCoy." She put on her Mae West voice. "And my radar equipment's fine. I located a blip just last night."

Euwwww. Get her off this subject. "I can't think about men this morning. Gotta focus on landing this job."

"The job's yours. The man's yours." Gram slapped her butt like an athlete and headed out with the clean glass. "Now go get 'em, Chickie-boom." She stopped at the door. "By the way, things are all arranged with Carlton and Simone. An evening of dining and dancing."

"You're the best," Jade called after her.

"I know," came the answer.

Jade had already laid out her ensemble for the day. She slipped out of her robe and into her newest purple bra and thong. She wanted to feel totally put together today and pretty underwear helped. She slathered on some moisturizer with a little bit of bronzing glimmer in it. She couldn't cover her back well and was relieved to hear Gram's special knock again.

Jade stayed behind the door so as not to expose her scantily covered derriere to the outside world and opened it to her back. "Would you get my back for me?" She held the lotion bottle out behind her with one hand as she swept her hair up with the other.

The lotion bottle left her hand, and she heard the obnoxious squirting sound. Then a hand started smoothing the lotion down her back. A hand much too large and warm to belong to Gram! Gasping, she spun around to face whoever it was she'd let in.

"Morning, beautiful. I didn't know you were expecting me." Adam Brock's eyes swept her up and down a few times, and each time his grin widened.

Jade fought an urge to run for her robe. Couldn't let the jackass get the best of her. Best to show him how little effect he had on her now. She remained still, letting him get an eyeful. When he worked his way up to her eyes, she met his gaze coolly. "What are you doing here?" She kept her voice level. No emotion.

"Feasting my eyes on Aphrodite in the flesh."

Jade rolled her eyes and turned around. His quick intake of breath let her know she'd surprised him, and she smiled to herself. She sauntered to her robe, swinging her hips ever so slightly, and slipped into it along with some flip-flops.

Adam had followed and was leaning against the doorframe of her bedroom looking better than ever. Costa Rica agreed with him. A few pounds thinner, lean and sinewy. Unshaven, shaggy blonde hair, cut-offs, tank top—the quintessential "boy-of-summer." The look suited him.

He grinned. "You didn't have to get dressed for me. I've seen you in less, remember?"

"But not lately, and now, not likely. Tell me what you're doing here." Much as she'd like to light into him, she would not allow herself to get riled this morning. She folded her arms across her chest and tapped her foot.

"I came to see you." He shrugged as if it were something he did everyday. "I thought we could talk."

"We don't have anything to talk about." Jade waved him back into the living room and took a stance by the door.

Adam stood there, but made no move to leave. "Then maybe you just need to listen." His eyes locked onto hers. "I was lonely in Costa Rica. I've missed you like hell and I think if you'd be honest with yourself, you've missed me."

"Like hell I've missed you, and that's not Yoda-speak. I don't know what would give you such an idea, but I don't have time for this." Much too snippy. She shouldn't let him get her worked up. He'd win if she did.

"Well, just a week ago, you were out with some Kai guy who didn't even know where you lived. That tells me there's nobody else, and if there's nobody else, there could still be me."

"You always think it's you—about everything." She took his arm and turned him toward the door.

"Jade, listen..."

"Nope, no time. Just send it to me in an e-mail. You're good at those." *Tsk, tsk. Showing weakness. Be adult.*

"Hey, I tried for a week to call you. You blocked my calls."

"You could've come by and broken up with me officially in person."

"I did come by. Twice. Gram met me on the deck both times and said you weren't home."

Jade studied his face. He appeared to be telling the truth—at least his eye contact remained steady. "Well, however it was done, it's done. Now, I have an appointment to get to."

She'd have to talk to Gram about this. It wasn't the first time she'd intruded in Jade's love life. Another reason to get this job and get an apartment of her own.

Adam pushed the screen door open. "I don't think it's done, and I don't think we're done." He turned and gave her a wink. "I'll see you later."

"Yeah, I'll have my people call your people."

She made to slam the storm door, but he caught it by the knob. "That's not acting very neighborly."

Jade clenched her jaw to keep from saying anything. What was he talking about?

Adam gave her that smirk he always reserved for gloating. "Did I forget to mention that I bought the house next door?"

****

Adam pulled the door closed in the middle of her shriek and waited a minute on the landing. *Any second now.* Thump! That would've been the flip-flop she launched at the door in frustration. Same old Jade. He put his hands in his pockets and whistled as he descended the steps. At the bottom, he killed the whistle in mid-toot. A man in a lime green polo was crossing the deck, headed for Jade's staircase. At this time in the morning?

Adam waited, curious. The man stopped right in front of him. The orange monogram on his shirt read Techtron. Malone's company. After Kai's phone call, Adam had done his research. He'd learned a lot by Googling the millionaire software golden boy and his company. From everything he read, Malone was definitely somebody Jade could get caught-up with. Well, he didn't want that kind of competition. He needed Jade fast. Or rather, he needed her money fast. He was in too deep to let some asshole screw it up for him now.

He leaned on the banister, effectively blocking the stairs. "Can I help you?"

The guy pushed his glasses back to the bridge of his nose and eyed him. "I'm looking for Jade Bartholomew. Does she live here?"

"Yeah, but she's indisposed," Adam whispered the word with a wink, "at the moment. Can I help you?"

"Well..." The stranger tightened his lips. "I don't know. Who are you?"

"I'm Adam Brock, her boyfriend. I live here, too."

The young man's eyes grew wide and his Adam's apple bobbed. "Her boyfriend?"

"Yep, that's right. So can I help you?"

The young man shook his head. "No, no I don't think that will be necessary." He started backing away. "I was just, uh, just checking some addresses." He wrote down Adam's name on the notepad he carried. "That's all. Thanks."

Adam chuckled as he watched the young man hightailing across the deck. He'd be reporting that news to Malone any minute. Malone would call, ask why a guy's leaving her apartment early in the morning. At the least, a seed of doubt would be planted. Best case scenario, Malone may even smolder for a few days.

Jade was going to be pissed when she found out, but she'd been pissed at him before. He knew how best to subdue her.

At any rate, he'd bought himself a little bit of precious time.

Feeling very smug, he stuffed his hands in his pockets and whistled all the way to his new home.

Chapter Nine

Stubo chewed his bottom lip, questioning his own sanity with calling Kai. It was one in the morning in Tokyo. But the big guy had ordered him to call as soon as he had Jade's number. Well, technically he didn't have her number, just the news about her living with someone.

"Hello?" Kai's voice was alert. No sound of sleepiness.

"It's Stube. Did I wake you?"

"No, I couldn't sleep." The familiar growl. "Did you get Jade's number?"

"No." He heard Kai's sigh and pushed ahead. "I found her house, though. Just now. Some guy came down the steps. Said his name was Adam Brock."

"Brock? What was he doing there? What time is it?"

Stube could hear the anger in Kai's voice. "A little before nine." The big guy had to know what it meant for a man to be leaving her house this time of the morning. "Said he lived there. With her, Kai."

"Sonofabitch!" Kai exploded into the phone.

Stube held the phone away from his ear until he was sure Kai had finished. "Sorry, big guy."

"This doesn't make any sense. She can't be living with him."

Kai would be running his hand through his hair by now, making it stick out in all directions, making him look like a crack addict. Stube could picture it well. He'd seen him do it often when he was angry or worried or upset. "That's what he said."

"Did you talk to Jade?" Now the voice had an

77

accusatory tone to it.

"No, but..." Talking to Jade hadn't seemed appropriate at the time.

"Okay, Stube, this is what I want you to do." The logical Kai was back in charge. "Order flowers. A big bouquet of calla lilies. Pink. Make sure they're pink. Here's what I want the card to say. Write this down..."

****

Adam sat near the window with his laptop, watching for Jade's car. She'd left that morning dressed to the nines in a business suit and carrying a briefcase. She mentioned an appointment. It all added up to a job interview. If she came home in a good mood, with a smile on her face, he'd be there to congratulate her and help her celebrate. A scowl would indicate news that wasn't so good. That would mean she'd need consoling and a shoulder to cry on.

He could feel her arms around his neck in both scenarios. His arms around her waist, hugging her, holding her, kissing her. God, she looked hot that morning in her purple bra. And when she turned around and showed him her nearly-bare ass with just that purple strip up the middle and across the top, he'd thought he was going to bust his zipper. His erection needed a hammer now to beat it down just imagining her in that outfit.

She'd been toying with him. Teasing him. A good sign. She obviously wanted him to still want her. It didn't take much imagination to conclude she still wanted him. She had him in her cell phone all this time. Wasn't involved with anyone else...yet. Pranced around in front of him half-naked in provocative underwear. Oh, yeah. She was definitely still into him.

And why shouldn't she be? They'd always been perfect for each other...until the Costa Rica thing came up. Man, what a mess that was. And it still wasn't over. His throat constricted at the thought of the debt he owed for the failed land development and now this house.

But Jade was loaded, or would be when the old bitch next door died. How much longer could Damn Gram last? Two or three years? Didn't matter. They all gave Jade whatever she wanted. If she wanted money, say to bail his ass out of the failed plan, they'd give it to her.

So the project-at-hand was to win Jade over again. A "piece-of-cake piece-of-ass." He snickered at his humor.

Oh, he and Jade had had their ins and outs. All couples did. But he always managed to get her to see things his way. This time wouldn't be any different. Before the week was out, he'd have her panting like…like that hot chick on his favorite porn site. He tapped the mouse to bring up the video of the dark-haired beauty with the humongous breasts, sprawled across the hood of the Ferrari, fondling herself. He unzipped his pants. Relief was just a…few…seconds…away.

He tossed the wad of tissues into the trash just as a van pulled up in the alley behind Jade's. "Bloomers." He read the sign on the side. Shit! Somebody was sending her flowers. If it was Malone, he had to head him off at the pass.

Adam zipped his pants and sprinted out the door and across Jade's deck, checking to make sure Gram was nowhere around. Wouldn't do to let the old bitch see him. She was always so suspicious of everything he did.

Gram didn't appear to be home. He slipped his hands into his pockets and let out a nonchalant whistle as he rounded the corner by the stairs leading to Jade's apartment.

He met the delivery girl at the bottom of the steps. Cute. A tiny blonde. Early twenties. In low-slung cut-offs and a v-neck tee shirt two sizes too small that read "Feelin' lucky?" She carried an enormous bouquet of cut flowers.

"Hey. Let me help you with that." Adam took the flowers from her and put on his most concerned look, eyebrows drawn in, bottom lip puckered slightly. "You're too tiny to handle this."

"Thanks." Her eyes traveled down his torso and back up, and she cocked her head. "But, I can handle big things very well, I assure you."

Adam grinned. This gal didn't waste any time. "Well, maybe I'll need something big handled sometime soon. Where you going with this?"

"Jade Bartholomew's. This address." She nodded to the door at the top of the steps.

"Well, I'm, uh, Jade's neighbor. And uh, her best friend. I was headed to her place. Want me to take them?"

"That'd be great. Thanks."

"I'm Adam Brock, by the way." He held the vase in the crook of his arm and extended his hand. The corner of one of the flowers gouged him in the eye. "Ow!" He swatted at the offending blossom.

"Careful. I don't want to have to re-do that arrangement." She stepped nearer him, pushing her breasts against the side exposed by his raised arm. "Here, let me see." She stretched his eye open with two fingers and examined it closely. "Look up." Adam obeyed. "Look down." Her position gave him an unobstructed view of her most-probably-surgically-enhanced cleavage, and he no longer needed her fingers to keep his eye stretched. "You're fine. It's not cut or anything, Adam Brock."

"I'm glad." Adam kept his eyes riveted to her chest as he spoke. "I'd hate to miss any of this glorious scenery."

"My name's Dori Lane." She reached into her pocket. "And here's my card with my number. If you ever need anything…" She headed back to the van, tossing him a wink over her shoulder.

Adam stuck the card in his back pocket. If things didn't move as quickly with Jade as he planned, he might just have to take advantage of that offer. Whacking off to the porn site was getting a little old.

He waited until the van was out of sight, then he sat down on the bottom step and pulled the small envelope out of the flowers.

"'Lost your number with my phone,'" he read. "'Miss you and would love to hear your voice. Call me and leave your number. 213-555-6752. Kai.' Awwww, how touching."

He returned the card to the envelope and threw away the plastic stick that held it.

He slid the envelope into his back pocket with the other card Ms. über-breasted Dori Lane had given him.

Hot-shot Malone no longer had Jade's number. This was a very interesting twist. Why was he sending people to her house rather than coming himself? Out-of-town maybe?

Oh, this was too good to even be believable. Like Jade was being handed to him. A gift. All tied up with purple ribbons.

Adam needed relief again. Very soon.

Chapter Ten

Jade walked as fast as her feet would allow in those damn needle-toe shoes. If she didn't get to the car soon, she might just fling them off and break into a happy dance right there in the parking lot. The interview had gone even better than she hoped.

She unlocked the door and grabbed her phone from the console. Two voicemails. Maybe one was from Kai. She punched in her code and waited, kicking the shoes to the floorboard of the passenger side.

"Hey." Beth's voice. "Just wanted to know how it went. I'll be in meetings all afternoon, but I'll call you as soon as I get free." She cleared that one and went on to the next message.

"Wanted to be the first to congratulate you, Chickie." Gram, always one step ahead of the game.

Jade would not let herself be dejected that neither call was from Kai. These people cared about her even if he didn't. She pulled out of the parking lot as she dialed Gram's number. When she heard the click, she didn't even wait for a hello. "Nothing definite yet, but definitely promising."

"With the man or the job?"

"The job. The man's still AWOL."

"So when do you start?"

"Well, they haven't offered it to me yet. He said they're in a transition right now. A new head-honcho starts July first. But he said I should hear from him in a few days."

"Sounds good, doll."

"Yeah, I think so, too. The interview went well."

She paused debating whether or not to tell the other news. Better from her than somebody else. "Gram, you're not gonna believe who our new next-door neighbor is."

"Is it somebody fabulous like Humphrey Bogart or Gregory Peck?"

The excitement in her voice made Jade giggle. "I hope not. They're dead, you know."

"It's Tom Selleck, isn't it? I knew he couldn't stay away."

"Actually, it's Adam."

A long pause. "You're birdturdin' me."

"Would I birdturd you about something like that? It's Adam. He bought the Langston house."

"So he's trying to get you back, is he?" Ever Gram. Straight to the heart of the matter. "The self-absorbed little sonofabitch."

Was what he'd said this morning about Gram's interference true? "He said he came by to see me twice before he left for Costa Rica and both times you told him I wasn't home."

"You weren't. You were at Beth's."

That was true. She'd felt frustrated, depressed, elated, free, and a little scared of being free again after two years of monogamy. Going to Beth's for a few days gave her some brooding time away from Gram's all-too-logical analysis. "But you didn't ever tell me he came by."

"You didn't ever ask. The second time, I caught him snooping around trying to see if I was lying about you being home. Whooooeeee, I was on him like ugly on an ape. Ran his ass off for good, or so I thought."

"Gram, listen to me." The tone of her last sentence left no doubt Gram was gearing up for battle and needed to calm down. "You don't have to fight this for me. I've no intentions of letting him in my apartment or my life."

"Yeah, well, the road to hell is paved with girls who swore they'd never again put out for their exes."

"Speaking of the road to hell, I'm at the 405. I'd better get off so I can concentrate."

"I don't have to concentrate so much any more to get off."

"Gram, you're sick." Jade switched lanes and cut off a woman in a blue Mercedes. "I'll see you when I get home."

"I'm shopping now, Chickie-boom, and I'm staying at Marvin's tonight. But I'll see you tomorrow. Stay clear of the Brat, you hear? Don't go getting horny and stupid."

"Back atcha. Bye."

Merging onto the highway, she should have been concentrating on her driving or at least the interview. Instead, the conversation turned her thoughts to Adam. Gram was right. She needed to steer clear of him as much as possible. He had a way of sensing her vulnerability, and she was feeling plenty vulnerable right now, still smarting from the sting of Kai Malone's rejection.

She couldn't beat Adam at his game. Like this morning. She'd had the upper hand for a time, but he'd won the battle with his parting announcement. He was quick to assess every situation and always managed to work it to his advantage. He was especially good at it when it involved sex.

He lived and breathed sex. It was his raison d'être. He went to great lengths—or heights, like in the hot-air balloon—to play out fantasies. Without a doubt, he made her feel like the sexiest woman alive. In bed.

And she couldn't deny a soft spot for him was still there in a nurturing sort of way. He'd had a tough life—losing his parents at seventeen in that plane crash. He'd had to grow up fast in some respects but had completely stalled in others, like giving and taking. And compromising. That word wasn't in his vocabulary.

She understood him better than other people, though. She'd seen his guard down. She knew the over-confident mask he wore covered a host of insecurities. But she wasn't up to filling the gaps any more. There was somebody out there who would think he was fabulous; it just wasn't her. Somebody he wouldn't have to lie to in order to get his way.

And His Hotness was out there somewhere, too. He would see through her stubbornness, think she was perfect. She remembered Kai's words at the bar that first night: "You sound perfect." Though she'd tried to convince herself otherwise, she hadn't completely given up on Kai Malone yet. She re-lived their three evenings together the rest of the way home.

Pulling into the alley behind their row of houses, Jade scrutinized Adam's new home—geez, that was going to take some getting used to—before pulling into her garage. There was no movement next door, no sign he was home, and she let out a sigh of relief as she retrieved her shoes. She'd had this nagging feeling he would be watching for her.

Coming around the corner of the house, she met Adam at the bottom of her staircase. He held a stunning bouquet of pink calla lilies. A lump rose in her throat. Had he really remembered her favorite flowers? He'd rarely bought them for her before.

Adam peeked coyly over the top of the huge display and then held it out to her. "These are for you."

Jade was stunned, suspicious of the unexpected gift. "You got me flowers? Why?"

"You said you had an appointment and from the way you're dressed," his eyes roamed over her appreciatively, "I assumed it was a job interview. If you got it, these would be for congratulations. If you didn't, they're to cheer you up."

"Thanks. That was sweet of you." Jade reached out to take them, but he pulled them back.

"They're kind of heavy. I'll carry them up for you, if that's all right."

Jade had her hands full with shoes, purse, and briefcase. "Okay. Sure." So much for keeping him out of the apartment.

He followed her up the stairs, and she made a definite effort this time not to swing her hips although she could feel his eyes on her derriere.

Once inside, she dropped everything else on the chair and took the flowers. "I can't believe you did this. You were never much of a flower person before." She'd have to add a few points to his journal page for this.

"Well, anything to score points on your Hotness Scale."

Jade turned away quickly to cover her shock that he'd seemingly read her mind. She placed the flowers in the middle of the dining table and stepped back to admire them—right into Adam's arms.

Pulling her tight against him from behind, he nuzzled her neck. "I've missed you, Jade."

The warm breath on her neck made her shiver and her nipples tighten. What was with that? It'd been so long that now her nipples were spring-loaded? Thank God she was wearing a suit.

"I've missed your face." He started down the outside of her ear with a line of kisses. "I've missed your smile. I've...missed...your...voice."

No. Don't let this happen. Jade pried the clasped hands loose from around her waist and turned to face him. The table was against her back, so she couldn't retreat any farther. Bodies still touching, she read the hope in his eyes and shook her head quickly. "Don't Adam. We can't. I can't."

"Yes, we can. Yes, you can."

He made to put his arms around her again, but she put her hand against his chest and moved him back, giving her room to sidestep away. "You're right. I can." She met his gaze and held it. "I don't want to. I don't want to be involved with you again." He opened his mouth to speak, but she wasn't finished yet. "We're not good for each other. We're only good in bed and that's not enough to build a relationship on."

"It's a start." He gave her a lazy grin.

"No, it's not. That's where we started last time, and we never got beyond it."

"And I've never gotten beyond you. I think about you, and dream about you, and fantasize about you."

A knot of over-vulnerability formed in her throat at his words. She went to the fridge and grabbed a bottle of water to wash it away. Kai's rejection still stung, and she was in bad need of a pacifier. But she wouldn't be sucking on Adam—figuratively or literally.

"I love you, Jade." His voice was little above a whisper.

Jade shook her head. "No you don't. You just want to love me."

Adam shoved his hands into his pockets. "I've changed. The old me would've stood here and argued." He strolled to the door then turned back to face her. "The new me is gonna give you time to think." He nodded toward her bedroom and gave her a wink. "Now, go add my points to your book."

She heard his whistle as he went down the stairs, and she waited for his steps to come back up. No sound.

He'd be back. He never gave up this easily.

Still no sound.

She stopped by the door on the way to the bedroom and peeped out. No sign of him. He was actually gone. She shook her head in amazement.

It was silly to believe he'd really changed, wasn't it? Jade took off the skirt and jacket and hung them carefully back in the suit bag. Nobody changed that much in nine months. She put the shoes back in the box on the shelf. He was just good at conning people, and he was trying to con her now. She slipped into some shorts and a tee and sat down at the desk.

Wasn't he?

The Hotness journal lay on the corner of the desk. She hesitated, then reached for it and flipped to the last entry: Kai Malone. She held the corner to tear the page out but decided against it. She could wait a couple of more weeks. Once she was sure he was home from Japan, if he still hadn't made any attempt to call her, she'd rip him out. Maybe. She might leave him in as a reminder of what it felt like to be rejected by someone she was totally into. Definitely a learning experience.

Turning back two pages, she added three notations under Adam's name. Still a smart-ass -5. Flowers +3. Changed + ?.

We'll see.

Chapter Eleven

For once, Kai Malone was at a loss for a good idea. He ran his hand through his hair to try and stimulate some creative brain cells. Jade would have gotten the flowers four days ago, and he still hadn't heard from her. Surely Stubo couldn't have been right. It didn't make sense that she and Adam Brock were living together when she couldn't stand to mention the guy just a few days before. Unless that had just been an act for his benefit...unless she was a gold digger, after anybody who might take care of her.

Kai had known fickle women before, but this went way beyond fickle. This went to...to absurdly fickle or...or absurd lengths of fickleness...or too much fickle.

He could almost hear Hazel laughing at his inept vocabulary. He sighed in frustration. The woman he wanted to call wouldn't, and the woman he didn't want to call had called constantly for years.

Why couldn't relationships be like business transactions? Why couldn't the terms be worked out beforehand and negotiated? Start with everything on the table and work toward a compromise everybody could live with and be happy. Of course, he hadn't exactly started out with everything on the table.

And Jade had come across so honest and open, but hadn't been honest with him about living above Gram. Other women had seemed totally sincere, at first, and then had become more enamored with his position in the boardroom than in the bedroom.

This Jade/Adam Brock thing was just further

confirmation he needed to keep his guard up. Damn it! Something wasn't right here. Something just didn't ring true.

But he'd put Stube through enough on this matter. He needed to give it some thought and come up with another plan. He rubbed his head harder, this time with both hands.

It might just have to wait until he got home. The thought of two or two-and-a-half more weeks in this limbo seemed like an eternity.

And the negotiations. He sighed. Most of the sticking points were small ones. They were asking for a consultant for a year, either him or Mark. Neither he nor his partner had anticipated that one, though it made perfect sense.

His phone rang. He snatched it up, hoping Jade was on the other end, and he could get the nonsense cleared up one way or another.

"Kai." It was Mark. The disappointment at not hearing Jade's voice vanished completely, replaced by an over-whelming sense of excitement. Could Mark and Jilli have made a decision so quickly? Kai held his breath. "We've decided to do it."

Kai's breath gushed out in an explosive sigh. "Are you sure? Are you positive about this? It's going to be a big change."

"Yes, we're sure. Jilli's all excited about it. Says she's always wanted to live in a foreign country. We've been reading up on Japan, and we talked to a neighbor from Kyoto..." Mark's words tumbled out. Kai could hear Jilli in the background, prompting him.

"What about the family plans?" Since the miscarriage, Jilli had been wanting to get pregnant again. That was what...two years ago? The time to try again would be about right. And Mark *had* volunteered for the consulting position. And it *did* mean nearly an extra million in salary for a year in addition to the sale.

"It's only for a year. We can wait that long. Her biological clock's not gonna run out in that length of time. Hell, with the money this means, we'll buy her a new biological clock." Kai could hear Jilli's near-hysterical laughter in the background.

"Mark, you're not going to regret this. This is going to cinch the deal. It's going to make it happen!" Kai paced the floor, trying to work off the excess energy that threatened to make his voice shake. "I'm calling a meeting for this afternoon." He needed one last confirmation. "You're sure? You and Jilli are positive?"

"Absolutely. Call the meeting and tell 'em I'm their man."

Kai spotted the bottle of Dom Pérignon in the wine cooler of the suite's built in bar. "Hey. Go buy a bottle of expensive champagne, and, what-the-hell, take tomorrow off."

"Already done, and already done." A loud pop sounded from the other end almost simultaneous with a squeal from Jilli. "Here's to us and future ventures." A clink against the phone. "And many more Memorial Days to remember."

Chapter Twelve

Jade's hands flew through the motions of typing
the edits to the memoir, but her mind wasn't on the
project. She couldn't keep from wondering what
Adam had up his sleeve. Since last Wednesday, he'd
been true to his word, not bothering her, leaving her
alone, except for the presents she'd found outside her
door every day. Thursday, there had been a giant
box of Godiva chocolate truffles. Friday, a Starbucks
grande latte and warm bagel with cream cheese
were waiting as soon as she returned from her run.
Saturday, a gift certificate to Daysprings Spa
appeared tacked to her door. And yesterday, a
basket with special edition DVD's of several of her
favorite movies arrived with boxes of Junior Mints
and gourmet popcorn.

And all had been accompanied with small tags
that simply read, Love Adam. The absence of a
comma made Jade wonder at the message.

A sharp knock at the door startled her, making
her miss a key. Probably another one of Adam's
surprises. She'd have to tell him to stop—again. Not
that it would do any good because it hadn't yet.

She opened the door to find a small ivory
envelope pinned to her screen door. It looked like
some kind of invitation. The card inside was of heavy
stock with an embossed B at its center. She
recognized Adam's tiny, distinct handwriting.

*Jade, it's Memorial Day. I have something
special to do—something I should have done long
ago. I'd rather not do it alone. If you can spare some
time, let me know. Thanks, Adam.*

The serious tone aroused her curiosity. And the fact that he said "thanks" not "love" this time. What could be so important, and why wouldn't he want to be alone? Probably just a ploy to get her somewhere romantic and sentimental. The thought made her angry. Did he really think she was that easy? She laced up her shoes, planning the most effective way of telling him to lay off.

Crossing the deck, she couldn't keep from noticing the large bouquet sitting on the table on Adam's patio. So that was it. More flowers. She sighed in exasperation.

Adam must have been watching. He came out to meet her, opening his gate in welcome. "Thanks, Jade." She opened her mouth to tell him she didn't have time for any of his games, but he kept talking. "I knew I could count on you. In addition to everything else you are to me, above all, you're a friend."

Jade noticed the red, puffy look to his eyes. Had he been crying? She was confused. "What's this about?"

Adam closed the gate behind her and motioned to the flowers. "I want to go put these on my parents' grave. I haven't been to the cemetery since the day we buried them, and I feel so guilty." He started to cry, little gasps at first. "The plane crash happened ten years ago yesterday." The gasps eventually built into long, pitiful heart-wrenching sobs.

This reaction was so unlike Adam. She'd never seen him cry before. Her heart ached as she imagined what he must be feeling. My God. He really was different. She folded him into her arms and hugged him tight. Warm tears dripped onto her shoulder. She realized the ones falling on his shoulder were her own. "Of course, I'll go with you." She stroked the back of his head, feeling the quivering of his body start to subside. "You shouldn't be alone at a time like this."

Adam pulled loose from her grasp and wiped his eyes on the bottom of his shirt. He took a couple of deep breaths that helped him regain his composure. "It's a four hour drive up there, so it's gonna mean making a day of it."

"It's okay. I didn't have any plans." She gave him what she hoped was a reassuring smile. "Can I have half an hour to shower and change?"

He nodded.

Jade swept away a last tear making its way down his cheek, then kissed him lightly. "Be right back." She hurried, not wanting him to have to wait on her. She wasn't looking forward to the task, but it made her warm inside that she could be there when somebody needed her like this.

Adam watched until she disappeared up her steps. So far so good. If she remembered his parents' bodies had been cremated and their ashes scattered on the Pacific, he'd have to wing it, but everything else was set: restaurant, B&B...hell, even the weather was cooperating.

He went inside for one last look. The computer screen still displayed the map to the cemetery he'd chosen. He went over the directions a couple of more times, committing them to memory. A screw-up there wouldn't be a big deal, probably. Hell, it'd been ten years. But, if he couldn't find it, he'd lose the whole special effect.

He hurried to throw a bag of clean workout clothes in the trunk of the car. He would, of course, be a model of propriety, giving her the clean tee. If all went as planned, he'd have her naked in twelve hours. Or sooner.

He imagined her in the tee shirt, nothing on underneath, pressing against him. He'd slide his hand up the back and circle that hot ass of hers. Then back down between the cheeks, fingers easing gently between her legs. She'd moan—just like that chick on the website, throwing her head back and arching her...

"It's going to be okay." The hand on his shoulder startled him. Adam wheeled around to find Jade's eyes filled with pity and support.

This was going to be too easy.

He fought back a smile, choosing instead a long, slow, dramatic sigh. Jade was just too softhearted for her own good. She'd be back in his bed before she ever knew what hit her.

"Don't forget the flowers."

He nodded and opened the passenger door for her, even offering his hand to help her in. Her gaze questioned if these changes were for real. He still didn't smile or speak. Too emotional, of course. But he winked as he touched the back of his fingers to her cheek, then shut the door, hoping she didn't notice his raging hard-on.

Adam situated the flowers carefully behind her seat. The new 'Vette didn't allow much room. He hoped the front seat offered enough protection for the flowers with the top down. This was definitely a topless day.

Neither of them said anything for a while. He wanted to appear deep into his emotions and she apparently sensed that, leaving him to his thoughts. He put on the *I Am Sam* soundtrack, one of her favorites, and listened to her sing along.

She finally broke the conversational silence. "Where are we going exactly? I mean I know to the cemetery, but where is it?"

"About four hours north along the coast. The cemetery's called Greenmont. Overlooks the ocean. Not too far from Carmel."

"Why there? For your parents, I mean. Did they...um...choose that place? They both grew up in Malibu, didn't they?"

Shit! He hadn't anticipated that one. He'd been too worried about the cremation thing. Time to ad lib. "Yeah, well, they loved it up there. Spent a lot of time there when they were dating. Honeymooned in Carmel and, uh, they talked about retiring in that area. Don't think they realized retirement was going to be so permanent."

"So they'd already bought a plot?"

Was she just making conversation or had he piqued her curiosity? He needed to get her off the subject before she became too inquisitive. "No. Gerald, my godfather, suggested the place and made all the arrangements. I was too young to..." he made his voice break, then cleared his throat, "know what to do."

Jade patted his leg affectionately. "Sorry."

The heat from her hand crawled up his thigh and settled in his balls. He laid his hand on hers and fought the urge to pull it up to his crotch. That wouldn't do. He had to stay true to the plan. Instead, he lifted her hand to his lips and kissed it. "I'm glad you're here."

Jade squirmed and tugged at the skirt inching its way up those glorious thighs when it came to him: he had her out of her comfort zone with that comment. That was good. He didn't want her anticipating. Wanted to keep her guessing. The new Adam was full of surprises. Good ones. She fidgeted some more, adjusting her sunglasses and applying lip-gloss.

Adam turned the CD up a notch, distracting himself from the thought of how those lips would feel sliding up and down his cock.

"So, you haven't said anything about Costa Rica. How was it?"

"It was paradise." That was an exaggeration, but it had been pretty good for a few months until Lia's husband came home and caught them in the act.

Being chased naked through the condominium complex by a butcher-knife wielding husband threatening to cut his balls off and cram them down his throat had been motivation enough to make Adam consider moving back to California. Memories of Jade—or mostly memories of her money—had convinced him Manhattan Beach was where he wanted to settle for now while he worked to get the creditors off his back.

"So why'd you come back?"

Adam took a few seconds to formulate his answer. Obviously, it couldn't be the whole truth. Couldn't be overly sappy either. A little truth, a little innuendo, something she would remember to chronicle in her journal. He kept his eyes on the road. "Because what I want most out of life is right here." *Good one, man. A definite leg-spreader.*

They made small talk after that. He filled her in on his mortgage brokering business, and she told him all about the job she was pursuing and the interview. They watched the surf and caught up on nine months of news.

He slowed the car as they approached Carmel, relaxing at the turn onto High Ridge Road. He appeared to know exactly where he was going. They followed the curves, one hairpin after another, to Greenmont Drive and the edge of the cemetery.

The place was beautiful and serene—just like the website promised—and held an "eternally blissful view of the Pacific." He scanned the tombstones. Near the edge of the cliff, its green obelisk catching the rays of the afternoon sun, he found the one most suited to his purpose. Large enough to be imposing, far enough for the name to be obscured by the distance away and the sun's glare. He turned to Jade and kept his voice solemn. "Do you mind waiting here?"

She took his hand and squeezed it. "No, I don't

mind. But wouldn't you rather I go with you?" She took off her sunglasses to make direct eye contact, showing him how sincere she was in her support.

He pulled away and got out of the car, carefully maneuvering the flowers from the back and turning reverently toward the monument. "No. I need to do this alone. I won't be long." *Dramatic flair, don't fail me now.*

He started toward the obelisk at a rather fast pace then decided that looked like he was in too big a hurry to get things over with. He slowed his gait as he neared it, feeling her gaze on him.

He suppressed a laugh when he read the engraved name: Hassle. Boy, no shit. An eight-hour round-trip ride and all the planning and timing to make this work. The word hassle summed it up perfectly. He allowed himself a few shakes of the head as he placed the flowers in front of the grave.

He walked around the stone and brushed a few pieces of debris off the plot although it was obviously well-kept. Then he chose to stop and ponder it from just the right angle so that he could really watch Jade. She might decide to join him after all. If she got out of the car, he'd have to make a quick getaway, too over-wrought by emotion to stay any longer.

He stood for ten minutes or so, finally working up a few genuine tears by thinking about his parents' funeral. He wouldn't dwell on it long. Just long enough to streak his face a little and get a bit of puffiness to his eyes.

Satisfied at last, he sauntered back to the car and met Jade's anxious gaze with a half-smile. He slid into the seat and patted her leg affectionately. "I'm okay," he assured her and watched her shoulders relax as she let out a long sigh and brushed away a tear of her own. "I'm getting hungry. You?"

She nodded, digging through her purse and locating a tissue.

Part Two of plan engaged. "Let's go check out the places in Carmel."

****

As they strolled along the beach, Adam was struck by Jade's mellow mood. He'd never seen her so ... docile. She agreed with everything he said, complied with whatever he wanted to do. He considered abandoning the plan and suggesting they get a hotel room for a quickie. *Naw. Gotta think new Adam. She's got to think it's her idea.*

She sneezed a few times and, at last, made a suggestion of her own. "Let's go find a place and get something to drink. I need to take an allergy pill." Her nose was obviously stuffy from the nasal sound of her words.

Adam guided her up Ocean Avenue, then detoured down Delores Street, hoping she'd be enchanted by the cozy bed & breakfasts of the area.

He wasn't disappointed.

"This place is dreamy." She sighed. "So romantic."

Adam called her attention to the cottage surrounded by the English country garden and the white picket fence. He smugly and silently fingered the piece of paper in his pocket that had tonight's reservation number written on it. "Yeah. Made for lovers," he agreed. "Oooh. I see a restaurant sign over there. How does Italian sound?" Another of her weaknesses he knew.

"Fantastic." She nodded enthusiastically. Unlike most women he'd been around, Jade was always ready to eat and never seemed to gain a pound. He wanted to think about the ways he was going to work that pasta off her hips tonight, but he couldn't take the chance...yet.

It was barely after six o'clock, still too early for

the dinner crowd, so getting a table was no problem. Adam requested something cozy and intimate, near the back. If the weather website was right, he didn't want her near the window. And the damn thing better be right. All his plans for the rest of tonight hinged on it.

Jade needed to take her pill, so they ordered some Pellegrino water in addition to a bottle of chardonnay. While she eyed the menu, Adam had the chance he needed to wrap up a minor detail. "Know what?" He pursed his lips in a thoughtful manner. "I'm afraid I left the car in a one hour parking zone. I'd better go get it."

Jade looked up from the menu and frowned. "I don't remember seeing any signs."

"I'm not sure, but something keeps nagging at me. There're parking places all around here. I think I'd rather play it safe."

"You want to order first?"

"No. Just get me whatever you're having. I'll be back in a few minutes." He shrugged into his jacket and left before she had time to ask any more questions.

Adam found the car and moved it to within a block of the restaurant. It needed to be close, but not too close. When he returned, he found Jade sipping on her wine.

"I probably shouldn't be drinking this." She pushed her hair behind an ear on one side. "I took that pill, and the combination might make me goofy."

"Goofy is good sometimes," Adam assured her. "And one thing we both should have learned from today's experience…" he took a sip from the glass she had poured him, "is that life is way too short. We gotta grab it while we can."

Thus he started in on the mental list of all the conversational topics he planned earlier. The objective was to keep her engaged through all of the courses, and not let her notice what was happening outside. He, on the other hand, kept one eye on the front windows. When the light outside started dimming earlier than it should have, he relaxed and ordered cannoli and a glass of port for them both.

He asked the waiter for the check, then looked toward the front and feigned surprise. "God, it's dark out there." He checked his watch. "It shouldn't be that dark this early."

Jade turned in her seat, and her eyes grew wide at the sight. "It's foggy!"

The waiter returned with the check just in time to hear Jade's comment. "Yeah, it's weird how it sets in early sometimes. Gets thick real fast. You just never know."

"We better get outta here fast." Adam put his credit card back in his wallet, and dropped two bills on the table—a hundred and a fifty. "That should do it. We don't have time to wait. Keep the change."

The waiter's eyes bulged at the huge tip. "Thank you," he called after them, as they made their way to the door.

They stepped out into a world of gray. The streetlight was a hazy ball of yellow and only the cars right in front of the restaurant were distinguishable. The ones across the street were merely vague blobs.

Adam took Jade's elbow and guided her down the street. She leaned close into him as if she were afraid she'd lose him if they got too far apart. His silver car blended into the fog, and he didn't see it until they got right on it. Jade's quick intake of breath told him she was worried. He helped her into her side, then went around to his, making a point of dramatically adjusting his seatbelt. When the headlamps hit the fog, it was instant blindness.

"Adam, we can't do this." Jade's voice was tight.

"We can't drive home in this."

Adam eased the car out of the parking place and started down the street, barely touching the accelerator. "It's not like we have much choice." His timing needed to be perfect.

"Yes we do. We can stay here some place. Both of us work at home. It's not like we have to be somewhere early tomorrow."

Adam took his foot off the accelerator, letting the car move at idle speed. "Spend the night here?" He kept his eyes glued to the street.

"Yeah. Why not? Let's find a place and just stay here. Please?"

Her pitiful little whine came at just the right point. He eased the car into a turn that just happened to be the driveway of the cottage B&B they'd admired earlier. He pulled up close to the front door and put the car into park with an exaggerated sigh. "I'll see if they have anything available, but don't get your hopes up."

Once inside, a cheerful English gentleman greeted him. "So glad you made it Mr. Brock. I should have warned you this morning of the possibility of the fog."

"It was no problem," Adam assured him. "We've actually been here for several hours, so we beat the fog."

"Very good. Cottage number seven is waiting for you then." He handed Adam the key. "Breakfast is from seven to ten, either in the courtyard or brought to your cottage. Just ring down in the morning to let us know which you prefer. And enjoy your stay."

Adam winked. "Oh, I intend to."

Chapter Thirteen

"Glad my workout clothes were in the car." Adam held up the gym bag proudly as he worked the key into the lock.

Jade wrinkled her nose. "Euwwww."

"No euwwww. I just washed 'em." He pushed the door open with a foot, revealing a stylishly comfortable living room of over-stuffed couches and chairs.

"Nice." Jade turned on the nearest lamp and looked around approvingly. "Not a bad place to get stranded." She wandered around, turning on more lamps, then disappeared into one of the bedrooms at the back.

Adam went straight to the gas fireplace, and soon the chill of the night dissipated into a warm coziness. He uncorked the bottle of cabernet he'd asked the manager to have waiting, and held out a glass to Jade when she joined him. "Classy place. Excellent complementary wine."

She hesitated. "I probably shouldn't. My lips are feeling a little numb."

"Maybe I can help you get the feeling back into them." Damn! Wrong thing to say. Nothing sexual yet. He watched her eyes narrow suspiciously. Mayday! He had to do something. Quick! Reaching out, he puckered her bottom lip between his thumb and forefinger, and wiggled it gently. "A good lip massage is what you need." He alternated from top lip to bottom a couple of times before Jade surrendered to laughter and took the glass out of his hand. Whew! Crisis averted.

Jade covered a yawn and settled into one of the chairs before the fireplace, propping her feet on the footstool, stretching out those long, gorgeous legs.

Adam would have much preferred the couch where they would have been within touching distance, but he hid his disappointment and got comfortable in the adjacent chair. He needed to soften her up before bedtime, maybe remind her of why they'd made the trip today. "How are your parents?" he asked. "I don't think I've even asked you about them since I've been back." Jack and Linda had never cared for him very much, but they'd been more diplomatic than Gram and always cordial.

"They're in Provence right now with Mimi, but they'll be back next week for the wedding."

Adam sipped his wine, waiting for her to say something about his parents, running the plan through his mind again. When she did, he'd start to cry, softly of course. She'd come over to console him. If he took up the room on his footstool with his legs, she'd have to sit on his lap to hug him. He did a quick mental calculation. From there, five minutes to get her top and bra off? Maybe slower, she liked foreplay...

"Whoa. I'm getting soooo sleepy." She didn't even try to stifle the yawn this time, but gave her head a shake. "Pryce says you're coming to the wedding with Caitlyn Treece."

Damn. She changed the subject from her parents. Okay, he'd have to go with this one for a few minutes, then ease back to parents. "Yeah. I ran into Caitlyn at a party. She was in a panic 'cause she didn't have a date. Practically begged me to go."

Jade's throaty chuckle caused him to grip his wine glass a bit tighter. "I'm sure you'll be nicely rewarded for your gallant behavior."

In their crowd, Caitlyn had always been known as Easy One, and she bore the nickname proudly.

He'd have a good time with Caitlyn that night. Find a dark corner somewhere or maybe his car, then get her mad so he could go home with Jade.

He stood up and stretched, spying the remaining half bottle of wine on the table by the window. He poured himself another glass, swirling the garnet liquid, breathing the dark, fruity undertones. A good cabernet was like a good woman: earthy, exotic, to be savored and tasted slowly, first with the tongue, then the entire mouth. Would Jade taste different to him after these nine months? He couldn't wait to find out. Time to get some action going.

He turned toward her slowly, hoping their eyes would meet in the flicker of the flame. Damn. Her eyes were closed and she let out a long deep sigh. Maybe more wine. He'd show her how attentive he'd become.

Bottle in hand, he walked over beside her, realizing too late the sigh was actually the deep breath of sleep. When he called her name, she jumped, spilling the last remaining swallow of cabernet from her glass.

"Crap!" She stood up and shoved her empty glass into his hand, scrutinizing the damage. No wine on the chair; all of it had landed on her, staining a large purple polka dot onto the crotch of her pink capris. Her voice was matter-of-fact. "Gotta get this out." She started unbuttoning and unzipping, sliding the pants down over her hips as she hurried toward the bathroom.

Adam followed, almost in a state of euphoria, as he watched her curvy ass appear, clad only in a pink lace thong. He stood speechless as she methodically blotted the spot, then rinsed it with cold water. Her white top was cropped, and when she reached to adjust the pants over the shower bar to dry, he was treated to the view of her finely boned vertebra running delicately up her back. His erection sprang up so fast he could almost hear the *yoiiiing.*

Jade turned, catching him in his appreciative gawk, and quirked an eyebrow. "So now would be a good time for you to produce some shorts out of your magic gym bag."

"Actually, right now I'm cursing the fact I *have* the gym bag." He heaved a dramatic sigh as he tore his gaze from the fetching sight.

"And make sure they weren't lying on some yucky, dirty jock strap!"

The gym bag was in the living room. By the time he returned, Jade had crawled under the covers and lay in the middle of the bed. A hint, no doubt. "I think I'm ready to turn in. I can't hold my eyes open." She yawned and snuggled deeper into the down comforter.

Adam tossed the clothes on the bed. One more quick reminder of why they were there. Then let the games begin. He sat on the edge, leaning down until their eyes leveled. "Thanks...for today." Her eyes widened as he leaned in. He brushed her cheek with his lips. Ah yes. Chaste and honorable. That should do it.

He left the room, closing the door.

He heard her rummaging around, slipping into his workout clothes probably. He poured the last of the wine and settled back in the chair to wait. Let her get to sleep first.

A few minutes of silence passed. She was pretty drowsy. Ten minutes should do it. He kept an eye on his watch. At the ten-minute mark, he moved to the door. He could hear a faint sound of deep breathing. *Okay. Make this good.*

Adam moved back into position in front of the fire and let out a few fake sobs. Soft at first, then a little louder. He stopped to listen. No sound from Jade's room. He sobbed louder, adding some jerky breath sounds, rubbing his eyes hard to make them water. Still no sound. Damn. He hadn't realized she'd sleep this soundly. Time to move to Academy Award worthy.

Adam set the wine glass down and began pacing the room—sobbing, sniffing, beating his hands on the furniture, virtually wailing at times. *C'mon, Jade. I'm a grieving man for God's sake.*

Finally, a noise caused him to catch his breath. All right. Ready. But the noise wasn't coming from Jade's room. It was coming from the door. A knock? *Who in the hell?*

When he opened the door, the manager he met at check-in stood on the stoop, eyes full of concern. "Mr. Brock. Forgive me, but I heard your sobs as I was passing, and I saw you through the window. Are you all right?"

Damn it. Jade slept through it all while the manager showed up to hold his hand. "I'm sorry to have been so loud." The knock might have awakened Jade, so he couldn't blow it now. He wiped his eyes on the bottom of his shirt. "I'll...I'll be fine...really."

The manager spread his fingers in a supplicating gesture. "Is there anything I can do?" He leaned to the side to see around Adam, scanning the room. "Is your wife...?"

"Sleeping," Adam assured him. "She's a very sound sleeper."

"Perhaps you'd like to talk. I'm a minister part time, and I counsel couples."

Adam suppressed the laugh that threatened, clearing his throat instead. "It's nothing like that. No problems with me and Jade. It's...well...you see, I visited my parents' gravesite today. I'm still just very emotional."

"Oh my," the manager's eyes softened in sympathy, "I am sorry." His eyes brightened then, and he added eagerly, "I also do grief counseling."

Why me, Lord? Of all the romantic hideaways he

could have picked... Adam took a deep breath and let out a long, poignant sigh. "Thank you. But I really need the time alone. That's why Jade's not out here. She knows I want to be alone."

"Well, if you're sure."

"Oh, I'm quite sure." *Damn right. I'm sure I want rid of you.*

"Well, all right then. Good night." He gave a nod of acceptance.

"Good night." It was all Adam could do not to slam the door, but he caught himself. Someone was watching him. Jade must have gotten up. He eased the door closed and turned to face her.

Jade's door was still closed. The manager's words came back to him then: "I saw you through the window." The creep was probably still out there, watching to see if he was gonna fall apart again. His jaws were tight with frustration—and all the fake crying. He wanted to march over there and just kick Jade's door in. How could she be sleeping through all this?

He started toward her room. The wine glasses still stood on the table where he'd set them. He grabbed his, downing the contents in one gulp. Hers sat empty...from the spill...when she'd taken off her pants...exposing her ass to him...that fine ass...those long legs.

He sighed. Better get some rest. She'd still be here tomorrow morning.

****

Jade was awakened by Adam's heart-wrenching sobs. She sat on the side of the bed, listening to his outpouring of emotion.

This was such a different Adam. What would be the best way to deal with him? He'd always been so stoic before about his parents' death. In fact, she'd never seen him cry about anything. Mister Tough Guy. Mister I-Can-Handle-It-Myself. Maybe the anniversary triggered something inside him.

Should she go to him? Her heart ached listening to him. She wanted to go out there and pull him into her arms and hold him and make it all better. She hated it when anything was in pain. Humans or animals or even characters in the books she read. Paisley's last bout with a kidney infection had nearly sent her over the edge.

But if she went out there now—if she held him—they'd end up in bed. She was sure of that. She was vulnerable and he was emotionally fragile. A combustible combination.

Would that be so bad? He needed her. And she could sure use some release of her own. Mr. Malone had seen to that. She hit the mattress in frustration. Kai again. Augh! She tried not to think about how hard his body had been when he pulled her against him. Such a contrast to the softness of his lips.

Adam's sobs brought her back to the present and made her stomach muscles tighten. Muscles lower down tightened at the thought of release being so near...like the next room. Or so far away...like Japan.

She took a deep breath. No sex with Adam. He'd just be Kai Malone's stand-in at that point, and that wouldn't be fair to anybody. But he needed a friend right then. She started toward the door, but stopped in mid-stride. There was a knock. And Adam was opening the front door?

Jade backed up to the edge of the bed and sat down, straining to hear what was going on in the other room. Adam was talking to...who was this guy? He called Adam by name, so maybe the manager? Oh, he'd heard him crying, too. Poor Adam. He must've been so embarrassed.

She tried to keep up with the conversation. He was a minister. He thought they were married. She chuckled. She'd better go out there and rescue

Adam. The guy sounded a little too zealous. She moved back to her door, had her hand on the knob. What was that? He wanted to be alone? He told the manager that she understood he wanted to be alone.

She heard the door close. She tiptoed back to the bed and crawled under the covers. She could hear him moving around. He wasn't crying anymore. He turned out the light, but she could still hear movements and see his shadow moving under the crack of her door. He moved to her door. She felt his presence on the other side. She started to call out and invite him in. No. If he wanted to talk, he'd knock to wake her up or come on in. She waited breathless, not exactly sure of what she wanted him to do.

Then she watched the shadow move away from the door and heard the sound of his bedroom door closing. She released her breath in a long sigh.

Hmph. I guess he really does want to be alone.

Chapter Fourteen

The ring tone of her cell phone woke Jade the next morning. It played "Tocata and Fugue" so it wasn't a regular caller. She groped around the unfamiliar bedside table, finally realizing the noise was coming from the other side.

She grabbed the phone and eyed the caller ID number. Not one she recognized. Was Kai calling at last? She sat up and cleared her throat several times, hoping to rid her voice of the raspiness of sleep. "Hello?"

"Hello, Ms. Bartholomew?" The voice wasn't Kai's, but it was one she'd heard before. Her mind raced to attach it with a face.

"Yes."

"I'm sorry to call so early." The clock on the dresser read 8:17. "This is John Levitt from Samuels Publishing."

Jade's heart made a gigantic leap and lodged in her throat. "Oh, yes, Mr. Levitt. How are you?"

"I'm very well, thank you. I'm calling in hopes that you can come in to speak with us again today. I realize this is short notice, but I've just found out I'm going to be out of the office for a couple of weeks."

"Oh yes! Yes, of course. I can come in today…" Yikes! She was in Carmel, four hours from home. "…er that is, as long as it's later this afternoon." She crossed her fingers and squeezed them tight.

"That would be best for me also. I have meetings that will reach into the afternoon, but I was hoping for sometime around 4:00?

"Four o'clock is good for me." She threw the

comforter back and drummed her heels into the soft bedding, glad for something that could muffle her exuberance. She didn't want to appear desperate or too overly surprised.

"Splendid. It's our intention to offer you the submissions editor position we talked about before."

Jade fought back the squeal, fearing it wouldn't come across as very professional. She curbed the sound to an enthusiastic gasp. "That's wonderful news."

"Yes, well, I'm glad you think so. I take it you're still interested, then." Jade could hear the smile in his voice.

"Oh, I'm definitely interested."

"Good. Then we'll fill you in on the details—salary, benefits, policies, and such, this afternoon."

"Sounds perfect. I'll be there at four."

"I'll see you then. Good-bye."

Adrenaline coursed through her body, and she sprang into motion. They had to get out of there pronto. Would Adam be up to it after the night he had last night? No time to worry about Adam's state of mind. If he needed to talk now, they'd have the long drive home. She ran for his room. "Adam, get up. Hurry! We have to get on the road."

Without bothering to knock, she flung open his door. He'd evidently been hot during the night. The covers were piled in a heap at the foot of the bed and he lay face up, sprawled across the middle. Completely naked.

Jade stopped just inside the door, gulping down her surprise and trying hard not to gawk. Her sudden intrusion brought him to a sitting position and, from the looks of his monstrous erection, he wasn't going to be pleased she interrupted whatever or whoever it was he'd been dreaming about.

"What? What is it?" He shook the sleep away and rubbed his face briskly a couple of times, not bothering to cover himself.

"I just got a call from Samuels Publishing." She pulled her gaze up to the ceiling fan. "I got the job!"

Adam jumped to his feet and was at her in two strides, pulling her into a tight hug. "Geez! Congratulations!"

His hardness pressed against her and the bouncing of his "Happy Dance" moves brought her target zone into direct contact. She gasped at the sensation that surged through her as well as at the renegade reaction of her body. Much as her brain wanted to continue the search for His Hotness, her body craved a who-cares-the-hell-how-or-why-it-happened release. She nuzzled her mouth into Adam's neck, then caught herself as she remembered the urgency of haste. "Thanks, thanks, but..." She maneuvered her hands between them and pushed away to gain eye contact. "I have to be in L.A. at four, so we've got to get on the road."

Disappointment registered in Adam's eyes. "Just like that? Don't we even have time for breakfast? It's included in the price."

She hated giving that up, also. It was sure to be sumptuous, and she was hungry. But there wasn't time. "It took us four hours to get here. Traffic will be horrendous today. Sorry. There's just no time."

He ran his hands through his hair with a frustrated sigh, and she took the opportunity to move out of his reach. "Hurry," she ordered as she scurried back to her bathroom and pulled the capris off the shower rod. The crotch was still wet, but so was she, she realized as she pulled them on...just from that brief encounter. Sheesh. She needed to do something about this low tolerance for hard naked penises rubbing against her.

She slipped out of Adam's tee and into her bra and top then threw the borrowed clothes back into the gym bag. Easiest packing she'd ever done. A quick once-over through her hair with the brush from his bag, a prayer of thanks for the disposable toothbrush sets left in the bathroom by the management, and she was good to go.

She met Adam in the living room. He looked none-too-happy about their quick departure. His smile was forced, not quite making it to his eyes, which were remarkably clear considering what he went through the night before. He patted his thigh absently, a move she'd learned long ago belied agitation. Probably still had some feelings from yesterday to sort through. She swallowed around the knot that formed in her throat and smiled. "Ready?"

He shrugged. "I guess."

When they got outside, Jade was relieved to find the fog had started to lift. She'd seen times, when it was heavy like the night before, it would take hours to burn off. She got in the car as Adam took care of the gym bag.

"Mr. Brock," a voice called, and Jade followed the sound by studying the side view mirror. She saw a man approaching Adam, waving something small.

"You're leaving without breakfast?"

She recognized the voice as the manager from last night.

"Yeah. We've had something come up, and it's put us in a rush to get back."

Yeah, Adam certainly had something come up that morning. And it certainly gave her a rush.

"Nothing bad I hope." The man watched Adam closely, eyes full of concern. Was he wondering if Adam was going to break down again?

"No, no," Adam assured him. "Good news about a job, in fact."

The man held out a card. "Good. Well, here is my card should you ever, uh, need my services."

"Thanks." Adam took the card and slid it into his back pocket, then he shook hands with the guy.

"The place is beautiful. I hope we can come again sometime."

"Yes, perhaps when you can stay longer." The manager continued to stand there and watch as Adam got in the car and buckled up. He waved as they pulled out of the parking space.

Adam waved back genially. "Silly bastard."

He spoke through his smile, reminding Jade of a ventriloquist. Now *that* was the same old Adam. She relaxed. This Adam she could deal with much better than the *getting in touch with his softer side* version from yesterday. But that sensitive side had earned him some points on the Hotness meter.

A couple of blocks into the return trip, Jade spied a Starbuck's. Her growling stomach reminded her she'd like a little breakfast, as long as it was to-go. "Could we just grab a bite and eat in the car?"

She saw Adam's jaw tighten as he gave a quick snort. He was certainly out-of-sorts about something, and it had to do with having to leave so quickly. Perhaps he'd wanted to go to the cemetery again on the way out. Her cell phone cut off her apology. "California Girls." Beth's ring.

Adam whipped into the parking lot. "I'll run in and grab us something." He slammed the door with more force than was necessary.

What was eating him? "Hey, Beth."

"Omigod, Jade. You've got to get a copy of today's Wall Street Journal." Beth's voice was low and hesitant, the voice she used when she knew something was going to be upsetting.

"Why? What's in it?" What could possibly be in the Wall Street that would be upsetting?

"It's Kai Malone! He's on the front page with these Japanese men. He's selling his company for mega-millions."

"What company?" This didn't make sense. How could a software salesman sell a company? "You've got to be reading that wrong."

"No, I'm not. I just called Pryce and he read it, too. Seems that Kai doesn't work *for* Techtron. He owns it. Or, rather did own it. He's in the process of selling it to this Japanese firm, for, for, 'an as-of-yet undisclosed amount reported to be in the tens-of-millions.'"

"But, why did he tell me he sold software?" A spark of anger flared inside Jade as she watched Adam through the window. Her stomach lurched. "Does he think I'm some kind of opportunist? Worried his money is going to make me chase after him...throw myself at him?"

"Listen to yourself, Jade. Lots of women would do just that." Beth's heels clicked across the pavement of the parking lot. Even in a hurry, her logic never missed a beat.

Jade was hoping for some support here to rid herself of fantasies about Kai. She didn't need her best friend pointing out that caution was a good thing for a man of his wealth. "But, I'm not a lot of women. And all his money doesn't make him any less of an ass."

"I dunno. He's obviously been really busy." An elevator dinged in the background. "I mean, the whole world can see that. Maybe there hasn't been any time to call."

"Hi. How've you been? Hope I can see you when I get back. Wow! That took all of seven seconds." Jade spotted a newsstand on the opposite corner from Starbuck's. "I'm going to grab a copy of that Wall Street so I can read the article."

"Where are you anyway? We stopped by last night to drop off your shoes for the wedding, but you weren't home."

"I'm in Carmel."

"Carmel?" Beth's tone grew suspicious. "With whom?"

"Adam." Jade said the name quickly, then held the phone slightly away from her ear.

Instead, Beth's voice dropped to a whisper. Jade had to push the phone hard against her ear to hear. "...your freakin' mind? I have to be in a meeting...damn, ten minutes ago, so I don't have time for this now. But don't let him convince you he's changed. He hasn't. Tear his page out and be done. Gotta go."

Adam was headed toward the door. She needed to hurry. She dropped the cell phone into her purse and grabbed her wallet. The stack of Wall Street Journals lay near the door. Jade recognized Kai in the picture without even looking too closely at it. Her stomach did a flip-flop. She snatched up a copy and tossed it on the counter along with a large bag of peanut M&M's. This was going to take some chocolate.

While she waited for the clerk to return to the counter, she scanned the picture. Kai smiled back at her with his gorgeous teeth and squinted eyes. He looked tired, like the morning after he slept on her couch. Puffy eyes, slight crease in the forehead. But this time he'd shaved. Negotiating a business deal had to be tough. Maybe time had been short, and he'd been too busy to call. Maybe Beth was right. Her anger ebbed slightly.

But a more thorough look at the picture revealed a small gleam on his hip. His cell phone. Right there in plain view. There had to have been times when they took breaks from the negotiating. The talks couldn't go round the clock.

He said he'd call and he didn't. He said he was a software salesman and he wasn't.

He lied to her about his company.

Adam lied to her about Costa Rica.

Men were liars.

Her anger descended on her again in full force.

****

"Hello. This is Kai Malone." God, he was tired. Kai sat on the edge of the bed and loosened his tie. If this was another reporter...

"Kai? Stube. You're quite a celebrity, man. Front page Wall Street."

"Yeah?" Right now, his body ached from sitting in those damn chairs for so long. After all the calls tonight, the picture was old news. Besides, the sake had him reeling. He lay down and stretched out, eyes closed.

"Yeah. Good picture, too. But hey, I didn't call to brag about your photogenic smile. I got her number."

Kai bolted into a sitting position, immediately regretting the fast move. His head felt like a cherry bomb had gone off in it.

"Yeah, man. When they figured out who it was requesting that call history, they moved it to the front burner."

"I hated being such a bastard about it, but it was *my* list for *my* phone. It shouldn't take an act of Congress..."

"Well, whatever it took, I have it now. You ready?"

Kai already had the pen poised over the paper. "Would you hurry up?"

****

Where in the hell was she going now? One minute she couldn't get out of there fast enough. Now she what? Had to have a friggin' newspaper? Adam watched Jade moving down the street toward the newsstand. He blew into the drinking hole of the to-go top. He wanted coffee in the worst way. His head felt the size of a basketball from all the wine last night. He'd been rushed out of bed with no time, no coffee, no breakfast. And no Jade.

Her phone started ringing. One of those annoying ring tones of badly done Bach or some such nonsense. He tried to ignore it, but the friggin' voice mail wouldn't pick up.

Unable to stand the irritating noise any longer, he snatched the phone from the open purse. "Hello?"

"Ummm, hello. I was trying to reach Jade Bartholomew."

The voice was deep. Very, very deep. Adam's instincts went on alert. It sounded like what he remembered of Malone's voice, but it could be that guy from the publishing company. Couldn't take any chances. "She can't come to the phone right now. May I ask who's calling or take a message?"

"This is Kai Malone." The voice was almost a growl this time.

"Malone, this is Adam Brock. It's good to speak with you again. I've been wanting to thank you."

"Thank me?"

"Yeah. For taking such good care of my girl that night. That allergic reaction must have been vicious. If you hadn't been there, she might not have been here waiting for me when I got back from Costa Rica."

"Oh. Yes. I see. Well, um…you're welcome and um…just tell Jade I called to say hello."

Adam watched Jade as she paid for her purchases. "I'll tell her as soon as she gets out of the shower."

"Well…um, goodbye then."

"Goodbye." He slid the phone back into her purse as she stepped off the curb, heading back to the car.

By the time she got there, he was all buckled in. He sipped his coffee and held one out to her. "No chocolate croissants. I got you a scone instead."

"You eat it. I'm not hungry," she snapped.

"I thought you were starved." Women were so exasperating.

Jade ripped open the bag of M&M's and poured

herself a handful. "Not anymore."

****

Adam wasn't sure what exactly had gone wrong, but Jade had been pissed the whole way home, ever since the coffee stop. She was obviously craving chocolate, but shit, how was he to know an orange scone would send her over the edge?

When he tried to draw her into conversation, she answered in monosyllables when she could, short answers when anything more was required.

He skirted around the subject of the reason for the trip without actually mentioning his parents. She barely responded, so that wasn't the problem. Jade would have lit into him if she'd remembered the truth about his parents. So she hadn't figured out he'd lied to her. Again. And she couldn't have seen him on the phone with Malone. He'd been too careful.

She seemed preoccupied, maybe nervous about the afternoon's interview. He decided not to press his luck. He quieted down and left her to her thoughts for a while.

Eventually, she fell asleep, and that was fine with him. It gave him the chance to peruse her at his leisure without her being aware. His eyes were drawn to the still-visible wine stain that disappeared between her legs. His erection grew taut and his finger itched to rub that stain. He imagined slipping his hand down her pants and caressing her, sliding his thumb around her clit until she was moaning. She wouldn't be able to stand it, and she'd wiggle her pants down and get herself off for him as they zipped along the highway. Just like Hot-Porn-Video Chick. He pushed the accelerator and watched the speedometer jump up near a hundred. Getting home fast might leave time for some heavy-duty playtime.

They neared LAX and Adam's erotic images dissolved as traffic slowed to a crawl. What should have been a ten-minute drive took fifty.

Jade woke up as they turned into the drive behind the houses. "Geez. Sorry. I haven't been much company. You should have wakened me." She yawned and stretched, arching her back, breasts thrust toward him.

He needed to be smooth. Shouldn't get her riled again. "I enjoyed watching you. You're beautiful when you sleep."

A blush crept up her neck and into her face, but she flashed him a smile. "What time is it?"

"2:13."

"Crap! I've got to run." She gathered her purse and paper. "Thanks for last night. The cottage was really lovely." She leaned to give him a quick peck on the lips.

What the hell. With Malone effectively out of the picture now, he could throw caution to the wind. Running his hands through her hair, he caught the back of her head and pressed a soft but meaningful kiss onto her mouth that was partially opened in surprise.

She didn't pull away immediately, but when she did, her eyes were full of question. "I've g-got to go." She stammered the words. "I've got like twenty minutes to get ready and be on my way." Then she dashed from the car.

What the shit did that mean? If she hadn't had that interview, would she have stayed? Would they have been going to bed now? Adam's penis sprang to attention at the thought and he groaned. His erection had been almost constant for the past three hours. He needed relief and he needed it now. Oh hell. Any port in a storm.

He pulled out his cell phone and punched the first name in his speed dial.

"This is Dori."

"Dori, it's Adam."

"Hey, how'd it go?" Her voice softened with sympathy.

"It was the right thing to do. The flowers were perfect. Thanks for making such a beautiful bouquet."

"Anything I can do to make you feel better?" From sympathetic to hot in eight seconds.

Adam chuckled. "Well, that depends. Can you get away for a while?"

Her giggle wafted over the line. "I do have some deliveries to make. I could be there in, say, half-an-hour?"

"Not sure I can wait that long."

Dori gave a long, sensuous sigh. "Well, I'm already dripping. Don't you dare start without me."

Adam whistled a tune as he got out of the car.

Chapter Fifteen

"I let you out of my sight for a month, and your whole life changes. You start a new job. Start a new relationship." Her mom's tone was wistful and a little sad.

"I've done neither, Mom. That's Gram's version." The azure tablecloth unfolded with a quick flick of Jade's wrists and settled neatly onto the table. Mom followed behind, setting places with festive lemon-colored stoneware. "Don't ever put her on the witness stand. She reports the world the way she wants it. Through sex-colored glasses."

"Okay." Her mom laughed, setting the vase of petite sunflowers and blue delphiniums in the center. "So tell me the truth, the whole truth, and nothing but the truth."

"I don't start until July 1st. That's the beginning of their fiscal year. Then there's a month of what they call training, but I call probation. A new CEO starts today. Mr. Levitt says they're not sure what direction she'll want to take the company, but she made it plain she wanted all departments fully staffed soon, as in immediately."

"She sounds like a go-getter."

Jade nodded, following her mom's hands as they folded the napkins into neat little cones. Hers ended up bent to one side, and it collapsed when she set it on the plate. "Hope I figure out what the new boss wants quickly. If I end up waiting tables, I'll starve." She gave up and reached for the next tablecloth.

"You'll catch on quickly. You always have. You've got that competitive spirit of your father's.

It'll serve you well in the corporate world." Mom set the refolded napkin on the plate then drew Jade into a hug. "My baby working for a big publishing company. Where'd the years go?"

Jade laid her head on her mom's shoulder, enjoying the moment. She missed her parents when they took their extended vacations to France with her maternal grandmother. "I'm glad Mimi's surgery won't make you miss Beth's wedding."

"Me, too." A final squeeze, then Mom motioned with her head to the stack of plates, indicating what was still left to do before Beth's party. "I could tell she was hurting during the trip—every time we ate. But she was bound and determined not to have her gall bladder out until we were home and the wedding was over."

"Poor Mimes." Jade gave a sympathetic sigh. "Beth's disappointed, too. She told me to tell Gram she'd have to bring two dates since Mimi's place will be vacant."

"That's a dangerous thing to say to your grandmother." Mom shook her finger at Jade, widening her eyes dramatically to display the dark brown irises Dad called chocolate M&M's. "She would relish the idea of having a man on each arm."

"I dunno. She's pretty taken with Marvin. I haven't met him yet, but she seems to have a gooood time with him."

Mom took a vase of flowers in each hand and placed them on the remaining covered tables. "And is there anyone you're having a gooood time with? She mentioned that Adam moved in next door, and that you've been seeing Kai Malone."

"You know him?" Jade fiddled with the flatware, avoiding eye contact. "I only had a couple of dates with Kai before he went to Japan." She shrugged. "I guess he lost interest. I haven't heard from him since."

"That's a shame. Your dad was impressed. He says he's never heard anything bad about Kai Malone. Apparently he's not your typical corporate head."

"Well, maybe I was too typical, then." Jade used her miffed tone. It was okay to let her guard down with her mom. They'd always been open with each other when it came to her love life—or lack of it.

"And how about Adam? Has he lost interest?"

Jade heard the concern in her mother's voice. It said, "Please don't make that mistake again," though Mom would never come out and say it. Ever the lawyer, she would advise, she would counsel, but unlike Gram, she would never tell her daughter what to do.

That's what made them get along during those hectic teenage years when everyone else hated their mothers. That's what made Jade confide that she was going to lose her virginity to Jordan Thompson, page five in her Hotness journal.

Mom hadn't argued or pouted. She laid out the consequences of unprotected sex in a no-holds-barred manner. Then she'd made Jade an appointment with a gynecologist to get her on the Pill and bought her a package of condoms.

And that's what made Jade plop down in the nearest chair to spill her guts. "Adam's as interested as ever. Maybe more so. He claims he's changed. He acts like he's changed...bringing me flowers...not pressuring me." She ran her fingers into the hair at her temples and squeezed. "I know he could be lying. Probably is lying. But what if he *is* different, Mom? He was fabulous in bed. It was the other, the lies and the cheating that tore us apart. If that part of him were different..."

Mom sat down in the opposite chair and smoothed a non-existent wrinkle out of the corner of the tablecloth. "Adam was fabulous in bed because he's an actor, Jade. A chameleon. He can become anything you want him to be for that moment. He's not a man of character; he's a man of many characters. And if sex is what you're wanting, he's definitely your man."

"But, he's not a man of commitment, is he?"

Jade watched her mother's eyes get misty, saw the movement in her throat as she swallowed hard. "My baby's talking about commitment. Beth's getting married. It seems like just yesterday you girls started your Hotness journals, and now here you are." She waved her hand, indicating the tables of blue and yellow that dotted the deck.

"Mom." Jade waited for the chocolate M&M's to settle back on hers. "Pryce is definitely His Hotness to Beth."

Her mom's eyes broke contact and scanned the Pacific. "And yours is out there too, baby. Don't settle for fabulous sex. Wait for a fabulous man."

****

Beth's delighted squeal and hug was all Jade needed to confirm that Gram's idea for an authentic French café had been recreated right on the deck.

Jade looked around the scene with pride. Although Mom and Gram paid for most of it, she'd helped with some of the consignment money. The result was indeed pretty squeal-worthy. The place bloomed in yellows and blues. Along with the linens and flowers, bottles of Châteauneuf-du-Pape wine and bowls of Niçoise olives adorned the tables. The only thing missing was Monêt to capture the scene.

"Jade, how'd you get all this done? There was nothing here this morning." Beth bounced from table to table, tasting olives at each. "Now it looks—and tastes—like you broke off a piece of France and transplanted it. Yum!"

Jade proudly showed off the party-favor gift baskets of lavender and olive oil products hanging on the back of each chair. "Mom personally picked out everything in Provence and had it shipped over."

"I'm still amazed that I'm honeymooning in your parents' place in Villefranche, just like we used to dream about."

Beth's sigh was wistful, just like Mom's had been earlier. Jade hoped she wasn't about to get sentimental. No time for that. Guests would be arriving soon. She countered with something light to keep both of their minds off the fact that, in two days, things would be changed for them forever. "Just keep in mind that, married or not, Pryce's going to have a perpetual erection from all the bare breasts on the beach."

"Hey, I don't care what causes it." Beth shot her a wicked grin. "As long as I reap the benefits."

"Well, we reap what we sow, right? Actually, my lack of sowing might also explain my lack of reaping lately. But I've got a bagful of seeds, believe me."

"Just add water?" Beth chuckled.

"Chocolate martinis preferably."

They moved into the house where some of the furniture still waited to be scooted out of the way to make room for the dance lesson.

An idea had been bouncing around in Jade's head. Now seemed like a good time to mention it. "You know, I don't start the job until July first, so I was thinking about going to Villefranche the week after you guys get back."

"By yourself?" Beth's tone was aghast. Jade knew she wouldn't approve. They'd always agreed the south of France was a place for lovers.

Jade shrugged. "Why not? It's not some strange place. It's like home. I know everyone, and I think it might be good to get away for a little while." They edged the marble-topped cocktail table into a corner.

Beth read her like a book. "You're running away from Adam? That's not like you."

"Not running away. Just taking a break. I see him constantly. It reminds me of the great sex. I end up in a perpetual state of need." The rationalization of taking some money from her trust fund didn't seem nearly so threatening now that a steady salary would be coming in.

Beth cocked an eyebrow. "Well, you know what Gram says, 'An orgasm a day keeps the muscles in play.'" They rolled their eyes in unison. "But Villefranche is such a romantic place, Jade. I'm not sure I'd want to be there alone." She covered her mouth and gulped a quick in-take of air as her eyes widened. "It's Jean Luc, isn't it! You're gonna hook up with the cabana boy again!"

Jade's face heated. Jean Luc had come to mind occasionally the past few days. He'd been googley-eyed for her since she was thirteen, and they'd had a couple of flings over the years, whenever she was in Villefranche unattached. But she couldn't think of him as the cabana boy any more. He was definitely a cabana *man* now. Part owner of the beach club and hotter than the beach at noon in July. "Can you think of a better reason for going? I mean, it's not like I need to sightsee."

"The last time I saw Jean Luc, he was certainly a sight to see." Beth rolled the rug into a tight column and deposited it in the closet. "You haven't seen him in quite a while. Think he's still unattached?"

Jade pushed the sofa table against the wall and motioned for Beth to hold the lamp. "Jean Luc will *never* attach. At least, not longer than a couple of hours."

The knock at the door heralded Chef Carlton's arrival and effectively ended the conversation at precisely the right moment. If Beth had too much time to think, she'd lecture about the hazards of on-again-off-again relationships. So either the wedding really had Beth distracted, or Jade's neediness was more visible than she thought.

As Jade showed the chef around the kitchen, he explained his wife was on the way. She'd gotten caught in traffic but would be there soon. He fascinated Jade with his menu ideas for the night: caramelized pears, fresh mozzarella, and prosciutto salad; grilled grouper with fresh mango salsa, which the guests would prepare during a short cooking lesson, served on a bed of couscous; and lemon sorbet for dessert.

Jade and Beth prepared the ten small cooking stations exactly like he wanted. He'd planned one for each guest, complete with an apron and a set of recipes for everything being served.

"What a man!" Jade whispered as they worked. "He's thought of everything. And Gram says men who cook like to spice up everything."

"Well Pryce's specialty is spaghetti sauce from a jar." Beth nudged her in the side. "But he does add extra spices to it."

The guests arrived in ones and twos, Beth's two sisters and her six closest friends other than Jade. They ooooh'd and ah'd Jade's handiwork, and a couple wrangled a promise from her to do something similar for them when their time came. She didn't make any promises since Gram and Mom were footing most of the bill.

Jade offered French *pastis* for those who dared the strong aperitif, frozen margaritas for those who didn't. It didn't take long for the alcohol to weave its magic spell, turning the young women into giggling girls again.

Carlton's wife Simone arrived during the cooking lesson. She was a stunning redhead that Gram described as "built like a brick shithouse." She applauded the spacious living area-turned-dance studio Jade and Beth had created. "It'll be perfect, plenty of room for everyone to move around during the routine. Now," she clapped her hands to get everyone's attention, "while you're finishing up your salsa, I'll come around and take care of the preliminaries. First, you'll have to choose a stripper name."

Jade choked on the bite of mango she had just popped into her mouth. "Did you...did you say...stripper?"

"Stripper." Simone nodded matter-of-factly to the group. "I teach stripping lessons at The Westhoff Gym. That's where I met your grandmother."

Jade was too stunned and too embarrassed to speak. Gram? In a stripper class?

Simone went on like it was a perfectly natural occurrence for one to learn that one's grandmother was taking stripper lessons at the age of seventy-eight. "She's really good! It's a tough workout, but great for the body." She ran her hands down her sides suggestively to illustrate her point. "And it's fun. Makes you feel like a million dollars..." She paused, then added with a playful wrinkle of her nose, "Has been stuck down your g-string!"

Jade was aghast! She never should've trusted Gram with this. She was always so vague, every time Jade pressed her. *Beth's probably mortified.* But one glance at Beth told her the reaction was definitely not mortification. The smile on Beth's face spread from ear to ear and her eyes glistened with excitement. Jade's astonishment grew as she listened to the excited sounds run through the group, the titters and the giggles. They all loved the idea! Jade slugged down the last of her *pastis. Here's to you, Gram. You never let me down.*

"One fun way of choosing a stripper name," Simone was instructing as Jade's attention drifted back, "is using the name of your first pet and your mother's maiden name."

Margie Grogann erupted into a fit of laughter. "Popcorn Davis?"

Leah Bristol threw her arms wide in a dramatic gesture. "Well, it beats the hell out of Prettybird McVeigh!"

The conversation stayed alive throughout dinner. Jade's 'Goldie Russell' was given a thumbs-up, but cheers erupted at Beth's 'Bunny Calloway'. By the time the lesson started, wedged between the main course and dessert, the group was primed and ready.

When Simone announced the background music would be "Roxanne" by The Police, Jade surrendered to the moment. The strong, heady beat was sensuous, erotic, and one of her favorites from her vast Sting collection. Jade slid into dance mode, letting any and all inhibitions fall away. She picked up the moves easily. Soon she was bumping and grinding and thrusting and arching like a pro, and loving every minute of it.

Over dessert, Simone announced the winner of the Golden G-String Award. "The award goes to Goldie Russell. She may be a novice, but she's got the moves to go pro!"

Jade accepted the gold lamé thong and twirled it around her head to the cheers of the group.

When the noise died down, Beth stood up and raised her glass. "To Jade and Linda, who've given me the best bachelorette party ever!" Cheers and shouts of agreement ensued. "And to Gram, whose wish for every one of us, including herself, is a pole to dance around." She clinked her glass against Jade's with a wink and lowered her voice. "But not every pole's meant for dancing. Some are there for support and others should have red warning flags run up them."

Beth's voice was a whisper, but her message came through loud and clear.

Chapter Sixteen

"...so it looks as though we're going to be delayed, maybe up to an hour. Sorry for the inconvenience, but we don't have any control over Mother Nature. Our new ETA is eight-thirteen Saturday morning, Los Angeles time."

Arriving hours before you even departed was one great advantage of flying east across the International Date Line. Kai reset his watch to 11:13 then pushed earplugs into place to tune out the grumbles around him. The announcement gave him another hour to relax.

He pushed the seat back to a comfortable recline and stretched his legs onto the footrest. Even the spacious first-class seating didn't accommodate his large frame very well, but he was so tired, he didn't care. He deserved some rest without having to think or make any decisions. The month had been more strenuous than he could have imagined. Meetings. Breakfast meetings. Dinner meetings. After-dinner meetings. Phone calls. Conference calls. His head spun thinking of everything that had happened over these four weeks. He pulled the cell phone out of the holder and held the button down, turning it off. The world could revolve without him for the next ten hours.

He needed something to get his mind off business. He closed his eyes. The image of Jade lying in the sand their last night together, top pulled down far enough to expose her breasts, immediately popped into his mind.

Since talking to Brock, he hadn't allowed

himself to think about her.

He took a long drink from his scotch and water. Maybe it was his own fault. If he hadn't panicked that night she was at the Urgent Care and called Brock, maybe this would have all turned out differently. Then again, maybe it was karma he'd had a part in bringing them back together.

And maybe it was better he'd never slept with her. He'd had enough women to know quality when he saw it. He had a gut wrenching feeling if he'd ever had a taste of Jade, she'd be damn hard to forget. Hell, she was damn hard to forget anyway.

****

"Are you sure you're okay? Pryce and I are headed out. If you're ready to leave, we could drive you home." Beth shouted to be heard over the band.

Jade focused on the deep crease between Beth's brows. If she looked into her best friend's eyes she'd dissolve into a puddle of tears. "I'm good to drive. I only had one glass of wine and it was a couple of hours ago at the rehearsal dinner."

"You're not coming down with anything, are you? Please don't be coming down with anything." This time there was panic in Beth's voice.

"I'm not sick. Promise. But I think I'll head home too since you guys are leaving." Jade fumbled in her purse for her keys, avoiding eye contact. The muscles in her neck tightened into iron bands. Thank heavens they were ready to leave, too. If she didn't get away soon, an artery in her head was sure to rupture. "My feet are killing me, and I'm just exhausted. It's been a long day." That part was true. She planted quick pecks on Beth's cheeks. "I'll be at your place in the morning by eight-thirty."

The bartender called to Beth then as Pryce paid the bill, and Jade took the opportunity to get out the door into the relative quiet of the street. Her car was just a block away. She could hold it together that long. But as she lengthened her stride, the tears started flowing, gushing by the time she got the key in the ignition. She gave herself a couple of minutes of hard sob time before she pulled into traffic. Thankfully, Mungo's Bar wasn't very far from home.

God, this was awful. She'd known that tonight was going to be hard. She'd prepared to be a little weepy, but nothing like this. When solid-as-a-rock Beth lost her composure during the wedding rehearsal, it was the beginning of the end.

"Longer" was a great choice of songs, and Tad's voice was perfect for it. But the sentimental connection of Beth's youngest brother singing the song from their mom and stepdad's wedding caught up with the bride-to-be on the first note. She'd started to sniffle, then cry softly. Then her mom cried so of course, Bridget and Molly followed suit. With all the Cochran women bawling, Tad got choked up, couldn't finish the song.

The minister's suggestion of another song had been innocent enough. He didn't know Beth considered it a tribute to her parents, especially the stepfather she adored. Only Jade understood Beth's firmness in the matter. It had to be "Longer"—and she didn't want Dan Fogelburg's CD piped in; she wanted it sung live.

But it had been downhill from there. Every little thing sent Beth into a tailspin. Jade had never seen her like that and it was damn creepy. Fact was, she'd never expected the always-cool-never-flustered Beth to have pre-wedding jitters. But she did. Even after seven years with Pryce, and the last two of them, living together.

When Beth had shown Gram her new engagement ring two years ago, Gram looked Beth directly in the eye and declared: "Marriage is serious shit."

Jade had never really thought about how serious

a venture it was until tonight. Now it hit her in the stomach like a wrecking ball. This was forever. And not just Beth's marriage. *Her* relationship with Beth was changing. Forever.

Jade sobbed again, hurtling the empty tissue box from the console against the passenger-side window.

Being the only one at the rehearsal dinner without a date hadn't helped her mood any either. Couples. Everywhere, couples. And afterward, dancing at Mungo's left her lonelier than she ever had been in her life. Nobody special to be with. Losing her best friend.

By the time she got the car parked and into her apartment, the tears were under control, but the mood wasn't. She scooped Paisley up, hugging him tightly until he fussed and squirmed free. No use going to bed. Not with this restlessness gripping her. Sleep would be impossible.

She flipped on the stereo, and The Police CD blared from the speakers. The stripper workout had provided a fun release several times that day. She'd played "Roxanne" time and again. But this time she let the CD start at the beginning.

Although a glass of wine sounded good, she hesitated. She'd heard alcohol was a mood enhancer, making whatever mood you're experiencing deeper. She doubted that anything could make her feel more miserable. *C'mon. Live life on the edge for once.* She poured a glass then went into the bedroom to wash her face and get out of the dress and heels. She set the glass on the desk and picked up the Hotness Journal—an especially poignant reminder of great times she and Beth shared growing up. The tears flowed again as she flipped through the pages.

"Kai Malone." The last page. When he asked her out, she'd let herself hope maybe he'd be her date to the wedding. Instead, he went to Japan, lied to her about the reason, and lied about wanting to call her while he was there. Would she ever get it through her thick skull to quit believing the promises men made?

She held the page by the corner, bracing the rest of the journal with her other hand, and tore the sheet slowly and dramatically from the book. A flick of her finger sent it to File Thirteen.

She went into the bathroom and splashed cold water on her face. Her eyes cooled and she felt better. Still miserable and lonely, but the tears and runny-nose were finished.

When she walked back into the bedroom, "Roxanne" was just starting. She closed her eyes and imagined a nameless stranger sitting in the chair in front of her. She began the stripper routine and imagined his eyes becoming mesmerized by her movements, squinting sensually.

Jade swayed across the bedroom, letting the music push her toward the chair, letting her body dictate where it wanted to be touched, touching without shame, feeling the power a woman's body can exude when she frees it from the usual inhibitions.

She performed an exotic lap dance on the empty chair, relishing the impact these movements could have on the man of her choosing. When the song ended, she was shaking. Those movements had an impact on her! Breathlessly, she touched her nipples, amazed at the tightness. She moved her hands along her body and between her legs where the moisture had spilled over onto her thighs. Her clit was so swollen it almost hurt to touch it.

The vibrator wouldn't do the trick tonight. She didn't just need an orgasm, she needed closeness with a body, needed to be held. Needed sex. Hot, wet, wild, uninhibited hours of lustful, meaningless sex.

And she knew exactly who would be willing to

give it to her. She bit her lip. Meaningless? Well, she'd deal with those consequences later. *C'mon. Really live life on the edge for once.*

She slipped on her shoes and pulled her dress back over her head, no underwear necessary for what was about to happen.

Hurrying across the deck, she checked Adam's lights. Yeah, they were on, but not the ones upstairs where the bedrooms were. He might have a date. She stopped in mid-stride. She hadn't seen any women at his house during the whole three weeks since he'd moved back. She forced her feet to move forward again. It was a chance she was willing to take. Yeah. It was time for her to start taking chances.

And with the mood she was in, she was willing to take whatever chance he wanted tonight. She knocked lightly on the door and heard movement. Somebody was headed to the door. She held her breath.

A petite blonde answered wearing nothing but a towel.

Jade's heart sank; her voice caught in her throat.

The girl's—she was hardly big enough to be called a woman, unless you considered the humongous amount of cleavage bulging over the top of the towel—expression was drawn, obviously not thrilled to find a woman at the door at 11:30. Then her eyes widened in surprise, and a smile broke across her face. "Hi! I'll bet you're Jade aren't you? I'm Dori." She held her hand out for a shake.

Jade made the handshake a quick one. She wasn't sure one of Dori's hands could handle the load of holding up the towel adequately. "Yeah, I'm Jade. I'm sorry. I didn't mean to interrupt…"

"No, no. C'mon in. You're not interrupting. Adam's gone to get beer. I just got out of the shower." She pulled Jade inside and shut the door behind her. "Adam's told me so much about you—how you guys have been best friends since college. I'm glad to finally meet you."

The ol' Best Friends story, was it? The lying sonofabitch. "I'm glad to meet you, too. But, um...I came to bum a beer." Lame, but all she could come up with on such short notice. "It seems I'm all out, and apparently you guys are too, so..." She hoped the wine on her breath didn't give away her lie.

Dori giggled. "My, my. We're all thirsty tonight. I'm afraid I just drained that man of every ounce of moisture in his body. Time to re-load."

This was way more information than Jade needed to hear. "Yeah, well. You guys enjoy your beer. I'll grab a soda instead." She got her hand on the doorknob. "See you later."

"Hey, I've gotta know..."

Jade stopped. Surely she wasn't going to ask about their relationship.

"...if the flowers worked?"

If the flowers worked? What was she talking about? Jade turned back around. "Flowers?"

"Yeah. The pink callas the Techtron guy sent you." Dori eased gingerly onto a barstool like she was expecting some long story. "The guy who came in told me all about it. How his boss had lost his cell phone with your number in it. How he was in Japan and frantic to get your number." She sighed, sounding like a love-stuck thirteen-year-old. "It was so romantic. I asked Adam if they worked, and he said he didn't think so, but I just couldn't imagine a woman not being turned on by a gesture like that."

So Kai had tried to get in touch! That was three weeks ago. And Adam. Knowing all along. Claimed the flowers were from him. Jade's fingers ached. She realized she had a death grip on the doorknob.

"So I've got to know. Did they work? Did you call

the number on the card?"

Aaaaaaiiieee. Jade screamed inside. There had been a card with a number. Adam must have gotten rid of it. She needed to get out of there, right then, before he got home. If he walked up now, within arm's reach, she was capable of physically attacking him.

She took a deep breath, swallowing the bile that had risen up in her throat. No use making a scene. Her emotions were too over-the-top tonight. And no use warning Dori about Adam. Jade could tell she was a short-timer. She gave the young woman the sweetest smile she could muster. "Yeah, it worked. Set Adam straight on that issue for me, would you?"

She eased the door closed, determined not to slam it, and started across the deck, her mind screaming at her stupidity. Halfway across, she stopped and slid into a chair.

She would wait for him. Would wait for him and confront the prick with his lying, cheating, sonofabitching mouth. She'd slap the smug smile off his face. Slap it so hard he'd think twice before he ever lied again. Slap it so hard he'd think...he'd think she cared for him. Think she loved him! And she didn't. She didn't love him. Not one bit. She felt sorry for him. And she'd wanted him. Wanted to use him for her pleasure. But she didn't love him!

The truth sank in. Everyone had always been able to see through Adam. Everybody but her. She thought she knew him because she slept with him. But she really didn't know him...because she slept with him! The sex had blinded her to everything else. But now she saw him clearly. He was a chameleon just like Mom said.

Footsteps on the walk jarred her to her feet. Adam stepped up on the deck, hands full with two six-packs. "Jade?" He stopped, clearly confused. His eyes darted back and forth from the door to her.

Jade could see the wheels turning to create a lie of explanation. It might be amusing to see what he came up with. Nope, she would be in control here. "Hey! I just wanted to borrow a beer." She walked over to where he stood and slid a bottle from one of the boxes. "Dori's a doll." She poked him playfully in the ribs, eliciting a grunt. Okay, maybe the poke was a little harder than necessary. "Don't worry. I didn't tell her that you're a lying sonofabitch. She looks street-wise to me. I'll bet she figures that out pretty fast on her own."

His mouth opened, but nothing came out. For the first time, Jade found him at a loss for words. "I'd like to talk with her more, but I've got work to do on my Hotness Journal." She popped the lid off the beer and took a long swig. "It seems I owe Kai for a bunch of points I mistakenly gave to you."

A sudden urge came over her. She reached down and grabbed Adam's balls with her free hand—didn't squeeze enough to hurt him, just a tight enough grip to say the choice was hers. "I could probably get you to tell me the whole story. Hell, I might even get you to remember the number that was on the card. But I don't want to spoil Dori's night. She did tell me the truth, after all."

Adam still hadn't moved or spoken, obviously feeling at a disadvantage. She let go with a wink and turned toward home, thoughts tumbling about in her mind, most of which involved fantasies of Kai that might require her vibrator after all. "Now, where in the world have I put that scotch tape?"

Chapter Seventeen

"Well, it doesn't change the fact that he lied to me about his job and who he is. But it does make me feel better about him. I mean, he made an effort."

Gram didn't say anything. She watched her granddaughter's bottom lip tighten up under the top one. That meant she was thinking, a gesture common to her father. She'd speak up again in a minute. Best wait. Let her sort out her thoughts. She watched the blush creep from Jade's neck onto her chin and spread to her cheeks until they glowed red under the tan.

"He probably thinks I'm a total ass-wipe."

That was a new one. Gram liked the sound of it. She filed it away in her collection of colorful descriptors. Snot-wad and fart-blossom sounded almost delicate compared to some of these newer ones. She pushed aside the temptation to make a mental inventory and turned her attention back to Jade. "You didn't get the note with his number. It was an honest mistake. Quit berating yourself." She held the coffeepot up in offer, but Jade shook her head.

"I need to leave for Beth's. We have appointments in Hollywood for hair and make-up."

Jade was unusually subdued this morning. Normally news such as this about Kai would have her hyped up. And she'd never been one to play games in matters of the heart. Like her dad, she was usually straightforward to a fault. Today she seemed totally confused. And the solution here seemed pretty obvious. "Did you call? Try to explain?"

"Yeah." Jade ran her fingers through the sides of her hair and gave an exasperated sigh. "I ran through my history of numbers just in case, and guess what I found? A strange number right after Mr. Levitt's last call. That was the morning I was in Carmel with Adam."

"And?"

"And apparently Kai called sometime that morning. I don't know how he did it, but I'm betting Adam took the call."

"And?"

"I called the number."

"And?" *Let's dole this out one bit at a time. More fun that way.*

"No answer. Just the voicemail. I tried to leave a message, but I think it cut me off. Then I called again, and it said the voicemail was full."

That was a letdown after all the hoopla. "Well, Chickie, at least you've got the number. You can try again later."

Jade drained the last sip of coffee from her cup. "I've got too much to do today. Can't deal with this, too." She stood up and stretched. "I've got a best friend to marry off." Her voice cracked a little on the last word.

So that was the reticence to talk this morning. Everything was crashing in on her. Beth getting married. Betrayal by Adam—again. Feeling like— like an ass-wipe. She was right. She didn't need to deal with this today. "Forget it, Chickie. The world'll still be revolvin' tomorrow."

Jade planted a kiss on the top of her head. "And Monday."

Gram watched her leave and fought back an urge to go whip Adam Brock's ass. She'd promised Jade she wouldn't talk to him. Did twisting his balls off come under that same category? Wouldn't have to speak to him to do it.

It was so hard seeing Jade down like this. They'd always been able to give her everything she needed or wanted. But relationships couldn't be bought, in spite of what the Brat thought. Loving someone took a special kind of magic.

She sighed. If only she had a fairy grandmother's magic wand.

Paisley jumped off the steps and headed toward the rose garden at the side of Adam's house. Gram couldn't hold back the chuckle as she watched the cat scratching around, making a spot to do his business. It'd been easy to train him to crap in Adam's flowers. Just sprinkle a little of his soiled litter in there each day so the smell stayed fresh. Kind of like a kitty outhouse. The plan was to keep moving it toward the gate until Paisley made some deposits right in the footstep zone.

Adam's door opened and the little blonde with Dolly Parton tits started out. She stopped in mid-step then hurried back in, leaving the door open. Gram had seen her there before a couple of times. A quick scheme came to mind. One that wouldn't require saying a word to Adam, but might let out some of the spitefulness she had built up inside toward him.

Gram jumped up and moved in the direction of the cat. "Paisley, get out of Adam's flowers." She kept her voice gentle, not at all the tone she would've used if she'd really wanted him to stop. This tone was for the girl's benefit in case she could hear. Paisley gave her a dismissive glance and continued the work of covering his pile with the surrounding mulch.

Gram gathered the cat in her arms and timed her turn to the quick footsteps she heard coming off the deck, through the gate, and onto the sidewalk. "Mornin', Lila. Sorry I didn't catch Paisley in time this morning. Couldn't see what he was doin' till too late. Don't have my glasses on." She squinted for effect. "I like the new haircut."

'Boobs' stopped, brows drawn in. "Um...I'm not Li—"

Gram patted her arm and squinted harder. "Now, now. I know you're not likely to put up a fuss. Leastwise, that's what you told me. But I promised you yesterday I'd try to keep him out."

"Yesterday?"

Gram let Paisley down and took Boob's hand, patting it in grandmotherly fashion. "Yesterday on your way out. Say, I must be confused. I thought you told me you'd be gone for a few days. I remember promising I'd keep an eye on Adam for you." Gram stroked the hand again, looked down at it, then back up to the face that was now a mixture of emotion. The eyebrows were still drawn in with question, but the eyes had started to narrow into angry slits.

"I see you took my advice." Gram continued her monologue. "Good. No need to be waving that two-carat diamond engagement ring in everybody's face on that plane. Don't know if you flight attendants get tips, but it sure wouldn't help your cause any if you do."

The Boob—that seemed a more fitting nickname—jerked her hand away, her face almost purple with rage. She looked like a little turnip in a blonde, spiky wig sitting atop two cantaloupes. "Engagement ring?" The words sputtered off her lips. She did a one-eighty and stalked back down the sidewalk toward the house.

"Are you gonna work after the baby comes?" Gram edged toward her, not wanting to raise her voice enough for Adam to hear. "I was thinkin' I might be able to keep Adam Jr. some if you needed me to."

The young woman nearly slid to a halt at the gate. "He's engaged? With a baby on the way?" She did an about face and started in the direction of her car again, charging by Gram, head down, muttering to herself. "Lying, stinking sack of shit. Calling me at all hours when he..."

"He'll do better," Gram promised sweetly. "He's really not a bad cat."

The reply came as a slammed door followed by a revved engine and screeching tires. Gram could see the Boob already on her cell phone. Instinct told her Adam was not going to be given a chance to explain. Gram chuckled with delight as she gathered the coffee pot and dishes and took them to the kitchen. It would take a second trip to get the rest. Just as she stepped onto the deck, a man whipped around the corner of the house at the bottom of Jade's staircase.

Gram let out a startled yelp but relaxed when she saw who the visitor was. "Kai Malone, you scared the livin' crap outta me." She took in his disheveled appearance. His clothes were wrinkled and he obviously hadn't shaven. His hair was doing a bit of its own thing, going several different directions at once.

"Sorry, Mrs....um...Gram. Didn't mean to startle you. I just got off the plane from Tokyo and was on my way home." He motioned toward the steps with his head. "I got a message from Jade. It was kind of garbled, so I decided to... Well, um, I was hoping to talk with Jade...um, for just a minute. I know it's early and her friend's wedding is today, but my plane got in sooner than we expected. I thought maybe I could catch her here."

His face reddened slightly. Embarrassed? Or did his ramblings have him all out of breath? "Oh, it's not too early at all. In fact, she's already gone." Gram watched his shoulders sag in disappointment as he dropped his head. She shouldn't go getting involved in this. They needed to work it out themselves. But, the poor thing. He looked like he'd been ridden hard and put away wet. Maybe she could make him feel a little better, though. "She tried to call you this morning."

His head shot up at that, but his eyes still held worry lines around them. God, he looked tired. "My phone was off during the flight."

"Yeah. And your voicemail's full." *Okay now, shut up. Quit talking. Don't screw anything up. Oh hell. At least find out if there's anything left to screw up.* "It seems y'all have a bit of a misunderstanding."

Kai rubbed his hands briskly through his hair a couple of times. "Yeah. I...um...realize that now. I didn't know she was still involved with the Brock guy."

One mention of the name sent Gram over the edge. She let out a hoot. This was too good not to meddle in. She plunged in head first. "The Brock guy is an ass-wipe." *That rolls off the tongue easily. Yep, a keeper.* "She's not involved with him. Hasn't been for almost ten months now." Kai's chest heaved a sigh. Of relief? Might as well tell the whole story. "Now go sit down while I make some coffee." She shooed him toward the table and chairs. "Then I'll fill you in on all the details."

Marvin, bless his heart, had left two full carafes of coffee before he went home, so she didn't have to wait on it to make. She loaded the tray with all the coffee essentials and Marvin's homemade lemon breakfast bars and hurried back out to catch Kai up to speed.

Once the coffee was poured and the breakfast bars served, she settled into her chair. "Now let me tell you what happened in this comedy of errors."

And tell him she did.

Kai listened intently, his face giving away all his emotions. He flashed that winning smile when he heard about Jade's disappointment after not hearing from him in three days. He scowled at Adam's deviousness. And he cringed and blushed when she told of Jade's hurt over his lack of honesty.

"I should have told her the truth about me at the very beginning." He made direct eye contact the whole time he spoke. Not like The Brat who'd never look right at her. "I should have told her the night we went to dinner. It was just that…"

"Women seem to get more interested in your money than in you when they find out who you are." She'd seen this happen time and time again.

"Yeah. And my gut told me Jade wasn't like that, but my gut's been wrong before. And our lawyer had advised us to keep our mouths shut about the business until the deal went through. My best friend—who's also my business partner—and I had a pact…" He finished with a little shrug that spoke volumes.

"Well, trust me. Jade doesn't need or want your money. She's got plenty of her own. Or at least she will have when I'm gone."

Kai took her hand and gave it a peck. "I've seen Jade when she talks about you. The money doesn't mean much to her. She'd rather have you."

Gram patted his cheek, already fond of this guy. She knew a winner when she saw one. "Yeah? I was just about to say the same thing to you."

Kai's smile came easily. His whole face kind of crinkled up in tiny folds of joy. He held his cup out for a fill-up. "So it's time we broke this stand-off. I know today's not good, but do you think I should call her tomorrow?"

Hmmm. Tomorrow? Jade had mentioned tomorrow or Monday. She thought back to Jade's mood this morning. She didn't seem too caught up in the excitement of today's joyous event. She'd really be bad tomorrow.

Then an idea occurred to her. A wave of a

grandmother's magic wand. "Kai, I have an idea." She proceeded to tell him her thoughts, watching his eyes spread wide.

"Do you think you can arrange it?"

Had they known each other longer, the doubt in his voice would've given her reason to call him by one of her snippy nicknames. As it was, she forgave this little slip. "Just leave everything to me."

Chapter Eighteen

One look at the wedding coordinator's pinched face told Jade something was wrong. How could that be? Everything was in place and perfect. She'd seen it herself before she came in to dress. She ran down the mental checklist once more. Flowers? Perfect. White callas that reminded her of the pink ones Kai had sent. She checked her phone again. Still no call. Maybe he couldn't even tell the message was from her. Or maybe he didn't care anymore. She took a deep breath. Not the time for that, or the place.

The place? Perfect. Gram's country club. Jade smiled, remembering how enchanted Beth became at the place during Gram and Grandpa's fiftieth wedding anniversary party. Beth made her wish that day, and Gram was good at making wishes come true. At least, most of them. She'd claimed Beth's date on the club's calendar as soon as Beth announced it. *This was also the place where I met Kai.* Jade pushed the thought out of her head. No more man-thoughts today.

Weather? Perfect. Cloudless and eighty-five degrees, a light breeze from the ocean. The meal smelled sumptuous. The cake was here, set up and stable. Ice sculpture? Check. Servers? Check. Annoying photographer? Check. Music, che—oh God. That was it! Something was wrong with Tad.

Jade moved quickly. She had to intercept the woman before she made contact with Beth who finally was calmly sipping champagne in the garden. The bride had nearly lost her composure a half-hour ago when she sat down for the first time in her fabulous Monique Lhulier gown. She'd never sat in it before, and when she finally did, the v-neck halter gaped open enough to reveal the push-up pads she relied on for cleavage. In a fit of frustration totally out of character, she pulled them from her bodice, double-stick tape and all, and threw them out the door of the bridal room into the garden. One had caught on a rose thorn and hung there still.

Jade thought perhaps there was a country song in the making. "I Gave You Real Roses; You Repaid with Bogus Breasts." No time for lyrics, though. She had a wedding planner to head off at the pass.

"What's wrong, Rena?" She didn't wait for a reply. Three more steps would bring them into Beth's view. "It's Tad, isn't it?"

Rena nodded only slightly, yet the effect was a head-butt into Jade's stomach. "He's sick."

"That's bullshit. He's not sick. I talked with him two hours ago."

Rena moved her pinky ring up and down her finger, but her voice stayed calm and smooth, practiced at making disasters sound trivial. "He's very nervous about messing up. His voice broke twice during his last run-through. He says he can't do it." Her voice rose ever so slightly. "I think perhaps we should use the CD, after all."

Tad was the closest thing Jade had to a younger brother, and she never pulled any punches with him. She moved her mouth to Rena's ear. "Tell him I said he'd better get over this stage fright now. At the appointed time, somebody better be singing 'Longer' or I'm going to tell his mom and dad where he really went last spring break when they thought he was skiing in Utah."

Jade clenched her teeth, remembering how he'd begged Beth for a loan to cover the forty-five hundred dollars he lost at the craps table in Vegas that week.

"I'm not sure that will help. He's—"

"Tell him." Jade cut her off.

Rena whirled and stomped off, obviously not thrilled to be part of Jade's blackmail scheme.

Jade took a sip of the champagne she held, letting the liquid bubble around her tongue a few seconds before swallowing. All was fair in love and war and in cases of potential meltdowns at weddings.

Her thoughts were cut off by Beth's voice, coming from the garden. "Jade, come out here. I want some candid shots of the two of us."

Jade noticed how warm Beth's hand was when she squeezed it. So the champagne Gram delivered had worked its magic. Gram had taken one look at the—what had she called it?—the "hanging falsie," and had disappeared, only to return with the bottle and several glasses. She'd whispered something to Beth, whose eyes had gone wide with surprise then had settled into a twinkle that was still there. Probably some new sexual position to try on the honeymoon.

Jade pointedly ignored the constant click of the camera's shutter. She wanted to enjoy this last half-hour of single life with her best friend, and maybe it would be nice to have it captured forever on film.

They kept the conversation light, having said all the sentimental stuff on the way to the make-up and hair session that morning. That's when she'd told Beth about last night. Her best friend had been all over the revelation, mad at her for even considering sleeping with Adam, pleased she'd threatened him with bodily harm but hadn't hurt him. She'd also made Jade promise to call Kai Monday to clear all this up.

They'd vowed then that, once the mascara was on, there'd be no more tears.

Now, laughing over the "falsie," Jade began to

feel like a champagne bubble herself. All light and airy, spirit soaring, giddy with Beth's happiness.

The pink bustier tops and long skirts Beth had chosen for her bridesmaids were stunning, and the make-up artist was a master at bringing out everyone's best features without overdoing it. Jade hadn't felt this pretty since...since the last night with Kai.

In the short time she'd been around him, he'd made her feel special. Maybe they could give it another chance. But what if he turned out to be a "falsie" too—like Adam? Only good at "pushing up" the sex drive?

She swallowed the thought with another sip of champagne, turning her attention toward Rena who appeared at the door. Jade shot her a questioning glance.

Rena smiled and nodded with a wink. "It's time. Check yourself over one last time, then I'll get you lined up."

Jade checked her chignon in the nearest mirror, towering over Margie who was applying one last coat of lip-gloss.

"Who's the hottie Gram's hanging onto?"

Hearing Marvin described as a hottie took her by surprise. She hadn't met him yet or even glimpsed him. Funny. She hadn't even considered that Gram was involved with someone her friends would label "hot." "That's Marvin. It was his chef who cooked for us Thursday night."

Margie smacked her lips appreciatively. "Whoo. Go Gram!"

Rena hustled them through the door where Weldon waited to take Beth's arm. He kissed Jade on the cheek and whispered, "You look stunning." Then his stepdaughter came through the door, and Jade saw his breath catch. "And you, my precious daughter, are the most beautiful bride I've ever seen.

You are positively radiant."

Jade held her breath. Would his comment send Beth into a blubbering meltdown? She got her hankie ready to dab any errant mascara.

"I'm so thankful to have you in my life." Beth's voice was low, but clear and unstrained. "And you'll be radiating when you get the bill for all this." She smiled sweetly and batted her eyes.

Weldon laughed and patted her hand as he placed it in the crook of his arm. "I'm sure you're right."

Jade let her breath out in a sigh. Everything was going to be all right. She was sure of it.

The wedding procession made its way among the large, potted ficus trees lining the porch. White tulle and tiny white lights wove through each tree, giving the effect of a fairy-tale forest. Tulle also scalloped the balustrade and down the staircase at the north end where they made their descent. The ceremony would take place on the lawn below.

Jade caught a quick glimpse of the grandparents and mothers already seated. Jeannie, the first bridesmaid, was on her way down the aisle by the time Jade came to a stop. She had to hand it to Rena—the coordinator kept things moving like a fine oiled machine. Maybe she would use Rena if she ever got married. Somehow the probability of that occurring seemed rather low.

When Jade reached the top of the stairs to start her descent, Adam was the first person she saw, seated directly at the pivot-point where she had to make the turn to proceed up the aisle. He looked her up and down, undressing her with his eyes despite the fact he had a date on his other arm.

His look, which she knew was supposed to be a come-on, had the opposite effect. The closer she got to him, the more it made her skin crawl. Oh yeah. She was so over him. She held the laugh welling up to a mere smile, and made her turn.

She spotted her dad seated about two-thirds of the way down the aisle. Mom was next to him, then Gram. She couldn't quite see the man sitting next to Gram, but she was about to get her first glimpse at the elusive Marvin. She slowed her pace ever so slightly when she reached their row, giving them a sly wink.

Gram winked back and patted the hand of the distinguished looking gentleman sitting next to her. He was broad-shouldered and large, but then everybody looked large next to Gram. His silver mustache matched his hair. As she moved on to her place, Jade saw his large hand cover Gram's.

Okay, he was a fine-looking elderly gentle for sure, but hardly one Jade would have described as a "hottie." Maybe Margie had a thing for older guys.

Jade puckered a kiss at Pryce as she took her place. His eyes swept over her, and he nodded in approval. It was exactly the same gesture Adam had made, but this one was genuine and sweet and made her feel pretty. It was the same way Kai had made her feel when he picked her up for dinner. Pretty. Why had it taken her so long to see Adam's leers for what they were?

When the music changed and everyone stood, Jade kept her eyes on Pryce. Everybody else would be looking at Beth, and there would be time for that, but she wanted to watch Pryce's face when he got that first glimpse of his bride.

She knew the instant it happened. Pryce had been standing with his hands clasped in front of him, a wide smile of anticipation spread across his face. Then the smile was gone with a quick in-take of breath, and his eyes grew wide and then even wider as if he needed more room to take in the image. She saw his eyes soften and knew he'd made eye contact with Beth. The smile broke again slowly, spreading more with every step that brought Beth closer. Now that was the way a woman wanted to be looked at by the man she loved.

Pryce's hands unclasped, curled into fists, then loosened again, and Jade feared his impulsiveness would cause him to rush down the aisle and pull Beth to him. Thankfully, he kept himself under control.

When Jade finally turned her attention to Beth, it was obvious her friend was totally oblivious to everything except the groom.

Pastor Downy made casual remarks that personalized the ceremony, finding the perfect balance between fun and seriousness. Beth and Pryce followed suit with their promises to not only be faithful and loving, but also to remain patient when he was watching a golf tournament or she was shopping.

Everything went so smoothly and quickly, Jade was startled to see them moving toward the vase of flowers to remove the roses they would give to their new mothers-in-law. As they did that, the introduction to Tad's song started and Jade held her breath, saying a silent prayer. *Please, God, let both of us get through this without throwing up.*

A beautiful, smooth baritone oozed out of the speakers. Jade relaxed and let out her breath then caught it again. *That's not Tad singing.* The voice had an oddly familiar quality to it though. Where had she heard it before? She dared not whirl around, but when Beth and Pryce moved toward the mothers, she could sneak a peak.

They had the roses in their hands. As Beth moved past Jade, she slowed and looked Jade dead in the eye with a wide-eyed stare. A tilt of her head indicted the point on the balcony above and beyond the seated guests where Tad was to have stood.

Jade turned slowly, trying to make her

movements a normal reaction to what was going on in the ceremony. She let her eyes drift slowly up to the area Beth had indicated.

Her stomach lurched.

Like a scene from one of the novels she'd edited, Kai Malone stood with the microphone to his lips, singing "Longer" directly to her.

If this were a Regency, this would be my cue to swoon.

Chapter Nineteen

It took all of about fifteen seconds for reality to set in. Damn him, Kai Malone. Why in the hell would he show up there at her best friend's wedding? Looking and sounding all gorgeous as somebody else's date. He was no better than Adam. Just another conniving ass-wipe. Jade mustered all the incredulity she was capable of into one icy glare then turned back to face the preacher as Beth and Pryce returned to their places.

Pastor Downy laid his hand on the clasped pair in front of him. "And now, by the powers vested in me by our Lord and Savior Jesus Christ and by the State of California, I pronounce you husband and wife. You may now kiss the bride."

Jade saw the mischievous gleam in Pryce's eyes as he swept Beth into his arms. In typical Hollywood fashion, he leaned her back over his arm and gave her a kiss neither she nor any of the women looking on would ever forget.

The crowd erupted into cheers and applause that greeted them all the way back down the aisle.

Jade and Pryce's brother Darren were at the mid-point of the recessional when something flashed through the air, coming straight at Jade's head. Her years of beach volleyball stood her well, and she threw her hands up just in time to catch Beth's bouquet.

"I couldn't take the chance that someone else might catch it later!" Beth called over her shoulder, barely audible above the din.

Jade threw her head back and laughed, noticing

Mr. Malone was no longer visible at the back of the porch.

As soon as they reached the top of the stairs, Rena whisked the wedding party to the garden for additional pictures. There was just enough time for the hugs and kisses and tears she and Beth had been holding back all day.

"Where did he come from?" Beth didn't even have to say his name.

"I don't know." Jade fought down the urge to sob, not sure if the tears were of joy for Beth or despair for herself. "It's pretty obvious though. He's somebody's date. And it's not mine."

"I don't know whether to hate him for that, or love him for saving the song." Beth sniffed and dabbed her eyes, careful not to smear her mascara. "The last time I saw Tad, he looked green. I was pretty sure he wasn't going to be able to follow through, but I didn't know what to do." She shrugged. "I just figured we were paying Rena enough to fix it."

So Beth had known all along! Jade shook her head in wonder at her friend's cool-headed logic as Rena shooed them into their places. Much to Jade's chagrin, posing for the pictures was a mindless task. She'd hoped to have something take her mind off Kai's presence at the wedding, but standing and smiling only required the mental aptitude of Elena Dellisio, the women's trainer at the club. Jade found herself chuckling at the name, realizing for the first time it was probably a made-up version of "delicious," aimed at the sexual implication.

The thought of sex brought her full-circle back to Kai, and she found herself having to force her smiles. She needed to get that under control quick though. They would be eating soon and, from the head table, there was sure to be a good view of him with his damn, hot six-five frame.

Through the remainder of the pictures and lining up for the grand entrance, she planned her strategy for dealing with the soon-to-be-torn-out-of-the-Hotness-journal-for-good-this-time Mr. Malone. She decided not to make eye contact until she got seated. She wanted to enjoy Beth and Pryce's entrance without any distractions. Once seated, she would scan the crowd, make eye contact with him, and then immediately look away to speak with Darren, dismissing Kai completely and letting him know what a minuscule part he once played in her life. It was, after all, a mere three days really, out of twenty-six years.

Jade swept into the ballroom on Darren's arm, head erect, chin up, proud of the position as Beth's maid-of-honor. Thank heavens the best man was slightly taller than she in her heels. That fact made this entrance easier, knowing Kai was watching. She felt his eyes on her, no matter who his date was.

Jade felt the stare continuing, running shivers up her spine, though not the pleasant kind. Beth and Pryce were announced and made their entrance, and still it went on. It became a reaction to danger at some level, and as Darren pulled her chair out for her, she couldn't take it any longer. She followed the direction of the perceived threat and looked straight into the glaring eyes of Adam. Caitlyn, his date, was doing some glaring of her own. At him. Jade slid her gaze away in as dismissive a gesture as she knew how to give. So much for the practice. Now for the ballgame.

Jade took a drink of water to moisten her mouth that was suddenly parched. Her eyes scanned above the heads of the crowd until she found the one that stood out above the others. Her glance met Kai's and came to a dramatic standstill. His eyes crinkled into slits and she knew it was time to pull away while she could—before she got lost in them. *Retrieve the anger, quick. Who's he with?*

Jade moved her gaze to the woman on his right. Gram?

The water in her mouth got sucked in faster than it should have by her gasp. She sputtered and turned, grabbing her napkin. Unfortunately, a concerned Darren got in the way, and his sleeve became her napkin, receiving the spewed water like the sink by a dentist's chair.

Luckily, Darren's sense of humor rivaled Pryce's. He brushed it away nonchalantly with a laugh. "Not quite the blow-job I had in mind."

Jade's face burned as she dabbed her mouth and offered her heartfelt apologies. Once the moment passed, she took up her scan again. Kai was seated at the table with Gram and Marvin and Mom and Dad! At a table for five!

Kai was looking right at her, amusement tugging at the corners of his mouth. She raised her glass in a salute and nodded demurely. He laughed and raised his glass in an answering salute.

"Jade!" Pryce's voice drew her attention reluctantly back to the head table. "Gram called this morning to see if Mimi's seat was still open...said she had an unexpected guest." He tilted his head toward the table Jade had been eyeing.

"And you didn't tell us?" Beth's tone sounded more amazed than irritated. She turned to Jade and shook her head. "The one time he decides to keep a secret."

Pryce shrugged, nonplussed by the pseudo-compliment. "I wasn't keeping a secret. I didn't ask who the guest was. Didn't figure it mattered."

Beth patted his cheek and gave him a quick peck on the lips signifying all was forgiven. "Well, can you tell me how Kai Malone came to be the soloist at our wedding?"

Pryce shrugged again. "I have no idea, but from

the looks of Tad, I'd say Mr. Malone saved the day."

Tad sat at the table with his parents—tie loosened, coat unbuttoned, hair disheveled. The poor kid looked like he'd been in a brawl. He shook his head at the offer of a glass of wine.

The music started and Pryce led Beth gallantly to the dance floor for their first dance as husband and wife. Jade settled back into her chair. So Kai was still interested in her, and from the way her heart was beating, she felt the same. Much as she wanted to rush over to him and Gram to get the whole story behind this surprise, there were too many ceremonial obligations to take care of first. Dances with Darren and Pryce, toasts, dinner. She sighed in resignation. It would have to wait. But she'd gotten good at that.

The prime rib was succulent and tender, but Jade couldn't take more than a few bites. Her stomach tightened into a knot every time she thought about how she was going to approach Kai. The moment would be awkward at best.

Throughout dinner, her family seemed to enjoy his company. Whenever she looked their way, which was about once every thirty-two seconds by her calculations, they were deep in animated conversation. She noticed plenty of laughter and glass clinking from their table.

The sight at Adam's table was not nearly so amiable. Jade only glanced that way twice, but both times Caitlyn's face seemed to be etched into a permanent scowl, and Adam's half-lidded smirk said he'd had way too much to drink.

Beth and Pryce finally left the table to dance and mingle with the guests, and Jade knew she couldn't put off reconnecting with Kai any longer. She wanted to make the first move rather than waiting for him to come to her. She owed him that. She excused herself from Darren and skirted around the edge of the ballroom.

About halfway to her destination, just as she passed the doorway, Adam stepped in front of her, blocking the way. "Hey, darlin'. How 'bout a dance?" His speech was slurred and he reeked of alcohol.

"I don't think so, Adam." Jade sidestepped to go around him, but, even drunk, he was fast. He stepped into her this time, caught her around the waist, and spun her halfway around.

Her hand went up to push him away, but instead, a large hand closed around hers, freeing her from Adam's grasp. With a gasp of surprise, she looked up into Kai's stern countenance. His slanted eyes, though normally pleasant, held a foreboding look this time. "Jade promised her first dance to me tonight." The voice was a threatening growl.

With no other word of invitation, Kai led her to the dance floor and pulled her against him into a slow rhythm. Her knees went weak at his touch and she grasped his hand firmly. "I want to introduce myself." His deep voice meandered its way down her spine like warm massage oil. "My name is Kai Malone. My partner and I own a software company named Techtron, which we are in the process of selling to a Japanese firm. Negotiations are almost complete. We are very wealthy and will be unimaginably rich when the final deal goes through about a year from now."

Jade lifted her chin and kept her face straight, trying to match Kai's somber expression. She swallowed, making sure the butterflies in her stomach wouldn't escape if she opened her mouth. "I'm Jade Bartholomew, only child of Jack and Linda Bartholomew. They're attorneys in L.A. I live with my cat Paisley in a small apartment over my grandmother's house on the Strand in Manhattan Beach." She concentrated on getting the words out. Only half of her brain seemed to be working. The other half wanted to concentrate on the feel of the arm around her back or the touch of the hand holding hers. "Currently, I run an on-line critiquing and editing service, but as of July first I will be employed full-time as an assistant editor at Samuels Publishing."

Kai's eyebrows shot up in surprise, and his lips twitched as they started to pull up into a grin. "I'm thirty-three years old, by the way, been divorced for four years. Just so you'll know, my ex-wife Hazel lives in New York and is also an editor of a small, but popular home décor magazine. Or at least that's what she was doing the last time I inquired."

His ex-wife was in the publishing business? Jade's back muscles stiffened involuntarily.

Kai must have noticed the sudden tension. He moved his large palm in a circular caress across the small of her back as he continued their steps around the dance floor. She felt the heat from his hand through the fabric of her dress. Her muscles loosened a bit at the warmth. "Hazel and I don't talk very often anymore...and your professions seem to be the only thing you two have in common."

So he was sexy, rich, and a mind reader. Jade relaxed into him; the large hand on her back moved on around her waist, pulling her closer. Head resting against his jaw, she could smell his cologne, a light scent with hints of green and summer rain. Had he really been away for almost a month? Her angst earlier that night had been for naught. It seemed like just yesterday he held her like this on her deck. She took a long, leisurely breath before continuing with her end of the introduction/confession.

"My ex-boyfriend, Adam Brock, was the guy you just tore me away from. Thanks, by the way."

"Well, it was either gonna be me or your dad. I just happened to be a little faster."

Jade took the lead for a minute and turned to

her parents' table where four pairs of eyes watched them. She winked at her dad and he returned the motion.

She picked up her previous comment where she'd left off. "Adam is a prick. He told me the callas were from him and threw away the card. I thought you went to Japan and forgot about me and I didn't find out the truth until last night. I tried to call you this morning—"

Kai interrupted her with a kiss to her forehead as the song ended. "You don't have to explain. Gram told me everything." He stepped back away from her and looked directly into her eyes. "I'm sorry I wasn't totally honest with you from the beginning. I would very much like another chance to be..." his eyes crinkled into slits, "...um, to be included in that journal of yours."

Jade squeezed his hand and laughed, all the nervousness and tension completely gone. "Well, it just so happens that I got your page out of the trash last night and taped you back in. And you know what they say about the third time being a charm."

They strolled back to the table arm-in-arm, arriving at the same time as Beth and Pryce. Jade kissed her mom, then her dad. "Thanks for almost saving me from Adam." She whispered it, but everyone around was talking, so she doubted she would have been heard anyway.

Dad chuckled in her ear. "I'm just glad there was someone younger around to take care of you for me.

Jade moved on to Gram with a hug and a kiss. Gram gave her a pat on the cheek and then made the introductions to Marvin. He was charming with a warm smile and a slight Irish lilt. Jade noticed that Gram absolutely beamed when she looked at him.

As Pryce pulled in extra chairs for everyone,

Beth motioned to the waiter with a tray of champagne.

"Kai, we would like to propose a toast to you." Pryce's eyes sparkled with mischief. "We've spoken with Tad, and it appears that he owes you a big one, and we will be forever in your debt. Here's to Sir Kai, the knight in shining armor who saved my bride's special song."

"To Sir Kai!" The group clinked their glasses together, along with some of the other guests at surrounding tables.

Jade had forgotten all about Kai's singing, but now her curiosity was piqued anew. "Would somebody please tell me what happened?"

All the surrounding fingers pointed to Kai. He shook his head modestly, but at Jade's prodding, finally threw up his hands in surrender. "Okay, once more, and then the subject is closed for good. I took my golf clubs with me to Japan, so I wanted to put them back in my locker. When I got to the locker room, it was deserted except for this poor kid kneeling by one of the stools, puking his guts up...with a bottle of Jagermeister sitting beside him. He'd evidently tried to boost his confidence with some shots. Some big shots. A bunch of big shots, actually."

He stopped, but Jade was determined to hear the rest. "Go on." She tapped his hand with her fingernail. "Total honesty, remember?"

Kai rolled his eyes. "He was crying, saying that Beth and his parents were gonna kill him...how he was supposed to sing this special song, but he just couldn't do it. Well..." Kai let out an embarrassed sigh, "in college, I made extra money singing at weddings. I knew the song, so I told him I'd sing instead if he wanted me to. I practiced a couple of times...and I sang."

He shrugged it off as no big deal, but Jade felt

her face beaming just like Gram's had been earlier. She gave his hand a squeeze and was rewarded by one of his gorgeous smiles.

The band struck up a fox trot. Gram and Marvin made their way to the dance floor and fell into a perfect rhythm. They made a truly stunning couple. A warm pride filled Jade. What other seventy-eight-year-old could pull off wearing three-inch gold stiletto sandals while dancing the fox trot?

Kai, Pryce, and her dad fell into easy conversation about the sale of Techtron. Jade and Beth proceeded to tell her mom about the wayward "falsie" that was still probably hanging on the rose.

Soon it was time to cut the cake and everyone gathered around to catch the moment on film. The sentimentality of the tradition was sweet and having Kai's arm snuggled around her waist made this time even sweeter. But the knowledge her best friend was going to be leaving soon on her honeymoon caught up with her, and with it came the emotion of the night before. "I think I'd like some fresh air." Her voice cracked, despite her willing it not to.

Kai rubbed his knuckles down her cheek in a tender gesture that made her eyes get misty. "Let's go take a walk."

The night was balmy with just a touch of warm breath from the ocean. They strolled silently down the porch and down the steps at the back. Moonlight shimmered on the swimming pool, covering its surface with thousands of diamonds. The twinkling drew Jade; she slipped out of her shoe and dipped a toe in, watching the diamonds scatter away in a delicate ring.

Kai held her arm as she bent to put her shoe back on. Raising up, she leaned into him, turning her face up to offer her mouth. She held her breath as his face moved slowly toward her. When his lips met hers, she closed her eyes and melted into the moment.

Muscled arms moved around her, pulling her against him gently and she glided a hand up his arm and across his shoulder to rest on the back of his head. His lips moved more firmly against hers. She parted her lips to allow his tongue entry.

He didn't hurry. His tongue brushed her lips then drew across her teeth, tickling its way on farther behind to the roof of her mouth and back. The sensation was exquisite and she arched against him, letting her head relax onto the hand that moved into her hair.

She sighed, keeping her eyes closed as his tongue left her mouth, wondering where it would land next. The wet nuzzle against her neck made her gasp, and then his mouth was back on hers, firm and insistent, tongue moving in and out to a slow rhythm. She became vaguely aware that it was keeping time to the music that filtered down from the ballroom.

Jade swayed to one side, then the other, and Kai took the hint, moving one arm down her back, directing her other arm into his as he curled it between their bodies in an intimate dance embrace.

When his mouth finally relinquished its hold, she opened her eyes to find his blue ones fixed on hers. They held the gaze for just a moment before he kissed her forehead. She rested a cheek against his chest, and they finished the song swaying side-to-side, feet never leaving the pavement.

Jade wished the song would go on forever, but it was over much too soon. Breathless with emotion, she tried to say "Wow!" but the word just came out as a croak.

Kai laughed his low rumble. "My feelings exactly. How 'bout I go fetch us a drink?"

Jade needed something she could gulp. "Make mine a Perrier?"

167

Kai nodded and started toward the steps. About halfway there, he stopped and rushed back, planting a firm kiss on her lips. "I'll hurry."

Jade rubbed her hands along her arms, luxuriating in the tingle remaining from Kai's touch. She'd never experienced a kiss like that—except maybe the last time they were together. Never even from Adam. His had always been firmer and, now she realized, more urgent.

Music drifted toward her, this time not from the ballroom, but from the ocean. A party boat out on the water, no doubt. She turned toward the breeze, barely able to make out the lights a little way offshore.

Footsteps coming up behind her heralded Kai's return. She smiled when she realized how fast her heart was beating just at the sound. Two arms came around her from behind and grabbed her breasts. "Whydn't you jus' lean over and let me fuck you righ' here?"

Jade didn't have to hear the voice. The overload of alcohol on his breath would have told her it was Adam. She grabbed his hands and tried to extricate them from her breasts, but he grasped tighter, pulling down, trying to make them pop free of the dress. All the while he ground his erection against her rear-end.

She bucked hard against him, hoping to jar him loose and hurt him in the process. "Stop it, Adam!" She let go of his hands and slapped wildly and blindly at his head.

His hands took the opportunity to yank down her top. He squeezed her bared nipples, causing her to yelp in pain. "Yeah, tha's it. Scream for me, baby."

Jade stomped on his foot, fighting to keep her balance in the high heels, and ground her elbow into his ribs. She heard glass breaking behind her, and then the hands left her body with a jerk.

She pulled her top up and swung around just in time to see Kai's fist connect with Adam's jaw. The force of the punch threw Adam a few feet. Head thrown back, he stumbled, trying to gain his footing and probably his equilibrium. Instead of landing on the hard concrete, he toppled into the pool.

Kai started toward the pool, but Jade took a firm grip on his arm and held him. "He's a good swimmer."

She checked to make sure she was properly covered then turned her attention to the figure breaking the surface of the water. Adam sputtered a few times and shook his head, then fixed the two of them with a threatening stare as he began to tread water. "Stupid slut." His words were not as slurred. Evidently the rush of cool water had sobered him some. He side-stroked toward the ladder.

"You okay?" Kai did a visual scan, but seemed satisfied she wasn't hurt.

"I'm fine, thanks. What about my hair?"

He pulled a dangling hairpin free and smoothed a piece of hair back into place, anchoring it again with the pin.

Their attention was drawn back to the pool as a dripping Adam emerged. He rubbed his crotch in a vulgar manner. "Hey, bitch!"

Kai's hands clenched into fists as he started toward Adam a second time. A pang of guilt squeezed her stomach. Kai was too involved in this already because of her, and Adam would be hell-bent on revenge. She needed time to think this out and decide what to do. She grabbed his arm. "Don't, Kai." She turned him toward her. "He's all talk."

Kai held her gaze for a long moment, and then nodded his agreement. "C'mon. Let's go back in." He pulled her in the direction of the steps.

Adam's laugh crackled with a sarcastic edge. "My parents were cremated!"

His words sank in with a thud. Jade knew she should feel anger or embarrassment; instead, there was only pity. For Adam, that he could never trust anyone to love him for who he was. And for herself—that she was never able to love him for who he was.

"We'll need to tell someone about the broken water bottles." Kai hurried her along the porch. "And Beth and Pryce are ready to leave."

****

The water pushed Adam a douse closer toward sobriety, and he rubbed his throbbing jaw. His anger dissipated gradually, replaced by a feeling of embarrassment. He sighed and ran his hand down his face. "Okay, buddy, face it. The Jade chapter is now officially closed. Better find a new source and get outta town."

Caitlyn had told him to get lost right before he went looking for Jade, so he didn't have to worry about her coming to look for him. No way in hell would he humiliate himself by going back into that crowd. He'd find some place to hide out until everyone was gone. He slapped his thigh. Yep. Keys were still in his pocket and not on the bottom of the pool.

He made his way around to the back of the clubhouse, the area close to the driving range and putting greens. The huge wooden door was heavy but unlocked, and he breathed a sigh of relief. He vaguely remembered the locker rooms were off of this hallway. That would be the perfect refuge. With the ballroom at the other end of the huge building, it was unlikely any guests would make their way down here.

He found the locker room door, stumbled through it and collapsed into the first chair. The roar in his ears stopped, replaced by a gasp that pulled his attention to the mirrored area on his right. Like an apparition unveiling before his eyes, a naked woman stood just a few feet away.

His eyes moved up from her hairless pubic mound to her gigantic, perfectly formed breasts and back down. She made no move to cover herself. "You from the wedding?"

Adam nodded mutely, not the least bit regretful that he'd stumbled into the women's locker room instead of the men's.

She leaned forward, head down and turned the hairdryer back on full force. "Just follow the big hall to where it turns left, then go straight all the way down."

Adam was enjoying the view much too much to leave. She finished drying her hair and raised back up. "You still here?"

He nodded again, this time letting his visual scan travel all the way up to her face. *Oh. My. God. It's Hot Porn Video Chick.* "You're the…the, um, you're the babe on my favorite website." The thought of the video made his cock want to burst its seams. He stroked it through the wet material.

Her face broke out in an obviously pleased smile. "Have you voted for me? I need your vote to get the movie contract, you know." The voice was a coo and it floated around his ear and made him feel lightheaded and giddy.

"Vote for you? Baby, I vote for you three times a day and have for the past month." He stood up and walked over to where she was standing within touching distance. "I'm Adam Brock." He held out his hand.

Rather than taking his hand immediately, she ran her hands through her black hair, thrusting her breasts toward him and giving her body a shake, just like on the video.

Then, she held out her hand. When she ran her tongue over her lips, it left a moist trail. "Glad to meet you. I'm Elena Delissio."

Chapter Twenty

Kai watched Jade as Beth and Pryce's car pulled away. She smiled, waved, wiped her eyes, sniffed a little. How was it that women could always get so many emotions going at one time?

He held out his hand, and she clutched it like a lifeline. A little tug and she came into his arms, relaxing against his chest. Her body jerked with a few more sniffs as he stroked her back. He sensed her resolve strengthen, those gorgeous shoulders squared, and she flashed him a smile that he read as gratitude. And hopefully promise.

"You okay?" He rubbed his knuckles across her cheek, wanting to kiss away her tears but wary of her reaction with the small crowd of people still milling around.

"Yeah, I'm okay, and I'm really glad you're here." She took the initiative and pressed her soft lips to his.

So she was the take-charge type, not the kind who sat around always waiting for the guy to make the first move. He had her pegged that way from the start, but the weeks in Japan of not hearing from her had made him doubt his judgment. Surprises were okay as long as they didn't come with huge price tags attached. A feeling in his gut told him he didn't have to worry about such shenanigans from Jade.

"Do you have any plans tonight?" She nibbled her bottom lip shyly, but at the same time the street lamp lit her eyes with a sparkle of mischief.

"Do I have plans? Yes, indeed. I have Plan A,

Plan B, and Plan C." He ran his fingertips across her back, finding a bit of skin exposed between her top and her skirt. She shivered. "And all three of them revolve around you."

Her laugh was soft and throaty. "Could we go for a walk? It's such a beautiful night, sort of magical, you know? I'm not ready to leave here."

A walk would be nice. A chance to relax. And there was one place that would be perfect for relaxing.

"You're gonna find I'll never turn down an offer to stay at a golf course a little longer," he confessed. Her arm looped through his as they walked. "And I've got someplace I want to show you. A special place."

Their path took them across the parking lot. Jade pointed out Adam's car to him. "Probably passed out somewhere."

Kai's stomach tightened. Could the guy be really hurt? He didn't want another confrontation, but he didn't want an assault charge either. "Do you think I need to go find him? Check on him?"

Jade pulled him onto the darkness of the cart path with a finger across her lips to shush him. "Look."

A half-clad, giggling Elena Delissio was making her way down the sidewalk at the side of the building with a staggering Adam Brock attached. One of his arms was thrown around her shoulder. His other hand explored inside her unbuttoned blouse.

Kai recalled the time he'd left the club to find Elena leaning against his car. She asked for a ride home, claiming her car wouldn't start, but all the way to her place, she'd leaned toward him, brushing her gargantuan, firm implants against his arm. He chuckled now, remembering the huffy way she slammed his car door after he turned down her offer to "come in for a while."

Jade and Kai stood still and watched the comical scenario of Elena prying Adam loose and tucking him into the passenger seat of his car. Apparently she had become his alternate date for the evening.

"Poor bloody bastard." Kai kept his voice low, though he doubted he could be heard over Brock's obnoxious singing.

Jade creased her forehead in question. "Feeling sorry for him now?"

"If he thought my fist was a jawbreaker, just wait 'til he tries to nibble on one of those."

Jade elbowed him in his side, drawing a "Mmmph." She was a strong one too.

Kai grasped the elbow, hoping to keep the weapon at bay and turned her back to their walk. "C'mon, Shank."

She laughed at his use of her nickname. "You know, the one that hit you may have been my best shot ever."

At the end of the cart path, he headed her across Fairway Sixteen toward the ocean. Walking in the grass proved difficult in heels, so she slipped out of her shoes and wiggled her toes in the grass. "Mmmmm. That...feels...sooo...good."

Kai's erection sprang up at the sound of those words. God, he hoped he could make her say that soon, just like that.

They strolled along hand-in-hand for a few more minutes before his "special place" came into view. The gazebo sat on the point of the highest cliff on the course. The way the ground jutted out gave the illusion that the white Grecian-style structure hung suspended out over the ocean.

A quick intake of breath accompanied the squeeze to his bicep. Jade obviously approved of his surprise. She slipped back into her shoes when they stepped onto the marble flooring. "This is beautiful! I never knew it was here."

"Most people just overlook it, I think. They assume it's decoration. I love to finish a round late in the evening and then sit out here and watch the sunset."

"Why, Mr. Malone." Jade moved against him, circling his neck with her arms. "I do believe you have a romantic heart under that rugged exterior."

The party boat she had heard earlier lingered, providing music. "Would you like to dance?" His arms circled her waist and he pulled her close, guiding her around the makeshift dance floor, humming the tune into the citrus scent of her hair.

"You know this song?" She murmured the words and her breath against his neck made him snuggle her closer.

"Yeah. It's one of my mom's favorites."

"Sing it to me."

Right at that moment, if she'd said, "Fly up to the sky and pull a star down for me," he would've tried. This request was easy. "Once on a high and windy hill," he sang, "In the morning mist two lovers kissed, and the world stood still…"

Never had a song been more perfectly timed to an occurrence.

When the last note faded, he didn't let her go, and she didn't object. Instead he found her mouth with his and the next few songs became background music to some of the most intoxicating kisses he'd ever experienced.

But then, with no warning, Jade moved her hands from around his neck to his chest. It took him a few seconds to realize she was pushing him away. "Did I do something wrong?" Damn! Not again.

Even without light, he saw her smile as she propelled him backward onto one of the couches. She shook her head slowly then turned and moved away from him. The exaggerated sway of her hips was a much better hypnotizing gimmick than a pocket watch.

What she was up to? A great song by Sting—"Roxanne" wasn't it?—carried over the waves from the party boat. She should be in his arms, not several feet away, dancing by herself.

Still, he couldn't keep his eyes off of her. Her movements tantalized him—hands gliding over her hair, head back, hips rising and lowering alternately to turn her in a slow seductive circle.

Her dress reflected the meager starlight, but her body appeared as a dark shadow. It gave a surreal quality to the image before him. Kai's breath caught in reaction to the erotic scene.

He sat mesmerized as her hands moved to the waistband of her skirt, unfastened the hook and slid the zipper open. The soft undulations of her hips moved the skirt to reveal the most perfect ass he'd ever seen, clad only in a pink lace thong.

His gaze moved with the skirt down the length of her long, sinewy legs. He could almost feel them locked around him. His breathing came faster. Her hands moved down and up and down her thighs in hypnotic circles, drawing his eyes everywhere at once. His mouth went dry, heat moved into his face. He had actually been sitting with his mouth gaped open. Hopefully, it was dark enough she didn't see.

Jade braced her back against the door post and lowered into a slow knee bend, hands smoothing over the tops of her thighs. Back up she went, hands moving erotically inside the thighs and up. Down. Up. Down. Up—to the slow, constant rhythm of the song.

His cock throbbed to the beat. She was killing him. He thoroughly understood the term "strip tease" now.

Oblivious to his aching need, Jade turned her back to him and unzipped the shimmering top. It fell away at the sides and dropped to the floor. She turned back to him, revealing breasts that threatened to spill over the top of a pink lace strapless bra.

His fingers twitched with the desire to unhook that bra and perform some teasing of his own. As if in response to his thoughts, Jade leaned forward, knees stiff, legs spread, moving her hands behind her. When she raised up, the bra was held in place only by her hands.

She moved toward him, emerging into the soft starlight, Aphrodite come to life. Instinct told him not to move. This was her show; she was in charge. He'd wait to see what she wanted.

One knee slid against the outside of his thigh. The other moved along the other side, and then she was astride him, not sitting on him, not even making contact with him, still moving her hips in slow circles and up and down to the final beats of the music.

He couldn't bear not touching her any longer, yet he was reluctant to break the spell she'd woven around him. Starting at her ankles, he moved his fingertips lightly up her legs, following the contour of the muscle lines so prominent in those amazing calves. He rounded the bend of her knee and moved up her thighs as she finally settled down on his lap.

His fingers traced the curve of her hips, and she shivered. She held his eyes with her steady gaze as she lowered her lips to his mouth. The bra dropped onto the cushion beside him as she moved her hands to caress his face. Her perfume mingled with the scent of her arousal as she positioned his hands on her breasts. He inhaled deeply, letting all his senses familiarize to her.

"I want you, Kai." Her voice was soft and husky.

"And I've wanted you for the past month." No lying. No pretense. Nothing but honesty this time around.

Her arms slid around his neck. She brushed her nipples across his lips, stopping just long enough to allow a slow suck on each one. He moved his tongue across the point and it drew tighter. Her fingers moved through the hair on the back of his head.

"My place is close." His brain was developing one plan while his erection screamed for something more immediate.

"No. I don't want to wait any longer. I want you here. Now." The words were breathless and urgent. "Do you have any protection with you?"

Thank God he'd listened to his cocky side this afternoon. It had convinced him that if Gram's plan went smoothly, he might be spending the night at Jade's. "Yeah, I do," he confessed. Their sighs of relief came in unison, and they laughed at their mutual need. "But here?" He looked for a piece of furniture that might be comfortable. No way would he make love to Jade on the floor. At least not the first time.

She slid from his lap, then stood and gave a saucy turn, holding his hand and pulling him toward an armless chaise. She adjusted the back so it was midway between sitting and reclining.

Then she turned her attention to adjusting him. She pushed his jacket from his shoulders and tossed it onto a nearby chair. He worked on his cufflinks as she unbuttoned his shirt. The shirt followed his coat. Fingernails tickled across his ribs then circled his nipples, replaced by gentle bites and then soothing lips.

She leaned down to untie his shoes, presenting him with the lovely heart shape separated by the strip of pink lace. He traced the delicate vertebrae down her back as they gave way to the soft roundness of her curvy ass.

She unclasped his belt and inched the zipper

down laying the waistband open. Her thumbs slid inside the sides of his boxers, freeing him of the underwear and trousers in one smooth move. As he rid himself of his socks, she stood back and took him in slowly but with an admiring smile.

As if understanding the seriousness of this inspection, his penis stood stiff and straight at attention. He was everything she'd imagined him to be. And more. She grasped him with a firm hold and stepped against him, sliding her hand forward and back along his length.

His quick intake of breath exploded into a groan of pleasure as his mouth engaged hers. His hands moved over and around her, everywhere at once, trails of heat lingering after each touch. With focused effort, she pulled herself loose from his embrace long enough to open the condom and roll it into place. "Why don't you sit down?" She kept her phrase short and to the point. Her tongue seemed to have a mind of its own and talking hardly seemed its primary function right then.

"No. You." He slid his thumbs under the strips of lace at her hips and slid them over the curves. The darkness heightened her sense of touch, making her acutely aware of the whisper of his fingertips and the soft material gliding down the length of her legs. She trembled with passion, keeping a hand on his shoulder as she stepped free of the panties.

Although her intentions had been to be on top, she didn't protest as he eased her onto the chaise. She was a piece of clay in the hands of an artist.

"My turn to give you a little of that sweet torture you're so good at." He pulled her hands over her head and settled them into a grasp on the back of the lounger. "Now, promise me you'll keep them there."

She was like a smoldering ember already. His warm breath would have her exploding into flame very shortly. "I promise," she whispered, "...until I can't stand it any longer." Her head relaxed against one of her arms. The rest of her body followed suit as she gave herself over to him, his to position as he wanted.

He took her legs, slowly massaging the length of each one. As his strong fingers kneaded the muscles, tension gave way to giddiness, making her feel loose and free.

"Is there anything more seductive than a woman wearing nothing but a pair of high heels and a strand of pearls?" His deep voice vibrated through her as he positioned her legs on each side of the chaise, opening her to the exploration of his lips and tongue. She'd never felt more beautiful or more desired.

His tongue caught the rhythm of the ocean waves lapping the beach below, and she imagined herself being carried away by his tide. The words whirling about in her head refused to congeal into any logical form as she submerged deeper. She managed "oh" and "ah" and allowed her moans and heightened movements to let him know when his caresses were on target. Thankfully, he read her body language as if he'd taught the course on it.

Whispered comments on the feel of her, the taste of her, floated around her ears on the breezes from the Pacific. Her breathing quickened. When it increased to panting, his assault became relentless.

The muscles in her arms constricted as her head pushed against the chair and her back drew into an involuntary arch. The signal shot upward into her brain and brought awareness that the tingling sensations had begun an undulating rhythm deep inside. She was getting ready to climax. Augh! Their first time should be together. She would have to move fast. "I want to finish on you." She spewed the words on a quick exhalation.

Kai wasn't sure what that meant, but her hurried movements indicated she wanted them to switch places. In five seconds he was on the chair and Jade's long legs straddled him.

When she slid down onto him, he felt the grasp of her muscles and then her meaning became clear. She was in the throes of an orgasm! Was there no end to the surprises this woman held?

Hands on his shoulders, she moved up and down the length of his cock, wet and slippery, tight and delicious. He brushed her nipples with his palms, pinched them and rolled them between his thumb and finger.

The fuse caught fire in his testicles and moved up the length of his erection, gaining speed and intensity. He held back, waiting for Jade. The muscles in her lean thighs pumped her faster and faster until her body stiffened and her back tightened into a slow, curving arch.

He let himself go then, rising up to meet her, pumping with thrusts of his own. The sweet fire made a final rush up through the length of him; he finished in a spectacular explosion as Jade collapsed against his chest.

He closed his arms around her, insuring she wouldn't get up too quickly. God, she felt wonderful—her head on his shoulder, soft breath against his neck. He'd gladly give one of his millions if it could make this moment last.

The breeze stirred around them and she shivered. Reluctantly, he let go with an arm long enough to reach his jacket and drape it over her.

"Will it disturb the greens keepers in the morning when they find us here?"

The smile in her voice made him chuckle, and when he did, his spent cock slid free of her. She groaned in response. "Sorry, ma'am. You'll have to give me half-an-hour to recycle."

That brought her to a sitting position. "You can do that again? In a half-hour?" She made it sound like a feat of magic. Obviously she had no idea how strong an effect she had on him.

He bent his legs to give her a back support, and she leaned back onto them, circling his stomach with her fingernails in rivulets of pleasure. His jacket hung open down the front, exposing the cleavage created when her arms moved. He became acutely aware that, in this new position, her wetness was warm against his lower stomach and his cock was being gently massaged by her ass. "A half-hour's gonna be stretching it if you keep that up."

She gave him a wicked smile and increased the clenching movements behind.

That was it. He wanted her this night, in his house, in his bed. The gazebo was exotic and exciting, but it couldn't take the place of a bed where he could stretch out on top of her and learn her inch by inch.

He caught her in his arms and swung his legs off the chaise. "This was your turn. Now it's mine." He pushed his jacket off her shoulders, wanting to feel her skin as he kissed her long and deep. Then he set her on her feet. "My house is only fifteen minutes away."

She let out a delightful squeal and hurried to gather her clothes and put them back on as he did the same. They cut across Number Seventeen fairway, moseying quietly toward the Number Eighteen. As they neared the green, an odd sound caught Kai's attention and drew it to the far edge where the green sat below a large bunker.

It took a few seconds for his brain to register what was happening, but eventually the form and the sound gelled—a couple, deep in the throes of making love, oblivious to anything else around them. The darkness hid their identity, but the sounds they were making were easily identifiable.

"So our idea wasn't a unique one," he whispered and guided Jade toward the opposite side so they wouldn't disturb the couple.

A few steps later, Jade tripped, her foot caught by some unseen object. Kai's quick arm caught her around the waist and kept her from falling. She balanced on one foot, hand on his back, as he leaned over and freed her high heel from another shoe with long gold ropes attached.

When he held it up to show her the culprit, she let out a startled gasp.

"Oh my God. That's Gram's."

He never would've imagined she could run so fast in a bridesmaid's get-up, but he found himself sprinting after her toward the clubhouse, laughing to himself and then out loud. He didn't know if he'd be able to keep up, but he sure as hell was gonna try. This one was definitely full of surprises.

Chapter Twenty-One

"Here we are." Kai pushed a button on the console, and the great bronze gates opened, revealing the mystery behind the ten-foot wall.

"Oh, wow!" The exclamation slipped from Jade's lips before she could catch it. She hoped it didn't sound too much like a star-struck teenager. Kai had simply referred to it as "my place." He hadn't prepared her for this ... this sprawling estate.

The house—no, this could definitely be labeled a mansion—appeared to be straight out of *Architectural Digest*, a work of art in buff-colored stucco with a multi-angled roofline in bronze tile. Windows of varying shapes and sizes were perfectly placed not only for dramatic effect, but Jade suspected also for maximum use of solar energy.

"Do you like it?"

It was more than just a question. Jade heard a need for affirmation in Kai's voice, a vulnerability she hadn't expected. And he wasn't watching her for a reaction. He was taking in the sight of the house as if he too were seeing it for the first time as they moved slowly up the long driveway.

"It's magnificent. It's breath-taking." Jade groped for an adjective that would adequately convey what she saw.

Kai slowed the car to a stop and scanned the house from end to end. He reached for Jade's hand and brushed it with his lips, letting out a long sigh of relief, maybe? "It was the first design we came up with on Techtron software, and we invested everything we had to build it as a 'spec' home." He shrugged. "When the time came, I couldn't bear to part with it."

Ah! Jade understood. "So this is your baby."

A smile lit his face and the pride in his look warmed her heart. "This is my life. Everything Mark and I have worked for—the abstracts, the intangibles—are encapsulated here into something warm and comfortable and tangible."

Funny, she hadn't really asked him too much about Techtron. But until a few hours ago, she hadn't known what a huge stake he had in the company. "So you're an architect, too?"

Kai shook his head as he shifted the car back into drive and headed around to one side. "No, Mark is. We're computer geeks, but he studied architecture, too. We decided to combine our talents."

There were three other cars parked in the garage. A black Mercedes and a couple of foreign ones Jade didn't recognize. "Well, the marriage seems perfect."

Kai turned the car off. "We do okay." He slipped his arm around her waist and pulled her to him in a warm, lingering kiss.

Tired as she was, Jade felt the stirring inside her. Arriving at the house with all its surprise brought her senses to full awareness, and Kai sent them into overload with the simple touch of his lips trailing from her mouth downward. She laid her palm against his cheek enjoying the sandpapery texture of his stubble starting to emerge, not willing to let go of the moment just yet.

"Ready to go in?" The words were murmured against her neck, so she felt both the heat and the vibration of them to her core.

The shiver that etched up her spine made her lose her breath, but she managed a quick nod. They entered the house through a room off the garage filled with sports equipment. The variety astounded Jade as she tried to take it all in. Fishing gear, skis, several sets of golf clubs, tennis racquets, and a wet suit hung around two of the walls. Another sported a kayak, and the fourth, a surfboard.

"You're a sports enthusiast." She smiled her delight. They had more in common than she'd dreamed, and it was a relief to know he didn't work all the time.

Kai nodded and led her through another door. "And I like to cook." A vast kitchen with stainless steel appliances and green granite work surfaces spread out before her. Warm mahogany cabinets and shelves balanced the industrial look and gave a homey feel. A cozy breakfast nook occupied an alcove surrounded on three sides by windows. Through an archway, a long rectangular table in the same mahogany as the cabinets presided over a large formal dining room. A crystal chandelier glistened in the center.

"Wine?" Kai guided her toward an octagonal island in the middle of the workspace and slid two glasses off the rack hanging above it. "I have an excellent Pinot Noir here."

Jade nodded. He'd surely read her mind. She needed wine. And a place to get out of these shoes.

He used the waiter's corkscrew with skill. Gram had a theory that men who used those easy one-smooth-step-push-and-pull gizmos were lousy in bed. "Women, like wine, shouldn't be uncorked too quickly," Gram would say. "A man who's willing to put a little work into opening a bottle will treat a woman the same way."

"Do you cook a lot?"

"Every night. At least, every night I'm home, which until a couple of months ago was most."

He twisted the screw slowly and deliberately into the center then angled the lever against the bottle. Her breath caught as the cork glided free of the opening. She and the pinot started breathing again at precisely the same time.

He poured a glass for each of them and handed one to her. "Would you like something to eat? I could fix you something."

His wide-eyed boyish expression told her he was serious. How sweet. "Not now. But maybe breakfast tomorrow?" she asked pointedly.

A deep chuckled rolled out. He leaned down and kissed her then clinked his glass against hers. "Just what I like, Shank; a woman who plans ahead, especially about eating. C'mon." He took her hand and led her into the living area.

Openness greeted her, obviously a design with entertaining in mind. She admired the expansive, high ceilings and one wall of nothing but French doors and windows that gave way to a large deck with the ocean beyond. Sectional couches and chairs in sandstone colors were scattered about, forming small conversation areas that would be a perfect setting for two or fifty. The focal point was a massive stone fireplace open on all four sides. She imagined the warmth generated by a roaring fire and Kai's arms around her as they lounged in front of it on a wintry night.

Her thoughts were way ahead of her. She drew them back to the present and the warm June night.

What word best described the house and the room? The size and the exquisite perfection of every detail stunned the first-time viewer. Or at least this one. But she found her word. Stunning. "This is absolutely stunning."

"No, Jade, this is just a house." Kai pulled her into a kiss that left her head spinning. Either that, or the bottom had just dropped out of her alcohol threshold. "You, on the other hand, are absolutely stunning." His lips seared down the side of her neck.

"You can explore the house all you want later. First, I want to explore you."

"Mmmmm. Has it been a half hour yet?"

He broke away long enough to check his watch. "One hour...thirteen minutes..." He gave his report, alternating between kisses and soft bites down her shoulder. "...and forty-six seconds."

She tried but failed to keep the chuckle out of her voice. "Then you've had time to recycle twice." The breath from his laugh scampered across her bare back and made her shoulder blades tighten in response.

"Well, Shank, if we're going to keep score, I might as well throw in the towel now. From what I could tell at the gazebo, you must've had me down eighteen to one."

Jade gave an overly dramatic sigh. "I'm just one of those lucky women." She shrugged. "You know what they say: easy come, easy come. Or something like that."

Kai brushed his fingers across her cheek. "I think that makes me the lucky one."

If she had known the way, she would have raced him to the bedroom. He led her through the foyer, a large formal area with pale green marble floors and a wide staircase.

"Four guest suites upstairs." He turned to her with a wink. "I'll give you the long tour later." He indicated a series of rooms off to the other side. "Library. Workout room. In-home theater."

A wide hallway at the back of the foyer led to another wing. A couple of large bathrooms. A room with a pool table and a bar. The hall ended abruptly at an ornately carved mahogany double door.

"The master suite, milady." Kai swung the doors open with a flourish.

Jade gasped in pleasure and surprise. It was as though she had stepped back in time about two thousand years. Before her lay a Grecian temple.

Four large pillars formed the corners of an enormous bed. Yards of soft, billowy fabric draped down and between the pillars, stirring sensuously in the night breeze. A bed designed for making love if she'd ever seen one, but it seemed more like a woman's fantasy than a man's. It didn't quite fit her perception of Kai. Like in the living area, one entire wall was made up of French doors about half of which were open.

The floor, bed, and moldings were creamy marble. Two large, overstuffed chairs, a couch of the same design, and all the walls were done in sandy brown. A few peach and salmon accent pieces were strategically placed.

No pictures hung on the walls, but her gaze was drawn to the numerous Greek statues scattered about—some freestanding, some atop pedestals. They certainly enhanced the Greek temple theme, but somehow they didn't say "Kai" to her either, unless he had modeled for them, which she doubted. She would have never thought of him as a Greek temple bedroom kind of guy. *There must be lots more layers of him to uncover,* she decided. *But the uncovering should be fun.*

A glass tabletop sat on two short pillars in one corner near a small fireplace. Peach and brown striped cushions adorned its chairs.

Just beyond the doors outside, wisps of steam curled from a small white hot tub. Big enough for only one, or maybe two? The room was suffused with intimacy, furnished with a couple in mind. That thought tightened her stomach a bit. As she uncovered Kai's layers, she hoped she didn't find the heart of a player.

"Kai, this is more amazing than the other side of the house, but I wouldn't have pictured this décor for you." She slipped out of her shoes and let the cool floor relax the aching in her feet.

"Yeah? Me either." He chuckled. "My sister Miranda's an interior decorator. She did all of this." He swept his arm around. "I think it's a bit over-the-top," he sighed with resignation, "but she's my sister." His mouth curled up on one side and he added, "She's gonna like you. They all will."

Jade smiled, secure that her instincts about him were pretty much on target after all. She gravitated to the one piece of furniture that broke the flow. A massage table. Obviously Kai's addition.

"Okay, you're sworn to secrecy about that." He moved behind her and whispered in a conspiratorial tone, "Miranda doesn't know it, but I leave that up because I have a guy that comes by three times a week to give me a massage."

"Ooooh. A massage three times a week. That must be heavenly." Jade rubbed her hands longingly over the crisp sheets, imagining how relaxing a massage would be after a long, hard day like today. She hadn't been able to afford a massage for a long time.

Kai's hands were on her shoulders, kneading the tired muscles at the base of her neck. His thumbs rotated in opposing circles across the top of her shoulder blades, plunging a tad deeper each time around.

Jade moaned at the sensation, not quite pain but not total pleasure either. The muscles were sore and tight. Her head fell back against his chest as the tension in her neck began to loosen under his tender assault.

"I have an idea." His hands left her neck, and the zipper of her top slid open. "A way to thank you for the sensuous dance you did for me at the gazebo." He laid her top on the foot of the bed and took the wine glass from her, setting it on a small pillar that acted as a bedside table. He unclasped her bra and dropped it on her abandoned top.

Her nipples pulled taut at the sudden exposure to the coolness of the night. She wasn't exactly sure what he had in mind, but it apparently required they be unclothed, so she was pretty sure she was going to like it. She reached up to unclasp the pearls, but his hands were back, pulling hers down to her side. "I'll do everything. Just relax."

"Would you take my hair down?" The touch of his hands had put every nerve ending on alert from the top of her head down. She longed to be free of the tightness of the chignon and the hairpins that poked into the back of her head.

He hesitated a moment, probably not sure how or where to start. A finger probed and then he located one of the pins and pulled it free. As he got the hang of it, he started using both hands and the pile of pins on the massage table grew. With every addition, more of her hair fell free from the twist until at last it hung in a heavy mass down her back.

Kai turned her to face him. Starting at the nape, he combed his fingers gently up and out, pausing to separate the tangles and the sections stuck together by hairspray. He took a deep breath and kissed the top of her head, her forehead, and her mouth. "God, you are so beautiful."

His hands left her hair, traveling down her shoulders and arms and back up to her breasts. His thumbs moved lightly across her nipples, but his eyes never strayed from hers. They held her as surely as if he'd locked her in a firm grasp. The blue-eyed hawk had her in his clutches. She had no desire to escape.

Every muscle from her neck down tightened at the touch. Relaxation was not in the cards for this night. She let out a tiny gasp and moved her hand against his zipper, feeling his erection.

Kai caught her hand and moved it back to her

side. "No, no, no. That's against the rules right now."

Being denied the touch made her want him even more. She wouldn't be able to stand it very long. But the wetness between her legs wouldn't allow her to deny the thrill of giving him total control.

He turned her around and undid her skirt, letting it drop in a heap at her feet. Then he slid the thong down her hips and legs, raising each foot to slip it off. He gathered up the abandoned clothes and spread them out over the back of the chair.

Now that she was naked, was he going to do his own version of erotic dance? Maybe strip for her? She hoped not. Guys were so awful at that. Kai was trying to be so sensuous, and she knew she'd lose it. She covered her laugh with a cough when he hit the button and a New Age melody filled the room.

He took his shirt off in a business-like manner, not keeping time to the music or even facing her, and hung it around the back of the other chair.

Well, at least he wasn't going to dance while he stripped. She breathed deeply in relief and ogled his powerful chest and shoulders and rippling abs as he moved in her direction.

"Up you go." Kai patted the massage table.

Not the place she would have chosen for their next round with the bed right there, but hey, she was game. She climbed up as gracefully as she could with his help.

The bed gave a couple of small pops as she settled her weight. That was not a good sign. "Are you sure this thing will hold us?" She hated to mess up his plans, but this really didn't seem like a smart idea.

Kai brushed his knuckles against her cheek and smiled. "It's not going to hold us. Just you. And trust me, it can do that." He pointed to the padded headrest. "Now, lay facedown and relax."

His intention dawned on her. "You're going to

give me a massage?" She hadn't been made to feel so special by a guy in a long time. On second thought, maybe never. This was truly touching. She leaned in and kissed him softly. "That is so thoughtful."

"The pleasure's mine, I assure you." Kai helped her lie down and positioned her face so it was comfortable. "I told you I wanted to explore you, and this is the best way I know how." He laughed his slow rumble. "Well, the second best way. But it'll lead to the best way."

The scent of the oil permeated the area as he warmed it in his hands. Tea tree oil and lavender. Two of her favorite scents, though she'd never thought about combining them. Invigorating yet relaxing, all at the same time. Mmmmm. Nice.

He started at the base of her spine, worked his way up with his thumbs pushing to each side and his hands fanned out. The pressure was perfect, and she could feel each vertebrae realign to its proper place. Sheer heaven.

He didn't talk but moved methodically up her back, and she soon learned why he had removed his shirt. It wasn't just for her viewing pleasure after all. He used not only his fingers, palms, and thumbs—thank God for those amazing opposable thumbs—but also, his forearms and even his elbows to relax some of those tough deep tissues in her thighs and calves and lower back. His touch was gentle but firm, like she knew it would be. Already becoming familiar.

He massaged her fingers and toes and the balls and arches of her feet and even her ear lobes. Her gratifying moans were met with kisses to whatever body part happened to be under his command at the time.

While her body gave way to subdued relaxation, her mind stayed acutely aware of the expertise of his fingers. She imagined how his oiled fingertips would feel coaxing her to climax. It made her eager, but the fabulous sensations moving through the rest of her body made it okay to wait. Hooray for extended foreplay.

The nondescript music in the background was subtle, no strong melody or rhythm, but its essence sucked Jade in. She got lost in her thoughts, imagining herself as a Greek goddess or priestess, a virgin, being oiled and scented in preparation to be taken by Apollo.

Kai rolled her over onto her back. He placed a bolster pillow beneath her knees; her breathing came faster in anticipation of what the second phase would bring.

He leaned down and kissed her, smoothing a warm oiled palm across her breast. He toyed for a minute with her erect nipple. "This is supposed to be relaxing. You don't seem very relaxed." Her eyes were closed, but she heard the smile in his voice.

She ran her fingers through his hair. "You're driving me crazy. Deliciously crazy."

"Let's see if I can get rid of the rest of the tension in your beautiful body."

His mouth moved to the nipple he had been fondling. The warm moistness of his tongue and the roughness of the stubble on his chin caused Jade to gasp at the conflicting sensations. Her hand found its way to his jaw line. The pinpricks of his beard made her fingertips tingle.

He let go of the nipple and ran a finger across the area where his beard had been in contact. His touch was hot on the sensitive skin and the feeling was exquisite.

"I'd better go shave." His husky voice blended nicely with the image of Zeus in her head.

No! Don't leave for even two seconds. Jade opened her eyes and took his head with both hands. "Don't even consider it." She pulled him to her, offering her other breast in pleasurable sacrifice.

Kai's gentle assault left her writhing, wanting to push his head further down to make contact with the heated area between her legs, remembering the feeling he'd given her earlier. She ran her fingernails down his back and the ripples shivered beneath her touch. The man had such self-control.

He stood up straight, placing a warm palm on each breast and rubbed her nipples in slow circles. His blue eyes stayed intent on hers, like he was reading the thoughts behind them.

His hands continued the slow circles down her ribs to her stomach and proceeded on downward. She moved her legs apart; his hand slipped between them only briefly and then moved on, massaging her thigh.

The slight contact sent a ripple effect up through her stomach and made her breasts tingle. "Nooo." She tried to make the whimper sound pitiful, but it changed to a moan and then a gasp as he finished the leg with small sucks and nips to her toes.

He started up the other leg, using both his mouth and his fingers, and her whole body quivered with excitement. His hand moved again between her legs, stroking just off-center, catching her wetness and blending it with the oil.

"I want to make you come now." His voice was almost a whisper. "It was so dark in the gazebo, it was hard to see. I want to watch your face when you climax."

His mouth moved onto hers, and his tongue made its plunge just as his thumb brushed over her clit. An electric current surged through her, connecting the two areas of her body. She tried to lock her arms around his back to gain as much contact with him as possible, but he was too broad. He straightened and broke easily out of her grasp.

His gaze remained steady on her face. Then the thumb brushed her clit again, and then again and again, setting a pace that her mind couldn't keep up with but her body fell naturally into, pushing into the touch greedily. She experienced another startling sensation as a finger moved deep into her, keeping the same rhythm as the thumb. Her own hands kneaded her breasts, pulled at her nipples, as the relentless thumb and finger quickened the pace. She became vaguely aware she was panting to get enough air to sustain her through the exquisite torture.

The autonomous vibration started somewhere deep within, and she arched her back to help push it to the surface. On it came, sweeping toward the surface. Her hands moved into her hair and held on tightly as her head thrashed to and fro. She felt the cry in her throat. She threw her head back, opening her mouth to release the explosion from within.

"Oh...oh...oh...oh...ooooh!" Her spasms tightened around the finger, wrenching a cry from her each time. His finger slid slowly out, and an involuntary whimper replaced the cry. The ceiling above her was spinning. She closed her eyes and relaxed.

One of Kai's muscled arms slid under her knees and the other under her shoulder blades. She felt herself being lifted and moved. His chest was hard against her side, and he nuzzled her neck as he laid her head softly on the pillow of the bed.

"I want to make love to you now."

"Okay." Her voice sounded breathy and weak. She certainly didn't want to come across as too tired, so she added a nod and a smile.

His eyes crinkled when he returned the smile.

He took off his trousers, boxers and socks. The thought of that long, perfect body pressed against her and into her made the breath catch in her throat. She released it with a sigh. He pulled a small knob on the pillar that she hadn't noticed before, and it opened, revealing a small compartment. Inside were a bottle of water, a book, and a package of condoms, which Kai deftly tore into.

He slid the sheath on and sat down on the bed beside her, leaning close, running his fingers through her hair. "You're incredible," he whispered.

"So are you." She slid her arms under his and gave him an encouraging tug.

He rolled above her then, keeping the bulk of his weight on his elbows. Bending her knees, she spread her legs and reached down to guide him in.

He paused then entered her, kissing her deeply as his length brought a gasp of pleasure from her. He pushed against her slowly, his body making contact with her already swollen clit.

She locked her legs around his back, and he groaned his appreciation as her body arched up to meet his thrust. She tickled his back and nipples with her fingernails, allowing him to set the pace he wanted, determined not to rush him no matter what her body was screaming for.

He started slow and long, pulling almost completely out before plunging in again. She nipped at his neck and shoulders, using her teeth and tongue, tasted the saltiness increasing as his strokes shortened.

Soon the friction became more than she could turn her mind away from. She met his thrusts halfway. Before long, he hardly left her body at all, stayed firmly planted within her, moved deeper and deeper, constantly in contact with her clit.

The sensation was overwhelming. Mind-boggling. He grew rigid...almost there. She gave herself over to pure reaction, allowed her climax to come, her muscles clenched and unclenched around his erection, drawing the rapturous cry from *his* mouth this time. "Oh God, Jade. Oh...God. Aauugghhh." His eyes stayed fixed on hers, the intense blue darkening with emotion. She felt as though she was being devoured from the inside out by some primordial, sex-beast. If he'd howled, it wouldn't have surprised her.

He stayed above her, panting to catch his breath, laughing softly at his inability to do so. At last he rolled off, wrapped in a groan of pure relief.

He made quick work of ridding himself of the condom, using some tissue that appeared from nowhere. He touched a button behind the bed and the room faded to darkness. Then he gathered her up against him, kissing her ear, cheek, and neck. "Now sleep," he whispered.

And she did for maybe a couple of hours.

She awoke to the warmth of his body behind her, spooned against her. She pressed back against him, surprised to feel an erection, then coming fully awake to the realization that his arm was around her, his hand stroking between her legs.

Without a word, she placed her hand on his to guide him to her wetness. Then she shifted to allow his entry from behind. He sighed his pleasure as she enveloped him. Her legs against his gave her leverage, and she thrust hard against him time after time.

They both stayed relatively silent, allowing their breathing to be their only form of communication. It was like they hovered in a dream world, and any voice would bring them to full awareness. By now, she could read the nuances of his body movements as he could hers. She squeezed his hand to let him know she was on the edge. He answered by wrapping his arms tightly around her as if to say, "Hold on and enjoy the ride."

They came simultaneously, quickly...and thoroughly.

His bottom arm came up under the pillow while his right arm stayed around her, his large hand cupping her breast. In no time his breathing was deep and slow, obviously in peaceful sleep.

Jade luxuriated in the totally relaxed feeling that infused her entire body. So the ten month dry spell was finally broken. She smiled. With Kai around, it shouldn't take long to get all caught up.

She thought about the past month and Gram's philosophy that everything happens for a reason. She and Kai had taken the blows and found their way back to each other. That was comforting.

Lying in the middle of a Greek temple, it was wrong to tempt the Fates. But this night was made for throwing caution to the wind. What could possibly go wrong with anything that felt this right?

Chapter Twenty-Two

"I'll call you later." Kai brushed his knuckles across her cheek then bent and gave her a kiss.

Jade breathed in his after-shave, hoping some of the crisp scent would linger after he was gone. The scent had caused arousal for her all weekend, but now it smelled like—mmmm, like contentment. She sighed, a long release of breath in utter, complete relaxation.

When he raised up, she stretched and gave her best imitation of Paisley's purr. That brought a smile to Kai's face and what she assumed was a wink, but his eyes crinkled so much, it was hard to tell.

She waved and blew him a kiss.

When she heard the door close, she kicked the sheet off and stretched again, letting the sun streaming through the window warm her naked body. Had there ever been a more perfect Monday morning in the history of the world? She scanned her memory and couldn't come up with one from the history of *her* world, at least.

And yesterday at Kai's had to have been the most perfect Sunday ever. Those delicious Monte Cristo sandwiches he'd fixed were the perfect brunch. And certainly the waves they'd surfed were the best she'd experienced since Hawaii. The dreamy lovemaking in his hot tub, and then again here at her apartment last night—definitely in a class all by themselves.

Jade sat up in her bed and pulled her knees to her chest in a hug. She'd never felt this way, so totally content. And, to be honest, it was a little disconcerting.

Was this the way people fell in love? If so, what she'd felt for Adam had never been love. What she'd felt with him was always exciting, a whirlwind that left her breathless, yet always waiting. For what? Something more...something more intimate. Yeah, that was the word. Something that united *them, their spirits, their souls,* not just their bodies.

Kai had been so tender and attentive and nurturing. The massage, his cooking, and countless other things throughout the day. She'd found herself responding to him in like manner. She wanted to do nice things for him, make him feel good.

Could Kai be His Hotness? The idea made her stomach flutter. It was a definite possibility. She needed to share this giddiness with somebody. If only Beth were here. She eyed the cell phone on her bedside table. *No. Don't even consider calling her on her honeymoon.*

She heard movement below on the deck. Well, when a girl's best friend wasn't available, she went to the next best authority. That would be Gram. Jade slipped into some shorts and a tee, going over which details she would share and which she would leave to Gram's overly-active imagination. Still deep in thought, she started down her steps, but came to a sudden stop.

Adam. Headed for his garage.

Something had been niggling at her since Saturday night. Now was as good a time as any to take care of it. Kai was a big man physically, and a powerful man in the business world with lots of money. A perfect target for Adam now that she could see her ex for the scum he was.

She took a deep breath, noticing she wasn't shaking or the least bit worried about what she was about to do. Kai had taken care of her. It was her turn to take care of him.

"Adam," she called and watched him turn to face her slowly, his movements hesitant. He didn't speak, just stood there, eyeing her levelly.

Not wanting Gram to hear, Jade didn't start talking until she was close enough to see the dark purple and yellow bruise coloring Adam's jaw.

"Jade, I..."

Jade shook her head to stop him. "I don't care what you have to say. I approached you. You didn't come to me. Now, I just want you to listen."

Adam closed his mouth with a small grimace and crossed his arms over his chest.

"Saturday night, you sneaked up behind me, jerked my top off, fondled my breasts, pinched my nipples hard enough to hurt, all the while making lewd remarks."

He opened his mouth, but she didn't give him a chance, continuing as if she didn't notice. "Kai stopped the attack by punching you, and I want you to know that if you even *consider* filing an assault charge against him, I will have my parents bring you up on sexual assault charges faster than you can come up with one of your sociopathic lies. Hell, considering what you said to me, there may even be a case for attempted rape."

She watched his eyes for the flash of anger that didn't come. That was confusing. "Do you understand?" Was he drunk? He didn't look drunk.

Adam nodded, and it hit her that for the first time she could ever remember, he looked like an adult, like he was taking this as a man.

"Good." She spun on her heels and started away.

"Jade." His voice was low, little above a whisper.

She spun back around to face him, loaded for bear this time. He'd hurt her, and used her, and humiliated her. But she'd be damned if he was going to hurt someone as nice as Kai because of her.

"I'm sorry." His arms were at his side, palms

open and facing her, the universal gesture of supplication. No weapons. Nothing to hide.

He probably really meant it this time, but she couldn't make herself care. She nodded then turned and went toward the front deck, walking away from Adam a free woman. No baggage. No guilt. No leftover desire. And she had handled it herself. Her own way. She truly was becoming Ms. Independent. For the first time in years, she had the urge to skip. She didn't, but she couldn't stop the spread of her cat-that-ate-the-canary smile.

Gram sat sipping her coffee with Paisley lolling in her lap, basking in the sun and enjoying ear scratches from Gram's long fingernails. Paisley's eyes were closed in contentment, but Gram's held a mischievous twinkle as she pointed to the unused place setting.

"For me?" Jade feigned surprise.

"Who else, Chickie?"

"How'd you know I'd be down?"

"I heard Kai leave. Beth's gone. Who else would you share all the juicy details of the weekend with?"

Jade laughed and plopped a couple of brown sugar cubes into her coffee cup and reached for the cream. The coffee smelled extra strong today. "Chatting coffee" Gram called it. The kind she would always make when she knew Jade wanted to chat.

"Soooo?"

Jade took a deep breath in and let it out slowly. "He's the most perfect man I've ever met."

"Now, now." Gram wagged a finger at her. "Don't go thinkin' he's perfect 'cause he's not. That line of thinkin' will get you into trouble. Tell me how real he is."

Images of Kai naked flashed in Jade's mind along with the memory of murmured endearments against her neck. Her hand trembled, and she wrapped her other one around the cup to hold it still.

"Gram, he's such an amazing guy. He's thoughtful and sweet and such a gentleman. And he cooks..." she nodded at the breakfast assortment on the table "...like Marvin, who gets two thumbs up from me, by the way."

"He gets more up than thumbs from me." Gram smiled a sweet innocent smile, wide-eyed, head cocked slightly.

Jade laughed at the inconsistency of the remark and the facial expression. Gram was a master at innuendo. "Uh-hum," Jade cleared her throat dramatically. "Can't switch to Marvin yet. I haven't finished extolling the virtues of Kai. He's into sports even more than I am. We had so much fun surfing and kayaking yesterday." She sipped her coffee, realizing she'd forgotten all about it in her excitement to talk about Kai. "He's built this magnificent house that he's so proud of. You can just see him swell when he talks about it." *And when Kai swells, it's a wonder to behold.*

She described the house and all the little extras Kai and Mark put into it. She went on, expounding on Techtron and the vision the partners had for their next venture.

"He mentioned a couple of new ideas at dinner, but only when your dad pressed him," Gram interjected.

"Yeah, he's really modest about their accomplishments." Jade agreed. "That's one of the things I admire most about him."

"Bet I could name the thing you definitely admire most." Gram's dimple deepened, and heat rose in Jade's cheeks.

"Well, I *am* your granddaughter." Jade raised an eyebrow and tried to look stern. "Don't beg because I'm not giving you any details." She paused dramatically. "Use your imagination, but kick it up a notch."

Gram grabbed the water pitcher and poured herself a cold one. "Whoooooeeee!" She took a big gulp.

Jade slathered butter on a croissant and forced herself back on the safe subject of Kai's business dealings. "Did he tell you about their idea for a new type of animation?"

"Yeah." Gram nodded. "He said it could change the industry."

"And they also have an idea for software that translates speech into different languages."

Gram's eyebrows tightened. "Doesn't that already exist?"

"Yeah, but this wouldn't be one of those word-for-word translations that are so awful." Jade smiled at her own enthusiasm. Kai had certainly sold her on the idea. The excitement in his voice when he talked about it was contagious. "This would have the nuances—the common slang and idioms and even inflection. You would just speak into the little phone-like machine, push the button, and voila! *Vous parlez français.*"

"Speaking of France, when are you leaving?"

Jade's stomach tightened, and she sighed. "I almost wish I hadn't made those plans to go, but Mom and Dad have already bought the ticket."

"Why don't you want to go, Chickie? You've always loved it so, and with the new job, it may be a long time until you get a vacation."

Jade heard the concern in Gram's voice. Might as well be honest. She was going to guess it anyway. "Truth is, Kai and I lost so much time…now that he's back I hate to be gone. And then I start the new job."

Gram shrugged matter-of-factly. "So ask him to go with you."

Jade nibbled on the croissant, which brought back memories of those in Villefranche. "Don't you think that's kind of presumptuous? We just got together this weekend."

"Would you be spending lots of time with him if you were here?"

"Yeah. At least, I hope so." Jade could see where Gram's logic was going.

"Then what difference does it make if it's here or there?"

A hint of possibility flared in Jade's mind, but it was immediately squelched. "He's probably too busy with the sale and all."

"He said that wouldn't be final for a year. Isn't that right?"

"Yeah, he and Mark will stay on as consultants for a year. After that, all the terms are finalized. That's why Mark and his wife Jilli, who's also Kai's sister, are moving to Japan for a year."

"Well, you could at least ask him about France. Sometimes, Chickie, you just gotta grab the opportunity when it's presented. You may only get one chance and you don't lose anything by trying, you know." Gram stood up and started clearing her dishes from the table. "Now, I've got a date with a strip class." She kissed the top of Jade's head as she passed on her way back in.

Jade brooded into her coffee, Gram's words echoing in her mind.

****

The efficiency of his staff amazed him sometimes. Kai glanced down the list of what two days ago seemed like the tasks of Hercules. Now, here it was Wednesday, and they were all completed.

Of course, some of them had demanded favors to be called in. Still others had to be bought...

But, the chance for a week alone with Jade made it worth a lot.

And the chance for Meg Prater?

He was willing to give whatever it took.

Kai glanced at the note from Stubo and chuckled. Stubo even managed to get Jade and him seated together in first-class on the plane. Meg would be on the following flight. That would help some. He wasn't sure how he could have gotten away long enough to pick her up and get her settled in the hotel.

His thoughts were interrupted when Mark barged into the office, slamming the door behind him.

"Juggling two women? In a foreign country where you don't even speak the language? Kai, me boy, you've lost your freakin' mind."

So Stubo had filled him in on the details. Kai sighed. He was hoping to do that himself.

He ignored the heaviness in the pit of his stomach that told him Mark was probably right. He went over the details aloud, trying to convince himself as well as his partner this was do-able. "I have a room at the Hotel Nigresso in Nice that Jade knows about. I've told her I'll have to work mornings there since I couldn't depend on a wireless signal in Villefranche. It's the perfect cover. I can be with Meg in the morning when she has her treatments, and Jade the rest of the time. Besides, it's only until Thursday when Prater gets there."

"At which point you'll collapse from exhaustion."

"I hope so." Kai laughed.

"Jade's a great gal, by the way."

Mark wasn't one to put a stamp of approval on anything very quickly, so his rating of Jade came as a surprise. Kai breathed a little easier knowing last night's dinner with the four of them had gone as well as he perceived it did. He'd never introduced them to a girlfriend this soon. With Jade, it seemed right.

"Jilli loves her," he paused, "and she says you do, too."

Kai rolled his eyes, running his hand through

his hair. Jade was special, that was for sure, but he could hardly call it love yet. And no way in hell was he even going to acknowledge the possibility to Jilli. She'd have them engaged and a date set by dark. "Like you said, Jade's a great gal."

"Don't lose her by doing something stupid, Kai. You need to just be honest with her about Meg."

The preachy tone of Mark's voice pinged at Kai's already stretched nerves. Mark didn't understand how Jade would react. "This is the same guy who, a few weeks ago, preached at me not to be so open and honest. Well, I'm taking that one step further. There are some things Jade is better off not knowing, and Meg is one of those things. If she knows Meg's there alone, I'm afraid Jade will insist on going to the treatments with her and staying afterward to make sure she's okay. You know how women are about support issues. Hell, they can't even go to the bathroom by themselves. I can just see her spending the last vacation she might get for a long time nursing Meg, and I don't want that." His voice had grown much louder than he intended, and he lowered it almost to a whisper. "I'm not telling her. I can handle this by myself. Now drop it."

Mark let out a low whistle. "Man, Jilli's right. You've got it bad."

Chapter Twenty-Three

The sight of the pale peach cottage with its window boxes spilling over with blooms in blues and pinks and purples brought a lump to Jade's throat. God, it felt good to be back. The scent of lavender growing in scruffy bunches all around the foundation mixed with the salty tang of the Mediterranean, catapulting her to the most wonderful summers of her life.

Stepping through the threshold of the house in Villefranche was like stepping into her childhood. The look of the house was more like pictures she'd seen of American houses in the 1950's, but it was memories that tugged her back through the years.

She stooped to pull back a lavender plant, exposing two carved sets of initials in the wooden siding. She pointed them out to Kai. "J.B.+J.P. and B.M.+J.P. Beth and I were both in love with Jean Luc that summer. We carved both of our initials with his. Whoever married him got to add a heart around hers."

"Hmmm. Guess Beth lost that one." Kai broke off a stem of lavender and slid it behind her ear.

She raised her eyebrows. "Hey, that's right. I'm a shoo-in to win this contest."

He pulled her against him and ran his fingers through her hair. "Not if I can help it." His lips pressed hers lightly.

The smile hadn't left Kai's face since they arrived at the Nice airport a little over an hour ago. She could tell he'd already been seduced by the Cote d'Azure, in love with its sights and sounds and smells and touches and tastes. He'd insisted on a pastry and espresso even before they left the airport. Jade knew one taste and he was hooked for life.

"C'mon." She unlocked the door and pulled him through. "Let me show you the house."

Kai followed her, stopping just inside the door to look around. "This looks like your apartment."

Jade had wondered if he would notice. "Gram and I furnished the apartment to look like this. The blues and yellows, and the whitewashed furniture. With the ocean, it has the same feel, don't you think?"

Kai nodded. "You must love this place."

"It's my favorite place in the whole world." She grabbed his hand and led him on a quick walk-through while they deposited their luggage in the large bedroom.

In the kitchen, Jade spotted a note left by Beth. Kai settled into a cane-backed dining chair as she read it aloud. "Jade, by the time you get here, we'll be seeing the sights of Greece. Honeymooning here was everything you and I ever dreamed it would be. And more! Oooo-la-la! Speaking of oooo-la-la, hope things are still working out with you and Kai." She paused and sat on Kai's lap. "Would you say things are still working out for us?"

He scratched his chin thoughtfully. 'Well, I'd say you're certainly working me out."

Jade wiggled her butt against him playfully and gave a dramatic flair to clearing her throat. "Jean Luc is hotter than ever. He's excited that you're going to be here…" Jade folded the note hurriedly, hoping Kai hadn't seen the words "all alone" that finished the sentence. Oh, crap! Beth had no idea she'd be there with Kai, or how things were with them. She'd probably primed Jean Luc all week, and he wouldn't like this set-up one bit. God, she hoped he didn't make a scene. Embarrassed at the thought, her cheeks started burning. The room seemed too hot all of a sudden. She jumped up to open a window and let in the breeze.

"Who's this Jean Luc I keep hearing about?" The nonchalance in Kai's voice sounded a bit forced, and Jade realized she had no idea whether or not he was the jealous type. She couldn't imagine he'd ever had much to be jealous of. But of course, he was divorced...

"Oh, just a childhood crush. Now a good friend." She chose her words carefully as she unlatched the next set of shutters. She wanted to assure Kai without sounding overly-attached yet. They were, after all, still getting to know each other. "He never quite hit the top of the Hotness scale." Lavender fragrance infused the room, and she took a deep breath, filling her lungs. Instant relaxation. Her muscles loosened.

She walked back over to Kai and pulled his head against her midsection, planting a kiss on the top of his head. The crisp waves tickled the end of her nose. Had they really only been together for a week? She was so comfortable with him. "You, on the other hand, are setting all new standards."

Kai ran his hand under her halter and caressed her breast. "Let me see if I can raise those standards again for this Frenchman."

"Mmmmm. Makes me want to break out in the Star-Spangled Banner." She untied her halter and pulled it down, giving his hands and mouth full access.

He made good use of both. He soon had her panting.

"Zhade?" An unexpected knock at the door sent her scurrying to get her halter pulled up. Her hands fumbled, trying to grasp the ties, and before she could get everything stored properly, Jean Luc strolled in like he owned the place.

"Jean Luc!"

No doubt the sight of her disarray and her breathless exclamation of his name brought an instant smile to his lips. *"Ah ma cherie, je vois—"* He stopped when his gaze took in Kai and the instant smile faded, replaced with a flash of something else too quick for Jade to read.

Two years hadn't changed his face, still long and thin with high cheekbones and chiseled features. But his hair had darkened a bit to a light brown, probably owing to him being inside the restaurant more rather than on the beach. Dark lashes and brows still framed those spectacular hazel eyes that could be read as easily as a street sign. He'd filled out too, and the weight was definitely in all the right places—much thicker through the chest and biceps, still lean through the middle. His damp shirt clung to his midriff, revealing the interesting ripples beneath.

Jade hurried to greet Jean Luc with a hug and a kiss on each cheek, but he had other ideas. His mouth swooped down hungrily onto hers. It happened too quickly for her to protest, but when her brain functioned properly, she pulled free with an embarrassed laugh. Couldn't let either of these guys get the wrong idea. "It's so great to see you." She meant it. Her fondness for Jean Luc was real. Her one and only foreign Hotness.

Jean Luc seemed to have forgotten completely about Kai, devouring Jade with his eyes. No doubt she'd be wearing nothing in a couple more seconds if she didn't avert his attention. She took his hand and tugged in Kai's direction, but the Frenchman stood his ground.

Kai came to the rescue, sliding a hand around her waist. The other he offered to Jean Luc. "Hi. I'm Kai Malone, and you must be Jean Luc. Jade's told me about you."

The hand around her waist touched only lightly, no firm protective hold. So maybe Kai wasn't the jealous type. But Jean Luc was. Had always been. More than once when they were teenagers, he'd threatened guys who showed her too much attention. She was sure green flashes were emanating from those hazel depths now.

Jean Luc shook Kai's hand finally. Jade stifled a chuckle as he pulled himself up to his full height, which was at least three inches shorter than Kai. He squared his shoulders and raised his chin. It was like watching a bad impression of a miffed Frenchman.

"*Bonjour, Monsieur Malone. Je suis enchanté—*"

Jade broke in. "English, please, Jean Luc. Kai doesn't speak French."

A condescending smirk settled on his curvy mouth. "No French? *Mon Dieu!* What ees the U.S. coming to?"

"He speaks Japanese," she interjected then felt stupid using such a defensive tone.

Kai chuckled. "But not very well."

The chuckle might have eased her discomfort some, but it was followed so closely by Jean Luc's derisive snort she couldn't be sure. Her stomach clenched. If only she'd had more time to prepare one of them, or herself, for this introduction. First Adam, now Jean Luc. Sheesh! How many exes could one relationship survive in two weeks?

"...But if you ever need anything translated from Russian, Mandarin or Gaelic," Kai continued, "I'd be glad to help."

Jade expected to see a mischievous twinkle in Kai's eyes, but it wasn't there. He was serious. "Russian, Mandarin, and *Gaelic?*"

"I needed Russian and Mandarin for the business." He shrugged and gave an embarrassed laugh. "I got interested in Gaelic while reading the

213

Outlander series, so I took private lessons."

Jade shook her head in amazement at all she still didn't know about this man.

Jean Luc's smug smile tightened, and he held Kai's unflinching gaze. "And eef *you* need German or Italian, *I* can help. I, too, need it for the business."

Oh God. They were actually one-upping each other. Childish as the behavior was, watching these two was entertaining, especially since it was done for her benefit. She could almost taste the testosterone in the air.

Jean Luc turned his attention to Jade and took her hand. "Beth deed not tell me you would be weeth anyone. Or did you just meet? On zee flight over, pairhaps?" She recognized the flash of hope as it brightened his eyes. He was thinking perhaps Kai was just a one-night-stand...someone he could dismiss.

Jade hurried to squelch this line of thought. "I'm surprised Beth didn't mention Kai. We've been seeing each other since the middle of May." It wasn't a lie, though not exactly the whole truth either. Kai's approval came as a pat on her hip.

"My coming was a last-minute decision, though," Kai interjected. "Beth and Pryce had already left before I decided to come." Jade glanced up at him. He smiled warmly and winked as he tucked a strand of hair behind her ear. "The thought of being away from her for a week wasn't very pleasant."

Icy daggers replaced the look of hope in Jean Luc's eyes as he shifted his gaze toward Kai. "We 'ave so much to catch up on, Zhade and I. I'm sure you will understand eef I steal her away from you for some time alone." He only needed to slap a glove across Kai's face to make the statement more of a challenge.

Jade fought the urge to laugh at this verbal sparring. If it got much deeper in there, she would have to change into some boots.

Kai's jaw tightened ever so slightly before he spoke. "Jade's a big girl. She can visit with whomever she wants. And I'll be working during the morning."

"Working?" Jean Luc's eyebrows shot up in surprise. "Every morning?"

"Kai has a room with wireless internet at the Hotel Nigresso," Jade offered in explanation. "He'll be taking care of business there in the mornings, but we'll have our afternoons free for sightseeing and lying on the beach."

Jean Luc's eyes narrowed. "We have a cybair cafe here in Villefranche. Weeth wireless internet."

"I checked into that. But I, um, needed more privacy than that afforded...phone calls and such."

Jade heard the edge in Kai's voice. Jean Luc was getting to him like he always got to the males around him. Women adored him; guys wanted to fatten his lips more.

"Kai's in the process of selling his company. You know, big business stuff." She leaned against Kai, but smiled at Jean Luc and squeezed his hand, hoping to break some of the tension gathered about them. It *was* good to see him, and she wanted to catch up on the past two years. She hoped Kai wouldn't object to what she was about to suggest. "Anyway, my mornings will be free. How about breakfast? Could we do that?" Breakfast together was nothing new. In fact, it had often been the perfect time since Jean Luc was always so busy with the restaurant.

The suspicion left Jean Luc's eyes and he beamed. "Pairfect! I cannot tomorrow or Monday, but 'ow about Tuesday?"

Kai gave her a little squeeze that she interpreted as a thumbs-up. He seemed relaxed again.

"Tuesday it is." She could breathe easily again. Crisis averted. Egos still intact.

Jean Luc insisted they have dinner with him at Chanson de Mer that night. Jade was anxious to see what he'd done with the restaurant, and he obviously wanted her to see it. He was like the proud papa of a new baby.

"Tonight then." Jean Luc kissed her forehead and shook Kai's hand.

They walked him to the door and watched his car round the corner before Kai spoke. "He hates me, doesn't he?"

"Yep." Jade circled her arms around his waist, resting her cheek against his broad chest. "You better have a taster at the restaurant with you tonight. And watch your back."

Chapter Twenty-Four

Jade arranged the still-warm croissants on the pretty hand-painted breakfast plates Kai had bought her yesterday in Sault. The delicate design of lavender stalks around the scalloped edges was a sweet reminder of their drive into Provence. Gram was going to love the identical ones he had shipped to her as well. "As a thank you for everything she's done," he'd said.

His thoughtfulness gave Jade a warm glow inside. He didn't show it just toward her. He was like that with everyone. He was forever taking care of something for one of his sisters or loaning them money. Jade suspected the loans were actually gifts. His biggest fault, Jilli had confided: letting people take advantage of him and his generosity. He always needed to take care of people. Jilli said that's what came of having so many younger sisters.

Jade wondered what his parents were like. They must be wonderful people to have raised such an unselfish son. And she wondered a bit about the ex-wife Hazel. What about Kai could Hazel have been dissatisfied with? He certainly was shaping up to be the ultimate His Hotness by her own standards.

The way he always put others first made her uncomfortably aware of her own spoiled ways. Until the last couple of years, she'd always looked to Mom and Dad and Gram for anything she wanted, and they had always complied. With the new job starting Monday, she would show them how independent she could be, and start giving back to the people who'd given her so much.

Adam was the only person she'd ever known more spoiled than she. It was weird that most of the time she gave into him. And no matter how much she did, it was never enough. He wanted his way all the time.

Kai wasn't like that at all. When he gave, it made her want to give back. More and more, she'd been putting him first in her thoughts, trying to pick out things she thought he'd enjoy. She had so wanted him to see the lavender fields in full bloom and was glad he'd finished up early enough yesterday to make the trip. She wished he'd get back early today, too. This morning, he didn't think so, but a girl could hope. So many places were still around she wanted him to see. It was hard to believe she wasn't tired of being with him even though they'd been together every spare minute for over a week.

Jean Luc's car screeched to a stop in front of the house. She needed to talk to him about driving so fast, another sign of the stress she sensed in him. He worked too hard, but Le Chanson de Mer was obviously a hit. Nothing but pleased comments came from the tables near them Saturday night. And the service had been impeccable.

Jean Luc had been aloof toward Kai at dinner, but that probably should have been expected. Sunday, however, when he visited with them on the beach, he'd been downright rude, carrying the jealousy issue to the extreme. While she hadn't expected him to jump for joy about Kai, the two of them had never tiptoed around their involvements with other people. In fact, most of their best conversations had been about just that.

She sighed in resignation. Setting him straight about her feelings for Kai wouldn't be easy, but she had to do it. Today. Now. Over breakfast.

She met him at the door. *"Bon matin, ma*

cherie." He kissed both her cheeks then pulled her into an uncharacteristic bear hug.

Jade hugged back, surprised by the solid feel of his arms around her. No groping hands. No kisses on her neck. This hug felt positively brotherly. Could it be Jean Luc had his own things he needed to discuss with her? A relationship perhaps? She relaxed, giving him a tight squeeze. Why hadn't he just said so?

"A-tu faim?" She indicated the table.

"Non, je n'ai pas faim. Peut-être seulement du café."

Jean-Luc not hungry? Odd. She hurried to fill their cups. She was starved and the croissants would get cold quickly.

"Eef you don't mind, I would like to speak English today."

Even more odd. Jade cocked her head in question.

Jean Luc smiled with just a touch of what she read as sheepishness. "I weesh to practice."

She wouldn't push it, but she'd bet money she didn't have that Kai's mastery of several languages brought this on. "Yeah? How come?" She couldn't resist the urge to needle him a bit.

He shrugged. "I theenk...for beezness."

She smiled to herself and gave him a nod. "Good. I've been finding the constant French kind of exhausting. I didn't realize how rusty I'd gotten with my idioms."

Jean Luc started in with small talk about the changes in Villefranche since she'd last visited. The *patisserie* around the corner had sold to new owners, but the pastries were as mouth-watering as ever.

"If I had a bakery this good around the corner from my apartment, I'd get as wide as this table." The warm center of the chocolate croissant bathed her tongue in rich sweetness as the bread flaked away into layers. "Mmmm." She closed her eyes and gave into a shiver of delight.

"But the fat content in your buttair and cream, she is not as high as ours. So unless the bakery imported those things, she would never make croissants like thees. And eef she did import those things, the price of a croissant, he would be very high."

It struck her as slightly surreal hearing Jean Luc talking about the content of butter and cream. The restaurant business was ingrained in him now. But he was hedging about something. He kept fidgeting—checking his watch, stirring his coffee, and talking about nothing.

His accent speaking English was easy to listen to though, so she let him talk, let him take his time to get to his point. The way he pronounced butter like buttair and swallowed the "r" in bakery—smooth and warm, just like the chocolate. Different from Kai's deep but mellow growl. That was more like the coffee. She took a sip. Strong and robust with a lingering taste. She pushed from her mind the connection she was about to draw about how nicely Kai had lingered that morning. But her face heated just the same.

"So thees Kai, how long haf you known him really?"

Ah. So they were getting to the good stuff finally. Jade took a fortifying gulp of her coffee. "We met around the middle of May."

Jean Luc raised his eyebrows in question. "But?"

Jade took a deep breath. "But, after a couple of dates, he had to go to Japan on business." She told him the whole story, start to finish, of their rocky beginning. He snorted a couple of times at the funnier parts but mostly just listened and frowned and sipped his coffee, constantly checking his watch.

"Zhade, are you falling in love weeth Kai?"

The question caught her by surprise. While she'd expected to talk about the relationship, she hadn't expected the term "love" to come up. Her heartbeat quickened for a beat or two. Could be the effect of the strong coffee. "I don't know." She shrugged. "Maybe...I mean not yet, it's too soon...but maybe eventually."

"But 'e has already lied to you. About who 'e is, what 'e does..." He finished with a circular hand motion that clearly meant "and on and on."

"Well, he had a reason for that. Not a great reason, but a logical one considering what was at stake. We started fresh at the wedding. No more of that." She repeated his gesture.

"'E still lies to you, Zhade."

She had the croissant poised in front of her mouth for another bite, but the pain she read in Jean Luc's eyes hit her like a blow to the stomach. What was he talking about? She set the half-eaten roll back down on her plate.

"What do you mean? What would he lie about? And how would you know?"

"I haf breakfast at Nigresso each Sunday morning. I see Kai. He come in weeth a woman around eight-thirty. A friend who works there, he tell me eet happened again yesterday around the same time." He glanced around the room, focusing on nothing particular before he locked his gaze back on hers.

Jade's mind whirled. Kai was bringing a woman to the hotel? Every morning? There had to be a reasonable explanation. He'd said he might be meeting with people. "She's probably a business associate." But why would he pick her up? She left the thought unspoken, but it hung in the air between them.

"I do not think so, Zhade. She does not look like business to me."

221

The concern in his voice cut through her, made a muscle in her neck tighten. She forced a laugh that sounded hollow even to her. "This is silly. It just doesn't add up. There's got to be more to this than what you're telling me."

Jean Luc stood up and held out his hand. "Come weeth me and we'll see if she happens again. Then you can decide for yourself."

****

Kai's hands tightened on Meg shoulders as the limousine swerved. He did his best to hold her stable as she retched into the plastic bag held against her mouth. Her blonde wig lay spread across his lap, thrown off to get it out of her way, now pinned in place by his strategically placed elbow. "Take it easy!" he yelled, taking his frustration out on the driver who was only following his instructions of "Hurry!" from two minutes ago.

Dr. Pineau had warned the nausea would probably be worse the third day. Still, Kai hoped they could at least get back to the hotel and get Meg settled before it hit full force.

Shudders passed through her frail body as she struggled for some deep breaths. In high school, her petite frame had been curvy, and after the first baby, voluptuous even. Now she could be on a commercial for "Save the World." Kai hoped to God this was worth what they were putting her through. Thinking back to the sinister conglomeration of needles, tubes, and IV solutions, Kai's body answered with a shudder of his own.

Meg knotted the top of the bag and dropped it into the trash container near the seat. She leaned back carefully as if weighing the risk of getting too comfortable. Apparently satisfied the nausea had passed for the time, she relaxed back into the seat with Kai's help, closing her eyes with a heavy sigh. "This is going to work, Kai. I can feel it—literally.

222

It's so much stronger than the other rounds of chemo I've had. It's got to work."

And if it didn't…what then? Kai wouldn't let himself think of the ravaging her body was taking from the mixture of chemicals. Or the cells that were in such multitude it took something like this to destroy them. It made him want to throw up his hands in frustration and cry out to God, "Why?" Instead, he pulled another trash bag loose from the roll and shook it open. It never hurt to be prepared. "If it works as hard as you work to make it work, it'll work."

Meg laughed and opened her eyes, drawing together the bony ridges where eyebrows used to be. "What?"

Her eyelashes were gone, too. God, what she'd been through, and yet, she could still laugh. It was nice to see her laugh, even if it was at his lack of eloquence. "I meant…"

She laid a small, icy hand atop one of his. "I know what you meant." She took the wig from his lap and held it out. "Would you help me get this back on? I'm too weak to hold my arms up that long."

Kai eyed the golden mass of curls skeptically. Was there a right way and a wrong way to do this? He turned it a few times viewing it from all sides, finally settling on what he thought was the front. He held it up, and Meg gave a nod of approval. Working together, he held the cap in front while she tugged the back snuggly into place. She wagged her head a couple of times, seeming satisfied it would stay on. "You're the only man other than Jake who's seen me without it. Outside of medical staff."

Tears welled up in her eyes when she mentioned her husband's name. *Oh God, please don't let her cry.* Kai hurried to bring up something that would make her feel better. He glanced at his watch. "Speaking of Jake, he's probably waking up somewhere over the Atlantic right now. Or maybe watching a movie."

Meg sniffed a little and wiped her eyes, but, to Kai's relief, the tears seemed under control. "I'm so thankful he's getting to come earlier. You've been great," she assured him, "but I really need Jake. I'm thankful for everything you've done, and I'm terribly grateful you're getting him here earlier than we'd planned."

The love in her voice was so evident and so touching Kai fought back the tears that threatened in his own eyes. How did Jake stand it? Watching the person he cared most about in this world going through this hell. If it were Jade... Kai couldn't even begin to think about that. It wouldn't do for Meg to see any of the emotion he felt about this whole freakin' business. She needed his strength and his assurance. "Well, he'll be here in a couple of hours." He took her hand and held it, covering his shock at the feel of cold skin stretched over bones. It was almost like holding the bones themselves.

She closed her eyes and swallowed hard.

Was she getting nauseous again? Kai held his breath and reached for the trash bag that had slipped between them.

"I'm okay," she whispered. "This one's going to pass quickly."

They remained silent for the last few minutes of the ride, but she surprised him when the limousine pulled up at the front door. "Kai, I don't want to use the wheelchair. People will stare."

She didn't have the strength to put the wig on, yet she thought she could walk to the room?

She must have read the doubt in his eyes and didn't give him a chance to answer. "Please, Kai. I've done this the past two days. I can do it today if you'll help me."

The plea in her voice made him bite off the protest on the tip of his tongue. Hell, with all she'd been through, if she asked for the moon, he'd start building a crane. "Okay, no wheelchair. We'll be just coming in from a night out." He smiled at her shocked look and hurried to explain. "Keep your arm around my waist and lean on me. I'll hold you up with my arm around your back and under your arm."

Kai and the driver each held an arm, nearly lifting Meg out the door of the car and onto the sidewalk. "Seven o'clock tomorrow." The driver acknowledged with a touch to the bill of his cap as Meg snuggled herself firmly against Kai's side.

The doorman held the door, and they passed slowly from the heat of pavement into the coolness of the hotel lobby. Kai prayed that the sudden change in temperature wouldn't turn Meg's stomach. Her hold tightened slightly, but she led with another step.

He shortened his stride so as not to tax her. "And miles to go before I sleep." The line came back to him from a poem he learned in middle school. He quoted it quietly.

Meg's strained whisper answered him. "I hope so."

He tightened his grip around her.

****

Jade was thankful for the dark corner table with the perfect vantage point to see the door yet remain unobtrusive. She and Jean Luc hadn't spoken three words since they left the house. Their café au lait remained untouched except for the constant idle stirs.

When the limousine pulled up in front, instinct told her it was him...them. She willed her breathing to slow down, but her lungs seemed to be taking orders from elsewhere. Air didn't seem to be able to get past the wad of cotton in her throat.

They strolled leisurely through the door, arms

entwined around each other's backs, bodies molded together. Jade's breath smashed into her lungs then in a full-force gasp. If she'd entertained any idea this was merely a business relationship, that broke apart when her heart hit the floor.

In some remote part of her brain, Jade registered shock at the woman's physical appearance. She was tiny, childlike even, with a head full of golden curls. Never would she have imagined Kai with someone so...so...opposite of everything she was. Jade slumped in her seated, suddenly feeling gawky and enormous.

During the ride to the hotel, she had imagined various scenarios of how she would react if Jean Luc's suspicions were correct. She saw herself rushing to greet Kai and his hussy with a huffy "Aha!"—perhaps accompanied by a dramatic slap across his square hawk-like jaw.

Another choice was to approach them with an indignant air and walk silently by, ignoring Kai's growls of apology and explanation. A variation of that was to manage to be in their path, locked in a romantic embrace with Jean Luc, and to look startled at "being caught."

But now, she simply watched the scene play out before her, a member of the audience detached from the action. And action it turned out to be. Halfway to the elevator, they stopped and the woman's free hand clutched at Kai's chest. He bent to her, and she whispered in his ear. He swooped her into his arms and bounded for the open doors of the closest elevator, obviously in a hurry to get upstairs.

Revulsion washed over Jade like a cold shower, chilling her to her core. She'd experienced betrayal before with Adam, so this shouldn't be anything new. But it *was* new. A pain she'd never felt so deeply. It seemed everywhere at once. Her eyes burned, her throat constricted, her stomach tightened. Even her legs grew weak.

With Adam, somewhere inside she'd always known betrayal would happen eventually and had built a shell his lies couldn't fully penetrate. But Kai had been different. She'd foolishly left her heart unguarded, and he'd settled there like some squatter, taking control of property that wasn't his by rights. She'd allowed it, encouraged it. Wanted it.

Worst of all, she'd allowed herself to believe His Hotness existed. She had only herself to blame. She was a fool. A dreamer. Still that sixteen-year-old at heart who dreamed someone would come along whose good points far outweighed his bad. She no longer believed in perfection, but she had so wanted to believe in goodness.

She felt violated. Used.

The last vestiges of girlish dreams dropped away as the elevator doors closed. Jean Luc's hand closed over hers. "Do you want to go upstairs and confront them?"

"No, I've seen enough" Her face and eyes burned with humiliation and sorrow for all she had lost. "I've got to get out of here, Jean Luc. Please take me home."

Chapter Twenty-Five

Kai made the curve much faster than was prudent. The back wheels slid sideways, and he fought the steering wheel to straighten it. In the past four days, he'd made the drive from Villefranche to Nice and back enough times to know better. This morning though, he couldn't get back to Villefranche fast enough. Back to Jade. He couldn't wait to feel his arms around her, hold her tight against him—against his chest and under his chin where he could protect her from anything out there that might try to harm her.

The last hour with Meg and Jake had left him reeling from the onslaught of powerful emotions. Watching the two of them had set off a series of reactions in him that ranged from head-spinning giddiness to the heart-squeezing realization that time on this earth is short. No matter how much time you had with someone you cared for, it would be never enough.

Jake's arrival had transformed Meg like a magical potion. After the initial tears and embraces, her frail body had come to life with animation, her color had risen from pasty gray to dull pink, her eyes had sparkled and looked beautiful despite their absent lashes and bare ridges. The nausea hadn't gone away, but it had eased up for a while. Jake's presence did something to her, *for* her. He brought a part of her with him, a part that was healthy and whole and cancer-free. With his news of the kids and life at home and all that was good in her life, Jake arrived just in time.

But the next three weeks would be hell for both of them.

Kai checked his watch. 11:13. Jade would be surprised he was back early again today. Hopefully she didn't have any major plans. A day just hanging out at the house sounded nice. Taking walks, cooking dinner, making love—any activity that wouldn't require her to get more than three feet out of his reach.

God, he'd never felt so needy. So vulnerable. A pain gnawed in the pit of his stomach. He'd have to tone down the emotions because Jade would see through him immediately and know something was up.

Maybe it was time to tell her about Meg. Kai sniffed. The vomit smell was still evident on his shirt from where Meg threw up in the elevator. Jade would catch that. He chuckled, reminded of their first date when *she* had been the one throwing up. They'd come a long way since then.

Yeah, it was time to tell her. He would just have to put his foot down about visiting too much. It wouldn't be right, cutting in on Meg and Jake's private time together.

His chest tightened remembering how sick Meg had been. She didn't need too much company, what with Jake and the hired nurses. But he and Jade could visit and give Jake a break if he was inclined to leave. Seeing the state Jake was in this morning, it was doubtful he'd want to leave.

Kai pulled into the driveway, relieved to be back to Jade at last. He shook his head at his hurried gait up the walk. If Jade had been in the yard, he would have swept her into an embrace.

His heart sank when he tried the door. It was locked which meant she'd gone out. He found the key atop the doorframe and worked it into the lock. "C'mon, Jade. Get home fast," he muttered to

229

himself.

The breakfast table was still set...for two? Oh yeah. It was Tuesday, the morning of the shittin'-ass breakfast with the I-wouldn't-piss-on-you-if-you-were-on-fire Jean Luc. God, he was a snot. And the way he looked at Jade, like he could serve her up hot by an egg timer... Kai forced himself to unclench his jaw and his fists and make sense of the scene. Two cups filled with undrunk coffee, croissants hardly touched. They left in a hurry...or were in a hurry to get somewhere.

"Sonofabitch!" he exploded, making it to the bedroom in record time.

His own audible sigh of relief echoed in his ears. The bed was made.

"Of course, it's made. Stop being a jealous jerk." What was the phrase Hazel used to use when she was mad at him? A selfish, uncaring dolt. Well, maybe she'd be right this time about the dolt but certainly not the uncaring.

At least he could shower and smell better by the time Jade got back. Or maybe she'd come in during the shower and decide to join him. That pleasant thought sent him to undressing pronto.

He took his time, leisurely washing his hair and lathering all over. The warm spray beating on his chest and back invigorated him. The morning had drained him more than he'd been aware. He finished showering.

Still no Jade.

It took him a couple of seconds to figure out what was wrong when he opened the closet door. He stared dumbly at the empty space. His clothes were there, but nothing else. Jade's clothes were gone. All of them! He checked the underwear drawer, the drawer where she'd placed her jewelry, the shoe rack on the back of the door. Empty. Every last one of them empty! And her luggage was nowhere to be found.

She'd gone off with the freakin' Frenchman! No good-bye. No explanation. No apology. Just gone. Just like Hazel.

The rage anchored in his stomach, moving out from there until a thin ringing sounded in his ears. He'd swallowed it the first time when Hazel left him. But he'd be damned if he would just stand by and take it a second time. He wasn't the perfect man, maybe not every woman's dream—or any woman's dream for that matter—maybe not Jade's His Hotness. But he was a human being, damn it, and he deserved to be treated better than this!

He grabbed the keys and slammed the door. He didn't know where Jean Luc lived, but he knew where the restaurant was. Somebody there could give him directions.

He was wrong about needing directions to the house. The sight of Jean Luc's car in the restaurant parking lot a few minutes later caused his stomach to roll into a knot. Probably stopped by for a bite since they never got around to breakfast. He could hear the blood pulsing in his ears as he made his way to the door.

The door was unlocked, but the place appeared deserted except for a light near the back. The office of the head prick? He and Jade might be back there right then, might be... Kai didn't give any sound of warning, just forced his legs in the direction of the light, dreading what he might find, but angry enough to have to know.

Jean Luc sat at his desk, hunched over some papers. Jade wasn't with him. The knot in Kai's stomach relaxed ever so slightly. Maybe he'd been wrong about the two of them. But what would make her pack up and leave with no warning? Had there been an emergency, and she hadn't been able to reach him? Oh God. Was someone hurt or sick at home?

"Jean Luc?"

The Frenchman gave a yelp of surprise as he came to his feet.

"Sorry," Kai apologized. "I didn't mean to startle you. Do you know where Jade is?"

Jean Luc's eyes narrowed as he came around the desk. "Yes." He nodded slowly. "I know where she ees. She ees on the aeroplane to go home. I take her to the aeroport myself."

Jade was on her way back to the States? Why? The fear that someone was hurt or dying caused Kai's head to spin. "What happened?"

"What happened?" Jean Luc gave a sardonic laugh as he stepped forward. "*You* are what happened. You...*et la femme à l'Hotel Nigresso.*"

Kai was still trying to make some sense out of the slur of French words when Jean Luc launched at him, burying his head into Kai's stomach. Caught by surprise, Kai stumbled backward, coming up against the wall behind him as Jean Luc's right fist flashed up and around toward his chin. Kai ducked, but not fast enough, and the knuckles found their way into his left eye accompanied by a string of French words, obviously expletives in any language.

Kai's mind raced to understand as he fended off the flurry of swings determined to loosen his teeth. Hotel Nigresso? Okay, he got that part. La femme? Femme? Woman? The woman at the hotel? Oh God! Jade had found out about Meg!

His roar of frustration stopped Jean Luc long enough for Kai to wedge his arms between them and shove. Adrenalin must have kicked in because Jean Luc sailed backward into the bookcase, sending its contents scattering. Trophies, beer steins, plaques, and books pummeled him as he covered his head with his arms.

Kai looked at his watch. A little after twelve.

"She probably went out on the same plane Jake came in on. Shit!" The frustration welled up inside him, and nothing would please him more than to take it out on this French *Cinderella Man*.

Jean Luc clamored unsteadily to his feet, eyeing Kai like a bull seeing red. Kai's depth perception was off—his eye already starting to swell shut—but his opponent's stance said he was ready to go at it again. They both knew the advantage of Kai's size now that there was no chance for a sneak attack.

Guilt washed over Kai. This was his fault, not Pepe LePew's. He was fighting for Jade's honor just like Kai did with Adam. She was special to him, and he couldn't fault the Frenchie for that.

Kai raised his hands palms out in front of his chest. "This is a misunderstanding I don't have time to explain now. But I will later if you want. I haven't been unfaithful to Jade."

Jean Luc moved his jaw slowly in a circular motion, reminding Kai again of a bull, this time chewing a cud. Then he jerked his head forward. "Pwau!"

Kai jumped back. The glob of spit aimed for his face splattered at his feet. He turned and stalked out.

Honor or not, it's lucky for him my reflexes are good. If that had hit me, I'd have ripped him apart limb by limb.

****

Jade took a deep breath, letting it out in a long sigh as she paid the taxi driver. His eyebrows drew together in a questioning look as she waved away the change.

She licked her lips, but the dryness of her mouth afforded no moisture. Her bottom lip burned where she'd chewed away the skin over the past three hours. Seeing the car in the drive made her hesitate, not at all sure she'd made the right decision. But it was done and there she was. She pulled her luggage up the brick walkway to the cottage. The rattles would warn him she had returned.

Sure enough, Kai met her at the door. "Jade! Thank God you came back. I can explain everything."

From the looks of him, he had a lot more to explain than just a lover in Nice. His left eye was swollen completely shut with a nasty bruise that reached under his cheekbone. His face and neck were covered in scratches and bruises. Had he and the pixie gotten into a brawl? Or maybe her husband caught them together.

Jade found herself wanting to laugh at his obvious pain, but she refused to sink to that. Instead, she kept her face hard and unflinching as she moved past him.

The door closed behind her.

She went straight to the bedroom to deposit her luggage. His suitcase lay opened on the bed, clothes in a pile in the middle, toiletries scattered about. "Good. I'm glad to see you're packing since you have somewhere else to stay. I don't want you here." It wasn't difficult to keep her voice flat. The muscles in her neck were so tight it was difficult to get the words out, much less any emotion.

"Jade, I'll be glad to leave if you want me to." His voice softened. "But first, I want you to hear me out."

"Fair enough." Her heartbeat slowed to something more closely resembling its natural beat. At least he wasn't going to make a scene about being sorry and wanting to stay. "I came back because I *wanted* to hear you out. I asked myself what Gram would do, and I heard her telling me to make you explain."

"The woman you saw me with at the hotel—"

"How did you know I saw you?" Had he seen her

after all? She didn't think so. He hadn't given any indication.

He pointed to his shiny black eye. "Jean Luc told me."

"Oh." How had Jean Luc already gotten involved? Had he gone back to the hotel after dropping her off at the airport? She quelled the questions. She needed an unencumbered brain to catch the loopholes that would no doubt show up in the story. She would be patient and attentive, and wait for him to hang himself.

Just like Adam.

"The woman is Meg Prater. She's the wife of one of my employees. And a friend."

The depth of such betrayal—not just to her but to an employee—turned her stomach. "You make me sick." She hissed the "s" sound to get her point across.

"Meg has cancer, and she's here to get treatments."

Jade could feel her cheeks burning with indignation. Of all the low-down, despicable scoundrels in the world, the man standing before her had to lead the pack. He made Adam look like an amateur. How could anyone take advantage of a sick woman? And her husband? Someone he saw every day? How could he face him?

"She and Jake have five children and were having trouble—"

"And she needed someone to lean on. How fortunate you were available, you son-of-a-bitch." Her hand connected with his unbruised jaw before she had time to consider the action, but she felt no remorse.

Kai's blue eyes locked onto hers. His jaw muscles twitched several times before he continued. "They were having trouble getting family together to keep the kids on such short notice, so I told them I'd take her to treatments until Jake got here."

What did he say? Jade heard his words, but comprehension still skirted the edges of her brain. "Huh?"

Kai pushed her back gently to sit on the bed. He sat beside her, pointedly not making any other physical contact. "I'm sorry. I should've told you from the beginning. We'd heard about these cancer treatments in Europe, so when you invited me here, my staff got on the ball, and we got Meg into a program here in France, at a clinic in Nice."

He's taking her to cancer treatments? Jade was too stunned to speak. Nothing could have gotten past the baseball lodged in her throat anyway.

"Jake called friends and relatives to get someone lined up to keep the kids. He worked it out to come Thursday, but then I found someone else, so he got to come today. He's here now."

Jade heard her pulse as it rushed through her ears. Her heart beat fast and hard. "But I saw you together...your arms... you picked her up."

Kai squeezed his eyes closed and massaged the bridge of his nose with his thumb. He let out an exasperated sigh. "Meg thought she could walk to the room. She didn't want to draw attention to herself, you know? But she got too sick to walk. I even tried to carry her, but we didn't make it." His voice cracked with emotion.

Jade's stomach tightened like she'd been punched, the wind knocked out of her. She remembered the tiny woman—emaciated... whispering to Kai, and his hurried reaction. Aaiieee! She was sick, didn't want to draw attention to herself, and he was trying to protect her dignity.

She watched his face blur as her eyes filled up with tears of sympathy for Meg and humiliation for herself. "Did...did she pass out?"

"No, she threw up." He sighed, and Jade noticed

how tired his voice sounded. "In the elevator."

God, she felt awful. For Meg. For Kai. For her doubting him. Thinking the worst of him. "Oh, Kai. I'm so sorry. I thought…" She choked back a sob.

His deep blue gaze pulled her into its tide. She was drowning in it, fighting for air as he spoke. "I know what you thought. Don't be sorry. It's my fault. I should've told you."

The sob escaped her then. "Yes, you should have. Why didn't you?"

Kai's knuckles brushed at the tears streaming down her cheeks. "I should have, but I was afraid it would ruin your vacation. And with the job coming up, this might be your last vacation for a long time."

Her emotional dam broke then, and all the frustration and anger and sadness plunged together over the spillway. "I'm not a child to be protected from the world, Kai. I know that bad things happen." She poked her chest, emphasizing her words. "I'm a grown woman, and I can handle pressure."

His mouth twitched ever so slightly. "I'm well aware that you're a grown woman, Shank. I was afraid you'd want to spend a lot of your time with her. And you only have nine days…"

"You should have trusted me to make my own decision about that," she shot back. "I don't need you making decisions for me!"

"You're right, you don't, and I apologize for that. But as long as we're on the issue of trust, let's get one thing straight right now." His business-like tone startled her. She'd heard him use it on the phone with work but never directed toward her. She straightened, readying herself for her comeback. "I'm not into any of that game-playing nonsense." He drug his hand through his hair back and forth a couple of times. "I'm crazy about you and have absolutely no desire to have another woman in my life. But, let me assure you…if I ever find myself dissatisfied with what you and I have, there will be a clean break-up before I go looking at anyone else. Is that clear?"

Jade sniffed and nodded, but his words brought a new swell of tears. *He's crazy about me. He feels the same way I do!* But she'd accused him of all those bad things. "Kai, I'm crazy about you, too. And I'm so sorry...f-for doubting you." She released another long sob, the culmination of the emotions pent up all morning. "I don't want anybody else but you."

Kai's eyes narrowed. "Not even Jean Luc?"

She gave her head a vehement shake. "Not even Jean Luc." She ran a fingertip lightly down his bruised cheek. "And if I ever made you feel differently, I'm sorry for that, too."

He turned his face and kissed the finger as it drug across his lips. "Then I'm sorry for doubting you, too. It won't happen again."

Jade took his hand, keeping her eye contact steady. She wasn't a fool for trusting him. She'd only been a fool for doubting him. He hadn't used her. He'd protected her. He'd restored her childish dream with his kindness, even kicked it up a notch. "You are so kind-hearted. You'd go to this length for an employee?" She hoped her voice conveyed all the awe and admiration she felt.

Kai shrugged. "Probably. But Jake's more than an employee. We go all the way back to high school. His dad was the head of maintenance at the school, and my mom thought he hung the moon." Kai took her hand and patted it. "Meg got pregnant in high school, so they were married young. Mom gave Jake a chance, and he worked as hard as his dad." He gave a little chuckle, and she watched his eyes squint in delight. "When we started the company, I snatched him out from under Mom's nose." He shook his head. "She still hasn't forgiven me for that."

Her emotions moved up and down like a rollercoaster. Happiness at the truth about Kai. Guilt for doubting him. Shame for slapping him. Sorrow and sympathy for Jake and Meg. She hadn't even asked about how the treatments were going. She threw her arms around Kai's neck and pulled him close. "Oh God, Kai. You must think I'm terribly callous."

He gathered her in his arms with a gesture that said he thought no such thing.

"How are things going for M-Meg?"

She felt Kai's breath catch in his chest. "It'll take a while before we know whether the treatments are successful. They'll go on for at least three more weeks."

"So, Jake is here now. Can he stay the entire time?"

Kai's nod wiggled the top of her head.

"Their families are keeping the kids?"

"Well, Jake's mom has taken off starting Thursday. Meg's parents are coming from Fresno for the last week. I found someone to keep them for these two extra days."

"Why does it not surprise me you'd be the one to do that?" His arms tightened closer around her, and she snuggled against him. "But five kids? How did you find someone willing to take that on?"

His laugh vibrated against her cheek. "You helped me there."

She leaned back and gave him a quizzical look. "How could I have helped? Who'd you get?"

"Gram."

Jade pushed out of his grasp to look him straight in the eye. "Gram?" That was the most preposterous thing she'd ever heard. Gram had never kept kids—except her—certainly never five at a time.

"I called to see if she knew of anyone." He smoothed his hand down her hair. "When she heard the story, she insisted on doing it. She said if she could handle you, five would be a piece of cake." The rumble of his laughter shook a smile to her lips at last.

"It appears that I...er, Jean Luc and I...were the only ones not in on this." She brushed a finger over the angry, purple patch of face. "He was trying to take care of me."

Kai grasped her hand and kissed her fingertips. "I know."

Jade took his face in her hands gingerly and kissed him. She'd let her mouth express what words seemed inadequate for, wanted to show him how wonderfully special he was. Her lips trembled with emotion against his. At last, she found the words that exemplified her emotions. "Would you unpack now? I really want you to stay."

Kai grabbed his clothes up and tossed them at the closet. They landed in a heap. "All done." He gave a quick nod of satisfaction. "Now, I've got three things I want to do today."

Jade stood and pulled him to his feet. "Anything you want. What do you have in mind?"

"First, I want to go apologize to Jean Luc and explain everything. He's a good friend to you, so I want to give us a chance to like each other. Then I want to take you to meet Meg and Jake."

Jade nodded. Anything top priority to him moved to that position for her. She could guess number three perhaps, but she wanted to hear him say it. "And the last?"

"I want to come back and take a loonngg time getting all dressed up to go to Monte Carlo tonight."

Jade circled her arms around his waist and pressed against him. "You want to go to the casino? Why?"

He tilted her face up and kissed her long and deep before answering. "Because today I feel like the luckiest man alive."

Chapter Twenty-Six

Jade leaned far over the table for the last sip of coffee. Couldn't risk getting anything on the exquisite pink silk Chanel suit Gram bought her for her first day at work.

She had to keep reminding herself to breathe. Making love to Kai this morning...first day on the job...the suit she had lusted after from afar but wouldn't even allow herself to try on. The reality of all these dreams coming true made her dizzy with excitement.

"And what will you be doing all day while I'm slaving away at work?" She jabbered away all through breakfast about the trip and the job, and mostly Kai. She hardly gave Gram a chance to say anything.

Gram's eyes twinkled with mischief. "I'm going to Disneyland!"

With that twinkle, there had to be more to the story. "You're what?"

"Yep. Marvin and I are taking the kids to Disneyland."

Jade could see now that the twinkle was partly caused by some tears held in check.

"They're just the sweetest little things. Nice and polite and well-behaved." Gram's voice thickened. "You just gotta wonder sometimes what the Lord has in mind. Why allow a fine young woman like that to get cancer, with five precious kids and a loving husband, while old farts like me somehow get off free and clear?" She shook her head and wiped away an escaped tear.

Jade stood up and wiggled a finger in a "come here" motion.

Gram stood up facing her, the top of her head barely clearing Jade's chest. Jade pulled her in for a bear hug. "I can't think of anybody more deserving of a blessing than you, Gram." A slight shudder ran through the small body. "And, if you get one tear on my new Chanel suit, I'll have to beat you."

Gram's body shook with laughter, and her hand reached around and swatted Jade's rear. "Oh yeah, Chickie? You just try it." Jade held her tight for a minute, knowing something else was coming. "I mean, you know how I've always told you everything happens for a reason? Well, I'm stumped as to what reason there could possibly be for Meg's cancer."

Jade planted a kiss on the top of her head and eased her back down in her chair. "I don't have an answer for that one, Gram. But you've also always told me that sometimes we only get one chance. Let's hope Meg's going to get two."

Gram poured herself another cup of coffee. "Have you heard from Jake?"

Jade shook her head and began gathering up her things. She needed to get on the road. Being late her first day would range in the nightmare category. "Not since we left on Saturday. She wasn't doing very well then, but he said the doctor told them that was to be expected. To treat her body, they have to break down the bad first, then build the good back up." She took one last look around to make sure she had everything. "Well, I'm off." She tried to make her voice sound smooth and confident. "Wish me luck."

"Break a leg, Chickie." Gram gave her a lopsided smile. "You and Kai have plans again tonight?"

"Yeah." Jade let out a long, satisfied sigh. "He's meeting me at work and taking me out to dinner to celebrate."

Her heartbeat moved into a higher gear. She'd made her announcement to Beth yesterday. It was time Gram heard it, too. She took a deep breath. "Gram, I'm in love." Just saying it made her giddy all over. Even her fingertips tingled.

Gram gave a snort. "That's old news, Chickie. I knew it a month ago."

Jade blew her a kiss and headed for the car, feeling like she could fly if she spread her arms. She slowed her steps when she spotted Adam outside his garage getting something from the trunk of his car. They hadn't spoken since she threatened him with the lawsuit. Well, now was as good a time as any to break the silence. She put on her best poker face and advanced to meet the enemy.

"Hello, Adam." She meant to push the button on her key fob to unlock her car but hit the panic button instead. The alarm sounded, drawing several neighbors to their windows before she found the wherewithal to shut it up.

When she turned her attention back to Adam, she wasn't surprised to see him grinning. He, of course, would enjoy watching her make a fool of herself. But the "For Sale" sign in his hand took her aback. "Are you moving?"

"Yeah. Well, *we* are. Elena and I. And I owe it all to you. Or maybe to Malone."

Jade stiffened, and she had to tell herself to loosen her hold on her car key before she snapped it in half. So he would blame them somehow for this, too? She didn't have to listen to his fabrications anymore, and she sure wasn't going to start today with one. "Whatever." She opened her car door and got in.

Before she could close the door, Adam caught it and wedged himself in the space. Her hand instinctively reached toward her purse and the pepper spray. She'd never been afraid of Adam, but after his actions at the wedding reception, she wasn't taking any chances.

"I mean it. I owe it all to you and Malone." Adam was smiling what appeared to be a genuine smile. No smirk, no over-innocence. "If I hadn't fallen in the pool that night, I never would've met Elena. And now, here we are, moving to Bangkok."

"Bangkok?" That jolted her more than Gram's coffee.

"Yeah. Elena's been offered this big movie deal over there. They've already paid her this huge advance." His eyes opened wide with wonder. "They make movies for the computer. People subscribe to the site. It's big business. *Really* big business. And they say Elena's the hottest thing around anywhere!"

The type of business he referred to wasn't lost on Jade. So Elena was going to be the Queen of Porn. Why was she not surprised? "Well, Adam, that must be so exciting for both of you." She reached out and shook his hand. "I'm happy for you. Really I am. And I wish you and Elena lots of luck."

Adam drew her arm around him and leaned down to give her a hug. "Thanks, Jade..." he whispered and gave her a quick peck on the cheek, "for everything."

He moved back and shut her car door, giving her a wink when she waved 'bye. She could hear him whistling as she backed out of the driveway. So Gram was right again. Everything happened for a reason. Elena was going to star in porn movies and Adam was thrilled. A His Hotness was out there for everybody.

When she got to the 405 Expressway, traffic was creeping at a snail's pace. She congratulated herself on having plenty of leeway on time. Even after inching along much of the way, she arrived at work twenty-three minutes early.

Mr. Levitt met her at the door with a warm handshake and a friendly smile. It helped calm the tumblebugs in her stomach. "We're glad to have you with us, Jade." He looked every inch the executive in his black suit, white shirt, and black and yellow tie. Her fears she was over-dressed were quickly put to rest.

"I'm thrilled to be here." Although her face was warm, her hand was icy, but he didn't let on that he noticed. Her emotions ran the gamut from terrified to elated, and all of them were manifesting through cold and sweaty palms.

Mr. Levitt led her to a small office, barely large enough to accommodate its desk, chair, and four tall file cabinets. A pile of multi-colored, multi-sized envelopes had been unceremoniously dumped in the corner below a plant stand holding a pot that contained a dried-up cactus.

"Slush pile." Mr. Levitt indicated the mound in the corner. "At least, the part of it you're responsible for." He must have noticed Jade's quick intake of breath because he quickly added, "But you don't need to start on it until tomorrow."

Jade forced a smile and swallowed the lump of panic that had formed in her throat. She could do this. She put in long hours with the editing business. How much worse could this be?

She looked around to find something to distract her from the corner. Her gaze dropped to the desk, and her heart skipped a beat. Her name on a nameplate in all its wood-look plastic glory! It shouted, "You've arrived!" to her in a kitchy sort of way.

She mentally sized up the office. About one-fourth the size of Gram's bedroom closet. About the size of the section Gram allotted to shoes.

"I'm afraid you won't have much time for settling in today," he apologized.

"Oh, that's okay. I didn't bring anything to settle in except myself, and the chair looks like a good fit."

"I've got you scheduled for back-to-back meetings with various people throughout the day, and we'll be having lunch with Roseanna Milford from the Excite—no, the Excitement—no, ah, the Excita Literary Agency." He pulled a small leather notepad from his breast pocket and flipped through several pages, scanning each one. "Our new Executive Editor wants to meet with you at 4:50."

What kind of person made an appointment at 4:50 rather than 4:45 or 5:00? She watched him for any sign that might clue her in to her new boss's quirks. A good start—no, a perfect start—was imperative. "Any words of wisdom on how to make a good first impression?"

He closed his notepad and gave her a grim smile. "Apparently, no one here has cracked that code with J.J. Whitney. But I *can* advise you not to be late."

His tone ran a shiver of anxiety up Jade's spine.

A young woman close to her own age appeared at the door. Jade tried not to show surprise at her strange get-up: black fishnet hose, white ankle boots, purple miniskirt, and a pink mesh off-the-shoulder top that showed a florescent orange bra beneath. Her short, blue-black hair stuck out at odd angles from her heavily made-up face.

"This is Cathy Wilson, one of the assistants. She'll be here to help you out and get you where you need to be today."

Cathy stopped chewing her gum long enough to flash Jade a brilliant smile. "Hi. Call me Cat. Last week, I was in the mailroom. Today, here I am." She extended her hand. Her grip was strong as a man's, but she didn't squeeze. Assertive. Confident.

"I'm Jade." Jade tried to return the confident air, but Mr. Levitt's comment had her worried.

"Well, Jade, I'll catch up to you about noon." He hurried out to catch up with someone else, leaving Jade still in Cat's clutch. When she let go, she gave Jade a quick smile and kicked the door shut behind her. She tilted her head toward Levitt who could now be seen through the window. He was speaking with a woman whose black hair was pulled back in a severe bun. "Levitt's porkin' Valerie Findlay."

The off-hand comment took Jade by surprise, and she had the distinct impression Cat was trying to shock her. She tried to keep her voice non-committal. "Oh." But she filed away the information. According to the novels she'd critiqued, affairs were always good things to be aware of.

"So, did Levitt fill you in about Hannibelle Lecture?" Cat's eyes widened as she gave a loud pop with her gum.

My, this person didn't waste any time. "Not exactly." Hannibelle Lecture? Was Cat trying to send her over the edge? Jade's stomach did a flip-over. What had she gotten herself into with this job?

"He didn't tell you about Ms. J. J. Whitney?"

Jade shook her head. Cat broke into a pretty good rendition of Elvis Presley's "Devil in Disguise," which Jade found both amusing and horrifying at the same time. It was becoming pretty evident that Ms. Whitney was considered by some people to be a royal pain in the ass.

Cat finished her chorus by curling her lip on one side. "Thank you. Thank you very much," she slurred then she pointed to the chair. "Have a seat and I'll fill you in."

Jade took the seat, thankful for the opportunity to catch her breath. The cubicles outside her office had filled up with workers, but without the usual morning chitchat she'd expected, except for the brief exchange between Levitt and Valerie Findlay. No gathering around the water cooler to talk about the news since yesterday. No doughnuts or muffins being passed. Everyone she could see was already diligently at work on something. "Is there a no visiting rule around here?"

"Naw." Cat shook her head and rolled her eyes. "There's just a work-your-ass-off rule. That's what I'm here to explain." She pointed to the envelopes piled in the corner. "Since Ms. Whitney's arrival, everybody here's a reader. And I mean everybody. Janitors, mailroom clerks, assistants. Everybody."

Jade wanted to ask if this was standard practice in the publishing world, but she bit her tongue. She would just keep listening for now.

"You're expected to keep up with your work, but you're not allowed to work on your regular stuff until your submissions' quota is finished for the day. That's why you don't see anyone talking. Everybody's reading on their slush."

Jade eyed the pile warily. She estimated seventy-five to a hundred queries waiting for her. "How do you get it all done?"

Cat's face broke into a mischievous grin. "Well, there's no way for anyone to tell what you've tossed, um, rejected. I just read the first page. Sometimes the first paragraph or even the first sentence will do it. And there's a whole lotta crapola."

"I know all about that." After two years of critiquing, this was familiar territory. Jade's stomach eased out of its knot. "I'd heard that's how a lot of agents and editors do it, but I never believed it."

Cat pointed to a six-inch stack of paper on the desk. "Those are rejection letters. Yours say 'I don't feel your work is ready to seriously compete in today's market.' Everybody's says something different." She waved toward all the offices on the fringe around the room. "The letters need your signature at the bottom then paperclip them to the

SASE. If there's no envelope, toss it. I'll fold, stuff, and mail."

Okay, maybe this was do-able after all. "What happens if you like something?"

Cat snorted. "Peons bring it to assistants." She pointed to herself. "Assistants bring it to submissions editors." She pointed to Jade. "You take it to the Levitt, and he takes it to..." she bowed her head reverently and growled, "Hannibelle."

Jade laughed. "Why do you call her that?"

"She talks you to the point of death, and then she eats you alive. You'll see." Cat grabbed a trash bag lying across the top of the filing cabinet and popped it open. She stooped down and began filling it with the letters from Jade's pile. "I'm going to take care of these today because in ten minutes you have to meet with the other submission editors."

Cat would have her own pile to deal with. It didn't seem right for her to take on a double load. "I'll get to them, Cat. Just leave them."

Cat gathered the bag into her arms. "Don't worry. Mail comes at eleven. There'll be another pile to take its place. Now." She pointed to what looked like a conference room at the other end of the row of cubicles. "You need to get your ass down there so everybody can look you over good before the meeting begins." She popped her gum before adding, "Great suit, by the way."

She hummed "Devil in Disguise" as she sashayed out of the office.

The day went by in a blur of new faces and too many names to remember. True to Cat's promise, another pile of envelopes appeared in the corner of the office—tomorrow's pile of dreams—just before Levitt whisked her off to lunch with the agent.

Neither of them had been impressed with the project being pushed. He complimented Jade on her "good instincts," and her confidence level rose to the

I'm-not-a-complete-moron level.

She'd spent the afternoon in meetings with people from PR, IT, and various other department initials as the clock hands fast-forwarded to 4:40.

She checked her make-up one last time before going upstairs. She'd received a text message from Kai that he'd see her around six. Just over an hour away. Knowing he would be waiting for her when she got out of it made the meeting with J.J. Whitney seem almost bearable.

No one else had spoken with Cat's frankness, but the guarded comments and insinuations indicated that Ms. Whitney probably wouldn't be nominated for Boss-of-the-Year by anyone.

Although Jade could have taken the public elevator, it ran the chance of meeting with someone whose name she should remember. Her brain was clogged with too much to deal with right then. She chose instead to take the private staircase leading directly to Ms. Whitney's reception area.

When she opened the door, she was greeted by a world vastly different from the one a floor below. Cool blue walls hung with modern art paintings, plush carpet, leather chairs, an over-sized ebony desk, and exquisite accent pieces in black and plum. Ms. Whitney had expensive taste.

The receptionist, Elaine Burch—according to the nameplate—looked up as Jade approached. Her smile vanished as her eyes gave Jade a quick but thorough scan from her shoes up.

Jade did a fast check. No stains from lunch or black ink marks that she could see. Perhaps Elaine Burch had an aversion to the color pink. Jade pulled her thoughts under control. "Hello. I'm Jade Bartholomew. I have an appointment with Ms. Whitney."

"Oh yes, Ms. Bartholomew." Elaine's newly resurrected smile didn't reach up to her eyes. "Ms.

Whitney's, um, expecting you. You can go on in."

Jade's hand shook as she glanced at her watch. Five minutes early, so Elaine's look of reproach couldn't have been because of her tardiness. Mr. Levitt had been most clear of the time she was expected. She gave a light rap on the door.

"Come in." The tone didn't give anything away except that it was female.

Jade made a quick entrance, checking to make sure the door closed well behind her.

A full-throated laugh met her, and she cringed, convinced by now that something was indeed wrong with her appearance. She turned to face Hannibelle. The petite woman who stood behind the desk was much too small for such a voice. Jade glanced quickly around to see if anyone else was there.

"Come in, Jade. Please have a seat." She indicated a leather wingback right in front of the desk.

Jade made her way to the chair, smiling and maintaining eye contact. J.J. Whitney might have been Hannibal Lechter's soul mate, but her looks certainly didn't give her away. Jade judged her to be about thirty. Her shiny, auburn hair lay in a smooth, chin-length bob swept behind her ears with fringe bangs across her forehead. She had a flawless fair complexion, eyes of an odd greenish-brown hue rimmed with thick dark lashes, and a smile that radiated with impossibly white, perfect teeth.

The woman was gorgeous. And she knew how to accentuate her coloring with her make-up and clothes. The pink suit she wore was stunning. Chanel, maybe? "Omigod!" The word escaped Jade's mouth before she could catch it as she realized the reason for the laugh and Elaine Burch's stunned look of disapproval.

"Well, I haven't been promoted to a deity yet, Jade darling, but I'm working on it." The accent was strongly New York and proud of it.

"I'm sorry, Ms. Whitney. Our suits..." Jade shook her hand.

Her new boss gave her hand a brisk shake then motioned for her to take a seat. "Don't worry about the suit. I'll donate mine to charity. It's up-lifting to me that someone else around here has taste. And it earns you the privilege of calling me J.J."

The compliment was a bit backhanded; Jade wasn't sure of the proper response. Mr. Levitt had been dressed very smartly in a well-tailored black suit and everyone else's attire—well, except Cat's—seemed suitable. She murmured a polite thank-you and hoped the suit conversation would die a quick death.

"So Jade, tell me, what is the source for your impeccable taste? I hardly expected such from someone who's been making a living running an on-line critiquing service." J.J. placed her fingertips together as her hands rested on the desk, head tilted at a slight angle, the epitome of self-confidence and intimidation.

"Um, my mother and both of my grandmothers have..." Jade leaned back hoping the support behind her would help her relax.

J.J. broke in. "Anyone in your family from New York?"

"No. My mother's from—"

"Ah, well then," Hannibelle showed her vicious bite as she interrupted a second time, "your good taste is bought rather than inherent." She sighed and rolled her eyes in disappointment. "What a pity."

The woman had an amazing knack. They'd been together for all of two minutes, and Jade already disliked her. She willed her hands to let go of their tight grip on the armrest. But maybe the armrest was a better placement than around the haughty bitch's neck.

J.J. spun her chair a quarter turn and focused her attention out the window. "Let me tell you about my vision for Samuels Publishing."

Those words opened an hour and a half near-monologue during which time Lecture droned on and on about her wants, dreams, wishes, desires, and hopes. Cat's nickname made complete sense after about ten minutes.

Occasionally, Jade interjected a sentence or two, but mostly her part was held to "Yes, I see."

If Lecture had made eye contact more often, it would have made it easier. Instead, Jade was afforded the luxury of watching the minute hand on her watch crawl toward six-thirty. Mmmm. At least Kai was waiting downstairs. In an hour, she'd be holding his hand, feeling his stubble on her cheek. And later...

"Well, I'm meeting with the realtor at seven, so I'll have to cut this short."

Is she kidding? My butt is so numb, I may never get feeling back. "Oh!" Jade jumped at her chance for escape. "You need to get out of here, then. Traffic will be terrible," she lied, knowing traffic would be lighter now than a half hour ago.

J.J. gathered her purse. "Won't we be a sight, walking out like two Twinkies in a package. I'll enjoy the look on the staff's faces when they see you wore my suit."

Jade gritted her teeth at the use of the possessive pronoun. Ten more minutes and she'd be rid of Hannibelle for the day.

They walked down the steps with Jade towering above the other woman like a giraffe. When they reached the bottom, J.J. waited for Jade to open the door for her. Yeah. Let her go first and fantasize about kicking her ass.

Jade opened the door, relieved to find everyone

gone. Except Kai. Thank God! He was sitting outside her office, near the stairs. He stood up when he heard the door open.

J.J. let out a breathless squeal, two octaves higher than her regular voice.

The sound stunned Jade. She stopped in mid-step and watched J.J. Whitney launch herself into Kai's arms. "Kai, darling! How did you know I was here? How did you find me?"

Jade watched his face contort with confusion when his eyes met hers. His Adam's apple bobbed as he swallowed. He licked his lips like his mouth had gone suddenly dry. He spoke, and his voice had an edge she'd never heard in it before.

"Hazel!"

Chapter Twenty-Seven

Kai struggled his way out of a veil of confusion. Why was Jade with his ex-wife? And why were they dressed alike? During one sickening moment of purely illogical thought, he looked around to see if Jerry Springer and a camera crew lurked somewhere in the immediate vicinity.

Hazel's arms around his neck and Jade's horrified expression brought him around faster than any smelling salts could have. He peeled Hazel's tiny frame off of him and set her on her feet. Her question cut its way through the fog, and he answered her honestly. "I had no idea you were here." He reached out for Jade's hand, and pulled her to his side. "I'm here to pick up Jade."

If he had slapped Hazel, her reaction would have been no different. Her face drew up in confusion that quickly passed, replaced by a flare of anger he recognized in the set of her jaw and the smirk on her mouth. "You're here to pick up Jade? Oh my!" She threw her head back and gave a forced laugh that carried a wicked edge. "It appears that clothing isn't the only taste we have in common."

Kai was still confused why the two of them were together and turned to Jade for an explanation. Eyes wide, mouth pinched, she looked almost fearful. Her hand trembled in his.

"This is Hazel?" Her voice sounded very small.

He nodded. What was going on here? Why was Jade acting so timid? It wasn't like her.

"Kai, darling, you're the only one who ever called me that." Hazel swept her hand around the office in a dramatic gesture. "My employees here at Samuels Publishing know me as J.J. Well, actually as Ms. Whitney."

Employees? No, this couldn't be happening. Surely Jade's dream job—the one she'd waited for so long—was not working for his ex-wife as her boss. Maybe he hadn't heard her correctly. "Your employees?"

Hazel was the epitome of composure then. "Yes, darling, my employees, like Jade here." She tilted her head in Jade's direction.

Another tremor ran through Jade's hand; Kai squeezed it for assurance.

"I tried to tell you my news the last time we spoke, but you were..." she let her eyes drift lazily up Jade's form before returning them to meet his gaze, "busy."

He'd seen this side of Hazel before. The jealous side. The side that viewed all women as competition and none as equals. It was an ugly side and he hated that Jade was being exposed to it. He put an arm around her protectively. She stiffened against his side, then relaxed.

"Well, to quote my grandmother: Won't wonders never cease?" Jade's light laugh filled the quiet office. She had her composure back, and her quick wink assured him she was okay. "If I'd read this in a tabloid, I would've thought they made it up."

Kai pressed a kiss to the top of her head. If it pissed Hazel off, too bad. She'd just have to get over it. Jade needed his support. "Truth is stranger than fiction."

Hazel's icy smile seemed frozen onto her face. It didn't match the fiery darts emanating from her eyes. Kai had known the heat from those daggers on many occasions. Amazing how they no longer affected him in the least.

"I'm hungry," Jade announced. "J.J., perhaps

you'd like to join us?"

Kai squeezed her shoulder again. Had the woman lost her mind? Maybe the stress of this was too much for her.

"Perhaps you should call me Ms. Whitney, Jade. We wouldn't want the other employees to think we're too familiar." Hazel's condescending tone seemed totally out-of-place considering Jade towered over her by half a foot, and she had to raise her chin to a preposterous angle to look down her nose. "And no thank you on the invitation. I have to get to my appointment." She turned her attention back to Kai and smiled warmly. "Kai, darling, could I have your new number? I seem to have lost it."

Kai held back the sarcastic snort and started to beg off with the excuse that he'd run out of business cards but would get one to her later. Jade's nudge in the side changed his mind for him. "Sure." He fished a card out and handed it to his ex, knowing full well the gesture was a mistake.

"Thank you, darling." Hazel dropped the card into her purse. "We'll talk later." She gave a coy wink over her shoulder as she turned to make her way back to the door she entered from.

When Hazel was gone Jade let out a long breath and turned toward Kai, batting her eyes in an exaggerated manner. The move was humorous, but by no means did it cover the worry evident in those green eyes. "Yes, darling, we'll talk later."

"Jade, I had no idea." Kai found himself apologizing but for the life of him he didn't know why.

He was interrupted by clapping from the cubicle directly in front of Jade's office. A strange looking woman with blue and black hair stood up, obviously delighted with the exchange she'd overheard.

"Oh. My. God!" She popped her gum in unison with her claps. "You are gonna be a legend around here."

"Cat," Jade's voice was school teacher stern. "You can't mention this to anybody. At least not any time soon. I want to keep this job."

"And I wanna keep you here. You're gonna make this place plenty interesting." Cat blew a giant bubble as big as her head.

Jade propelled Kai toward the door.

Instead of the celebration Jade had looked forward to all day, dinner was a strange combination of frustration and angst with a healthy dose of helplessness mixed in. She found it difficult to swallow around the lump of nerves in her throat, and what went down felt like bowling balls hitting her stomach.

J.J. Whitney was difficult to work with at best, and this situation was hardly best. In fact, it ranked right up there with the worst of the worst.

Beth and Pryce tried to make light of the situation. And it *was* pretty funny Kai nicknamed her after an old television sitcom character who always managed to come out on top no matter how she had bumbled things. According to Kai, that description fit Hazel to a tee. Jade had been sure the nickname was because of the color of J.J.'s eyes.

Jade held off until they got home on some of the more personal questions she wanted answers to. Snuggled with her back against Kai on the couch, the soothing weight of his arm draped across her shoulder, she finally felt comfortable enough to ask.

"So how did a nice guy like you come to be married to someone like J.J. Whitney? I mean, Cat calls her Hannibelle Lecture."

Kai pressed his cheek against the back of her head. "We were in college ... she was one of the fraternity sweethearts. Outgoing...fun. We dated over a year. And she seemed great."

"But..." Jade prodded.

"But, after we got married and I tried going pro in golf, I began to see another side of her. She stayed disappointed in me all the time. Nothing I did was ever good enough. When I wouldn't make the cut, she'd throw mad fits. Tell me how pitiful I was. She kept telling me how I wasn't trying hard enough. If I'd just put my mind to it I could do better." He sighed. "She was probably right about that, but my heart wasn't in it."

Jade pulled her knees up and scrunched around to lay her head on his shoulder. "Go on." She felt the tension in his arm and realized this was probably painful for him. But maybe it was cathartic too.

"Mark was talking to me about starting Techtron and that's what I wanted. She hated Mark, by the way, and the feeling was mutual. She also hates California, so I can't fathom what could possibly make her come back here."

Jade swiveled to look him dead in the eye. "You are joking, right?"

Kai raised an eyebrow in question.

"She's back here because of you. She's still in love with you, Kai." The words hung heavy in her chest.

"You said still. I don't think she was ever really in love with me. She was attracted to me, but she didn't love me. Didn't love who I am." The blue of his eyes seemed to darken with his words.

Jade pushed a little farther. Might as well get this all over with at once. "So how did the break-up happen? Big fight? Dramatic scene? What happened?"

Kai's thumb rubbed softly down her arm. "Nothing like that. The day we opened Techtron, we had a celebration dinner planned with Mark and Jilli. I came home early, on cloud nine and ready to take on the world." Jade watched him swallow hard. "She was gone. Clothes, pictures, most of the furniture. She called me a few days later. She'd taken off with one of the guys I'd been on the golf tour with."

Jade stayed quiet as he paused for a minute. "I was pretty distraught for a little while, and then one day it hit me what I really felt."

Poor Kai. How devastating. Her stomach tightened at the thought of the pain he must have gone through. "Betrayed?" She poured all her sympathy into that one word.

Kai shook his head and smiled. "Relief." One of his deep chuckles rumbled out.

Jade pushed away from him in mock frustration. "Kai, that's awful!"

"It's the truth." He gathered her back against him tenderly. "When my head quit spinning, I realized how terrible we were together. I could never be the man she needed. The man she wanted me to be. She's wants someone who'll stop at nothing to get his way. And hers. I'm not that man, Jade. I don't operate that way."

She leaned back to look him in the eye. "I know." She smiled and ran the back of her fingers up his strong jaw. The coarse stubble tingled against her sensitive skin, running a tingle of excitement through her arm that touched her heart.

He took her hand and pressed it against his lips. "You and I aren't like that though. We're good together. Hell, we're great together." He cupped his hands around her face and held her eyes with his gaze. His voice was husky and deep. "I want to be the man *you* need. I know you may think it's too soon for this, but I love you."

His words surged through her like an electric current. She'd been wanting to say the same thing for days now, but she'd been afraid of his reaction. Afraid of scaring him off. "Oh, Kai, I love you, too!" Her heart soared into the clouds as she spoke the words. The tension of the day melted away as his lips met hers in a kiss of urgency and need. And surrender for them both.

Before she could catch her breath, he scooped her into his arms and headed for the bedroom. She held on tightly around his neck, unwilling to let her mouth disconnect from his.

By the time he settled her on the bed, she was shrugging out of her camisole and drawstring pants. They came off easily. She raised up on her knees and loosened his belt and trousers while he made quick work of his shirt.

Words hardly seemed necessary. They'd said it all. She wanted to let her body speak to his. Wanted to show him how he filled the aching need growing inside her. Show him he was already who she needed. His Hotness.

He leaned her back onto the bed, and she drew him down with her, arms clinging to him, fingers in his hair.

His lips seared their way down her neck and started toward her breasts. She took his face in her hands and lifted it, shaking her head. Interlacing her fingers in his, she stretched her arms above her head bringing his body in full contact with hers. His arms covering hers, his cheek nestled against hers, his chest pressed against her breasts.

He bent his knees to relieve her of the bulk of his weight. She took the opportunity to arch her back and position herself under him. Then she pressed against him, gasping as he slid into her, raising her heat index to white-hot.

"I want to come together... in one... gigantic... mind-blowing climax." She groped with the words as she wrapped her legs around him, drew him in farther.

He responded by thrusting deeply, making her gasp in pleasure. "I love you, Jade." He whispered the words as their bodies fell into a rhythm of their own making, perfect and thrilling in its perfection.

The climax grew inside her—a slight twinge, then a tingling sensation that soon became an involuntary gripping. He grew rigid at the same time. It was going to happen together. "I love you, Kai." She tightened her stomach muscles and arched her back. His body became a solid, turgid mass of steel, holding her, pressing her, filling her, carrying her up the mountainside, and dropping...her...off. The seismic shock ripped through her body causing an avalanche. Wave upon wave of sensation, almost unbearable in its intensity.

Her tears of happiness and euphoria mixed with Kai's sweat on her cheek, and she smiled.

Later that night, lying in Kai's arms, listening to the sound of the crashing waves echoing their spent passion, she turned to him, compelled to ask, but dreading the answer. "Kai? About Hazel." She took a deep breath. "She hates me, doesn't she?"

Kai pulled her closer and wiggled his head against hers in a nod. "Yep. Better watch your back."

Chapter Twenty-Eight

When Mark walked into the office at two o'clock in the afternoon, it seemed odd. But one look at his drawn face, and Kai knew something was terribly wrong. "Shouldn't you be home in bed? What's going on?"

Mark collapsed onto the couch and ran his hand over his face. "Kai, I've got… We've got a problem."

Kai's mind raced and his heart speeded up to keep pace. A bomb scare? A virus that wiped out all the software? What could possibly warrant the look on Mark's face? He kept his voice calm and controlled. "What is it?"

Mark's eyes leveled with his. "Jilli's pregnant."

Kai let his breath out in a relieved whoosh. Mark, ever the joker. After all their years of trying for a baby, this was fabulous news. "Congratulations, man! This is fantastic. I'm going to be an uncle again!"

Mark shook his head and held up a hand to signal Kai to stop. He wasn't smiling.

He's not joking. Kai's stomached tightened in preparation for the blow. "What's wrong? Is she okay? Is the baby okay?"

"Jilli's okay, but the doctor says there could be complications because of the miscarriage two years ago. Something about some molecule in her blood that was different from the baby's. It's like the pH thing only rarer." He jumped up and paced in front of the desk. "Evidently some of that baby's blood mixed with hers and it had a different molecule, and now her blood is making antibodies to fight it off."

His voice cracked. "And they could attack this baby's blood. So they're going to have to keep a close eye on the level of antibodies in her blood. They'll have to monitor it constantly."

Kai came around the desk and leaned on the front of it. When Mark paced by, Kai caught him and made him stop. "They can monitor it, Mark. They take care of things like that these days. I'm sure the baby and Jilli will be fine."

Mark gaze was direct, unflinching. "It's not that, big guy. Jilli's terrified something will happen. She doesn't want to leave her doctor and I can't be away, leaving her to face this alone." He paused. "I'm telling you we can't move to Japan."

Japan! Of course! Kai mentally swatted the front of his head with his palm. So if Mark couldn't move to Japan for the year of consulting... The blow hit him full force and he fought not to show a reaction. If Mark couldn't go, he would have to go himself. And he couldn't dawdle. They were contracted to start that phase on August 5th. Less than a week away.

He put his hands on Mark's shoulders and shook him gently. "Quit worrying. I'll go. They don't care which of us it is. It won't make one bit of difference."

Mark swallowed hard. "But what about you and Jade? You guys are getting serious. A year, Kai. Think about it. You'll be in Japan for a year."

Kai was well aware of the length of time they committed to in the tentative sales agreement. And there was no question. He and Jade were in love. He didn't want to be away from her for a day, much less a year. The thought of it made him almost nauseous.

Jade would just have to go with him. It would mean quitting her job. But the job wasn't good for her anyway. She was working way too hard. And Hazel was being totally unreasonable with her.

No doubt about it. Jade would have to go with

him. "Jade and I will work it out. She'll go with me." He tried to convey his confidence to Mark whose expression said he wasn't convinced.

Kai pushed the button on his intercom. "Alice?"

"Yes, Mr. Malone?"

"Book me two tickets to Tokyo for August 4th." He released the speaker button. "It's going to be okay, Mark. I'll take care of it."

He flipped his phone open and called Jade, knowing he'd get her voicemail. He left her a message that he'd be over tonight. They had something very important to discuss.

****

Jade's hand trembled as she brought the bite of salad to her mouth. She set it back down on her plate without taking a bite. "It's making me a nervous wreck, Gram. This constant pressure. I always thought if I worked my butt off, it would be rewarded in some way. Maybe even appreciated. I mean, I don't need constant praise, but the harder I work, the more she finds to complain about."

Grams eyes narrowed in concern. "How much weight you lost, Chickie?"

"Seven pounds in the four weeks I've been there. I work through lunch usually and, by the time I come home, I'm so tired I don't have much appetite for dinner." Jade forced the bite into her mouth but had a hard time getting it swallowed. She was exhausted although it was only a little before nine. If Kai hadn't sounded so anxious, she would've told him to stay home, and she would have gone straight to bed.

"You can't keep this up, Jade." Gram never used her name unless she was deadly serious. "You're working fourteen and fifteen hours a day and not eating. Commuting adds another two or three hours. You're gonna collapse."

"My one-month review is the day after

tomorrow. I'm hoping after that, some of the pressure will let up." Jade pushed aside the salad as it no longer seemed appetizing. Nothing sounded good except hot green tea. At least that was good for her.

Gram let out a long breath. "You need to tell Miss New Yuck to take that job and shove it. She's not doing you right and you know it. And you know why."

"I can't do that, Gram. I've got to prove to myself and everybody else I can do this. I need at least a year's worth of experience in the field. Then maybe I'll look for something else. I can put up with anything for a year."

"Well, nobody's gonna want to hire you if...if..." Gram at a loss for words? "...if your hair and teeth have all fallen out because of malnutrition."

Jade fought back the laugh that would spew her tea until the liquid was safely swallowed. Then she laughed out loud. "I won't starve. Quit worrying. And I'm learning how to get around some of her nonsense, anyway."

Gram's eyebrows rose. "Oh yeah?"

"Yeah." Jade felt pretty smug with the plan she and Cat had worked out. "Ms. Whitney was turning down everything I sent up. Out of twelve possibles she only accepted two. But if I send them as Cat's finds, she takes almost everything. So most of my finds I send to her as Cat's. Not all of them. Maybe three-fourths."

Gram shook her head. "You shouldn't have to play games like that."

"I know. But when you're dealing with a game player, you've got to understand the rules and then manipulate them, don't you? Would you believe she even doubled my slush pile? Cat found that out from the mailroom. They were told to give me twice as much as everybody else."

"You've led a pretty sheltered life, Chickie. I hope you know what you're doing.

Gram's words hit Jade's already frazzled nerves. She wasn't a child any more. She could handle herself. And she could handle this job. And she could handle J.J. Whitney. "Trust me, Gram. I know what I'm doing. Everything happens for a reason. Remember? And sometimes we only get one chance to get it right." The deep, relaxing breath did nothing to loosen the knot in her stomach.

"Getting it right this time might involve telling her off."

"No." Jade gritted her teeth. "Getting it right this time might involve everybody leaving me alone and letting me—"

Kai stuck his head in the door, so she didn't finish. Going off on Gram would only give her regrets later.

Sheesh! This behavior was so unlike her. Especially with Gram. But lately, she'd been testy with everybody. A dull ache throbbed in her temples.

"Hey, babe. You look exhausted." Kai kissed her on the cheek.

What was with all this babe talk from everybody today? What happened to Jade? Or Shank? "Hi. So do you." And he did. He looked more frazzled than she'd ever seen him.

He kissed Gram on the cheek. "Hey, gorgeous. When you gonna leave Marvin and come live with me?"

Gram's dimple appeared and lightened Jade's mood a little. These two were such fun to watch. It was evident how they adored each other.

Gram stood up and gave him a pat on the cheek. "Oh hell, you're not foolin' me, Kai Malone." She stuck her stomach out, threw her shoulders back, and did a sultry model's runway walk to the door. "You only want me for my body." She blew them a kiss and was gone.

Jade dumped her salad down the garbage disposal and put her plate in the dishwasher. The movements sapped all the energy she had.

Kai was in a strange mood. Distant. Normally by now he was talking her leg off. With her headache, the quiet was rather nice though. He patted the space next to him on the couch. She plopped onto it with a heavy sigh.

Immediately, he turned to her and took her hand. Something about his touch startled her, and when she looked into his eyes his grim look confirmed her suspicions. Something was wrong.

"We need to talk."

Oh God. Those detested words. Her heartbeat throbbed in her temples.

Kai's words came out in a rush. "I have to move to Japan in the consulting position that was specified in the sales agreement."

"What?" He spoke so fast, she wasn't sure she heard him right, prayed she hadn't heard him right.

"Mark and Jilli can't move like we planned. She's pregnant. There are some complications. I have to go instead."

Jade squeezed her eyes shut, trying to block out the pain, physical and mental. Mark and Jilli pregnant? Complications? Kai had to move? "You're moving to Japan? Just like that? I mean, this is quite a bombshell to drop, don't you think? No easing into it. Just, "Hey, guess what?" Heat moved from her chest to her neck and into her cheeks. Sadness? Anger? Hurt? All of the above.

Kai cradled her hand. "I don't want to be away from you, babe."

Babe again. She cringed. "Please don't call me that."

Kai's lips pressed into a thin line, then the tip of his tongue grazed over them. "Sorry." She watched his Adam's apple bob. "But my point is I love you, Jade. I can't stand the thought of a year without you."

"You'll be able to come home some, won't you?" Kai's words had started a churning motion in the pit of her stomach. The churning increased when he shook his head.

"It's too far. I'll get time off, but I'll be on call 24/7."

"Oh, Kai, this is awful!" Jade blinked back the threatening tears as hopelessness engulfed her. Maybe she was a baby about things, but this was too much to take all at one time. First the job. Now this. "I don't get my two weeks of vacation until I've been with Samuels a year."

"I know and I know how much this job means to you, but..." He was holding her hand so tightly it was starting to go numb. "I want you to quit and go with me."

Quit? He wants me to quit? His words ricocheted around her brain. What was he thinking, making such a suggestion like it was nothing at all. "Quit? I can't quit. The idea is preposterous." She was incredulous. "I've just started. I'll *never* be able to get another job in publishing if I quit this one after only a month."

"I can get you any job you want. In publishing or any other field you choose. I've got money. I know plenty of people. I can pull strings—"

"No!" Jade jerked her hand out of his grasp and moved out of reach. He used to be so adamant about not being that kind of guy. Maybe he didn't know himself so well after all, and he sure as hell wasn't acting like he knew *her* very well. "I don't want your getting a job for me. I don't need you to pull strings!"

"I could talk to Hazel about giving you a leave of absence. She'd listen to me." The plea in Kai's eyes matched the tone of his voice.

His words cut through Jade like a knife and laid her wide open. "No! How could you even consider laying our problems at the feet of that woman? Like my happiness and my life is somehow her concern?" Anger spewed and she didn't try to hold it in check. The past month had been too long, the pressure too great.

"I didn't mean it that way." Kai approached her, arms outstretched.

She moved away, putting the table between them. A horrifying thought slammed into her. "Gram always told me everything happens for a reason, Kai. Nothing has been easy for us. From the first glimpse on." She tried to choke back the words, but the fears and insecurities that she'd pushed down for so long erupted. "We've been up against problem after problem from the start. They've been constant." A sob broke free. Her nose stopped up and she couldn't breathe. The pain in her head increased in direct proportion to her mental anguish. "Maybe we're not meant to be together. Maybe I'm just here to get you back with Hazel."

Kai came around the table faster than she could react. He swung her around to face him, holding her at arm's length in a grip of steel. "Jade, stop it. You can't mean that. I love you. I want to be with you. Nobody else."

He let go of her and she slid into the nearest chair, not trusting the strength of her own legs.

"I thought you felt the same." His tone wasn't accusatory. Just sad.

Jade ran her hand through her hair. Things were happening too fast. She was riding a giant wave, approaching shore at breakneck speed. She needed time. She needed rest. But the prospects for neither of those looked good.

Kai pulled a long, thin leather folder from his back pocket and dropped it on the table in front of her. She eyed it but didn't reach out to touch it. "What's that?" She kept her voice void of emotion.

"Tickets. To Japan. I bought them this afternoon."

He didn't know it, of course. She'd never discussed it with him she was sure, so he had no idea he'd just rung the death knell. It was déjà vu, and he was no longer Kai. He was another Adam. Making decisions about her future. Thinking he knew better than she did what she needed. Taking control of her life without even considering her feelings or thoughts about matters of the utmost importance. She'd been taken in once by a man like that. She wouldn't be so gullible again.

"I can't do this, Kai." She pushed the pouch to the other side of the table.

"Talk to me, Jade." The familiar growl had earned him plenty of points on the Hotness scale. Now it was pointless.

"There's nothing to talk about anymore. Please leave." Paisley jumped into her lap and bumped her chin. She was happy to have something to focus on besides Kai's ocean-blue eyes.

He stalked across the room toward the door. "We'll talk tomorrow when you've had some time to think this over."

She flinched at the slamming of the screen door. "I thought this over a year ago," she whispered as the tears started anew.

She sat for the better part of an hour, nuzzling Paisley, trying not to think. It hurt too damn much.

****

Kai's thoughts were racing miles ahead of him before he started the car. He thought of several ideas as he drove home. Several options. All of them painful. Some excruciating. The one he kept coming back to felt like he was cutting off one of his limbs.

By the time he pulled into his driveway, he was

praying Jade had changed her mind. He dialed her phone. No answer.

No answer at 11:53.

No answer at 1:07.

No answer at 3:28.

He showered and dressed and headed to the office. He had to talk to Mark about his decision.

Amputation.

Chapter Twenty-Nine

Jade moved about in a mental fog the next morning, unable to get the conversation from the night before off her mind. The headache was gone, but she felt beaten and numb. She considered calling and apologizing for her over-the-top reaction, but that would only give Kai hope when she didn't feel any.

She turned on her phone and checked her voicemail. Four calls from Kai. She deleted them without listening to them. She couldn't risk hearing his voice. Letting him leave last night was the hardest thing she'd ever done. The energy drained out of her just thinking about it.

God she loved him, but she had to stay strong. She had to think of her own future. A year from then when he got back, maybe they could pick up where they left off. She'd be able to move to another job by then. Away from J.J. Whitney. Thoughts of the woman made her jaw muscles tighten.

Last night, she'd been reacting. Talking out of emotion. But what if what she'd said actually were true? What if she was the catalyst in this bizarre universe, placed here to reunite J.J. and Kai? Maybe they would be the ones back together in a year. She shoved that thought out of her mind to make plans for the day and how to get some rest that night.

A large Marriott Hotel had opened across the highway from Samuels. She decided to spend the night there. Away from Kai, should he decide to come to her apartment looking for her. Away from Gram, who would know instantly something was wrong if she saw her.

A hotel room would give her privacy and rest. It wouldn't stop her thoughts, but it would stop any interference. She'd be able to get some rest and be ready for her evaluation scheduled for ten the next morning.

She packed a small bag of necessities and zipped an extra suit into a garment bag. Her cell phone rang. She checked the caller I.D. and gave out a long sigh.

Mark.

She hit the ignore button then turned her phone off.

****

J.J. Whitney opened the door to her office the following morning at precisely 10:00. "Jade, come in."

The low voice was no longer a shock, but it sent a little shiver through Jade. She dreaded this meeting.

"How are you this morning?" J.J. sat down in her chair and indicated the leather wingback for Jade.

"Fine, thank you." Jade reminded herself to unclench her teeth in order to answer. Her jaws ached with tension. She'd probably ground her teeth during the tiny amount of time she'd slept.

"You don't look fine. You look tired." The voice held no true concern.

Did J.J. know something? Had she talked to Kai? A flare of irritation burned in Jade's chest, and she felt the blush creep upward.

"Well, I'll make this brief. And as painful as possible." J.J. gave the wicked Hannibelle laugh Cat could mimic so perfectly.

Jade said nothing, concentrating on making her face unreadable.

"You, Jade Bartholomew, are one of the toughest

people to get rid of I've ever employed. Or perhaps your brain has been dulled by all of those God-awful manuscripts you edited."

The comment took Jade totally off-guard. *Tough to get rid of?* J.J. was known for being unpredictable. Maybe this was her inept attempt at humor.

"Despite that fact," J.J. continued, "I believe you are perceptive enough to realize I'm still in love with Kai." She arched a perfect eyebrow inquiringly.

Jade nodded in response, not trusting her voice.

"I was appalled at first when I learned it was actually one of my employees Kai was in love with. But I decided that might work to my advantage. He seemed much more willing to talk to me, knowing I held your career in check." She drew a long dramatic sigh.

Jade concentrated on keeping continuous eye contact with the other woman. To look away would be a sign of weakness she couldn't afford. As "Ms. Lecture" headed into one of her monologues, Jade was reminded of Gram's theory about people who talked too much. "People who monopolize a conversation are trying to cover up their own inadequacies," Gram had said many times. "That's the way they try to hang onto control."

So the more she talks, the more weakness she shows. Jade smiled and watched the petite redhead react to it by launching quickly into her next statement.

"Try as I might, I couldn't stomach the thought of working with you everyday right under my nose. Or under my feet as lay-out would have it." She squared her shoulders and raised her haughty little chin. "I devised a plan to make you quit by rejecting all of the submissions you picked and accepting all of the ones from your assistant, which, by the way, I knew were actually from you." Her head shook in mock sympathy as a smirk settled on her lips. "My

God, woman, have you no sense of pride?"

Remaining silent seemed a bad idea now to Jade as the flare of irritation that started earlier flashed to anger. To hell with staying calm and collected. If she was going to get fired anyway, she might as well say exactly how she felt. "You do realize, Ms. Whitney, that by discriminating against me, you've opened yourself up for a lawsuit. My parents are attorneys of the highest caliber."

J.J. gave a sarcastic chuckle. "I'm well aware of who your parents are, Jade dear. But any good attorney will remind you that you are working here provisionally. You have no binding contract yet. Just an agreement that stated, had you read it carefully, you are employed at the pleasure of Samuels Publishing—that would be me—and that you can be released at any time during the first thirty days with or *without cause*. And, oh yes, your signature is at the bottom."

Jade opened her mouth to speak again, but J.J. shook her head and waved her off. "Please. Let Hannibelle Lecture have her complete say, then she'll allow you to argue any point you desire." Her demeanor remained cool, unaffected by the nickname. "I didn't get where I am without knowing *everything*," she stressed the word, "that goes on within my company."

Jade settled back into silent mode. She would have her say when the other woman had talked herself dry.

J.J. continued her one-woman diatribe. "I doubled your slush pile and still you hung on. At last, I decided I would leave you to your own personal hell. You would have your one-month evaluation. I'd get rid of you then. End of story. But..."

The word jolted Jade from her stupor, gripped her stomach, and held on.

"This morning I received a call from Mark McCallister."

"Mark called you?" Kai had always made it clear how much Mark and Hazel disliked each other. She remembered the call she had ignored from Mark. Had something happened to Kai? She squeezed her hands together to quell the trembling, but it found it's way into her voice when she spoke. "Why?" she whispered.

"My thoughts precisely. Mark and I have never gotten along, so why would he be calling me? Well, he tells me that apparently you and Kai have broken up."

"That's really none of your business," Jade snapped. She'd found her voice again, and she'd had enough of this.

She stood to leave.

"Oh, sit down, Jade. Hear me out. It *is* my business. It is quite literally my business."

Jade sat back down on the edge of her seat. She could walk out at any moment of her own choosing.

"It seems that part of the Techtron sales agreement requires a one-year consulting position that must be filled by either Mark or Kai. Mark was scheduled to go, but Jilli's pregnant." She rolled her eyes. "They can't go, so it falls on Kai to move to Japan. As I understand it, he wanted you to go and you refused."

Jade remained silent. *Breathe,* she told herself.

"Well, your refusal to go has now precipitated Kai's refusal to go, which means the sale of Techtron will soon be history. Mark is disappointed, of course. I mean we are talking millions of dollars here. But he can live with that decision."

Kai wouldn't do that to Mark. Jade gripped the armrest to stop her hands from shaking. He probably was tired and making irrational decisions. Probably wasn't sleeping. He just needed a couple of days to get his thoughts back on track.

J.J. came around the desk and leaned back on it, directly in front of Jade. "What he *can't* live with is Kai's decision on how to make up the loss to him."

Jade shook her head. "I don't understand."

J.J. smiled an icy grin. "Noble Kai feels guilty for the money he's making Mark lose, so he's selling *everything* and putting it in a trust fund for Mark and Jilli's unborn child."

"What do you mean he's selling everything?" None of this made sense. "You said Techtron wasn't going to sell now."

"Not Techtron. His personal possessions. His house, his cars, his art collection... He's putting everything up for sale. He has a meeting with a realtor to put the house on the market this afternoon."

The reality of what J.J. was saying bored into Jade's mind. *Mark wants J.J. to talk some sense into Kai, so he must think they have a future together, too.* She took a deep breath and let it out slowly, hoping it would carry away some of the tightness that had moved from her stomach to her whole body. "So Mark wants you to talk Kai out of this."

"Not exactly. Mark and I both want *you* to convince Kai to move to Japan. Mark tried to contact you all day yesterday, but you wouldn't answer his calls. He called me out of desperation, knowing I'd have access to you. He reasons that if you are truly finished with Kai, there's nothing to stop Kai from making the move to Japan. But no one is going to be able to convince Kai of that except you."

Her chuckle ran a shiver up Jade's spine. She swallowed hard, knowing the answer before she asked. "And *your* reason?"

"The obvious, of course. If Kai moves away for a year, that should give me adequate time to regain his favor. I'm considering marketing some of our titles to foreign markets. Japan would be an ideal place to start." J.J.'s eyes opened wide in mock surprise. "And, of course, I'd have no reason to get rid of an extremely hard-working employee like you who has proven herself highly qualified. In fact, you've earned a promotion to Acquiring Editor in only a month's time. I see you moving ahead in this business at a record pace."

Jade held her gaze steady. "And if Kai stays here?"

"You can consider yourself dismissed. Let go at the end of the trial period because you weren't the right fit for the company. I mean, your assistant found more submissions than you did. And I gave you every chance. Even doubled your slush, so you had twice as many queries to find good material from. Tsk, tsk. Such a pity." No evil laugh this time. Just a short moment of stony silence. "Now, take the rest of the day off. I'll know the outcome based on whether or not you're here tomorrow."

J.J. gave her no time to respond. She went over to the door and opened it, effectively closing the door on further discussion.

So Gram's theory was right. Hannibelle had talked herself into a state of wide-open vulnerability and had to dismiss the enemy before the power exchange became apparent.

The power of this knowledge surged through Jade. She stood and followed close behind but stopped just inside the door, positioning herself so the petite woman had to crane her neck to make eye contact. "Ms. Whitney, before I leave I want you to understand that my personal life is really none of your affair, and no matter how much you wish it to the contrary, the relationship between Kai and me is none of your business. You won't have to look for me tomorrow. I won't be here." She started out but thought again and turned back around. "And by the way, if you're going to continue your tirades standing directly in front of the poor people who think they have to listen to you for whatever reason, you should seriously consider sucking on a breath mint."

The door slammed behind her.

Elaine Burch gave Jade a silent round of applause and a wink as she passed.

Jade had no time to savor the sweet victory or the relief. Her mind whirled in thought. Kai was giving up everything? To stay with her? There was only one thing to do. She had to set him straight. She turned her phone on and dialed his number.

He answered on the first ring. "Kai, we need to talk. Can you be at my house in an hour?"

"Sure." His growl sounded frayed around the edges.

"I'll see you then." She snapped the phone shut and speeded up her pace.

****

Kai beat Jade by a good ten minutes. A glance in his rear-view mirror as he waited showed he'd been running his fingers through his hair. He looked like an escapee from a mental ward. He was trying to get his hair back into place when Jade drove up. Seeing her made his heart skip a beat. She'd been crying. Damn, that didn't look good.

In spite of his best intensions to let her do the talking, as soon as she stepped from the car, he couldn't contain his words.

"Jade, I just can't do it. I can't move to Japan for a year and leave you here. I would be completely miserable and when I'm like that I can't concentrate, so I'd be a terrible freakin' consultant." She didn't respond, so he continued talking as he followed her up the steps into her apartment. "Bushido is spending an extra million for that position, and I can't take their money knowing I couldn't give them fair value for their dollar."

Jade still wasn't saying anything.

He kept going. "It's not Mark's fault this is happening, and the money I'm causing him to lose makes me sick. But you're worth more than money, and I think I've figured out a way to get some of the loss back to him."

He watched as she pulled a book from her desk drawer. He read the hand-lettered title. *His Hotness*. His next words caught in his throat. He watched her flip to a page that bore his name across the top and long pieces of tape where it had been attached back into place. As if in slow motion, she took hold of a corner and carefully tore the page free once again.

Pryce's words flashed through his mind: *"And if the poor guy's score ever drops below a sixty, his page is ripped out. Symbolic of a crash-and-burn sequence."*

Oh God, he'd lost her. No. He'd lost everything.

Jade's eyes were misty when she looked up at him. "Kai, I started my His Hotness journal when I was sixteen," she said. "I developed a scale to help me find the man of my dreams objectively. For ten years, I've rated guys on everything I could think of, trying to find out what's important to me."

Kai's sadness silenced him. He'd never been eloquent, and now words failed him completely.

"I was trying to find love using a whimsical scale. But love can't be left to whimsy." She tossed the journal onto her desk. "I learned a lot from Adam, and I tried to apply what I'd learned to you." She shook her head. "But you aren't Adam. I can't compare you to Adam. There's no comparison. In fact, you're not like any other man I've ever known."

She stepped near him and took his hand. The warmth of her touch moved through him.

"You are the most unselfish person I've ever known. You're honest and thoughtful and kind. And

I love you. I love you enough to follow you any place on this earth you want to go, whether it's Japan or the North Pole or Timbuktu."

She moved into his arms, and her grip tightened around him in a hold that said she'd never let go. He breathed her perfume and kissed the top of her head.

She lifted her lips to his in a sweet kiss of promise that said what her words so inadequately expressed. Euphoria moved through her at the mere touch of him. Kai's arms—wherever they happened to be—were the place where she belonged.

His lips were soft on hers at first, but she could tell when understanding of her words and their implication started to sink in for them both. His hands caressed her face, moved into her hair. His mouth devoured hers with exquisite tenderness then one hand moved to her back, crushing her against him.

She wasn't losing her independence. She was giving it away willingly. She eagerly surrendered her mouth to his tongue and met each thrust, giving and receiving the entitled possession represented by each. Body. Soul. Future.

Life.

The thought infused her with happiness, and for the first time she understood the unadulterated joy of commitment.

A warmth against her leg brought her back to reality. "Paisley. Will I be able to take Paisley?" She gathered the cat into her arms and rubbed her nose in his fur.

Kai rubbed his knuckles down her cheek and across Paisley's head. "I'm afraid not, sweetheart. There's a long quarantine period. Months. But if you'll accept my job offer, I think I can make that better."

"Job offer?" She gave him a look of severe

warning. "This better not have anything to do with J.J. Whitney."

Kai's eyes crinkled into a squint as he chuckled. "No Hazel. Mark and I have started on the language conversion software, and we think French would be the ideal language to begin with. We need someone fluent in French and English to work on the project. You're the perfect choice. In fact, Mark brought it up first."

The more the man talked, the better it got. She couldn't wait to hear what would come next. "And what's that got to do with Paisley?"

"Well, if you accept the offer, you'll have to come back to L.A. a few days each month to meet with the staff of the new company." Kai's smile broadened. "But I don't think Paisley will be too lonely anyway."

Her kitty rubbed his head against her chin, purring softly. "Well, I know Gram will be here."

"And the others."

What was he talking about? "Others?"

Kai's eyebrows shot up in surprise. "You haven't talked to Gram?"

"Not since the night before last."

"She called me this morning looking for you. She said she couldn't get you on your cell and had missed you before work." He held his palms up, and shook his head. "I didn't tell her anything about us, but she started telling me that maybe we should consider moving in together. When I asked why, she explained that Meg Prater is coming home next week."

Jade's breath caught. Was the news good or bad?

Kai's smile offered relief. "She's doing well, but she's still really weak. Gram wants to move Meg and Jake into your apartment and let the kids live downstairs with her. Jake can work, they'll all be together, and somebody will always be around to take care of Meg."

A small tear gathered at the edge of his eye, and she moved in to kiss it away. He caught her and gathered her to him with a contented sigh.

"Shank?"

"Hm?"

"Why'd you tear my page out of the journal?"

She broke away from him with a laugh and grabbed the book. "Because I'm throwing this thing away." She dropped it into the trash. "But this," she held up his page, "I'm going to treasure forever.

He kissed her then in a long, forever kind of way.

Chapter Thirty
Ten years later

Jade sat at her dressing table, eyeing the formal engraved invitation in her hand. As she read it aloud for the ten millionth time, her heart swelled in pride again. "Dedication Ceremony and Grand Opening of the Malone-Bartholomew Cancer Research Center." She dabbed at a tear. She and Kai and their families had found something of priceless value to invest their money in.

"Shank!" Kai's deep voice called from hallway. "The limos are here."

She glanced in the mirror and tucked a stray strand of hair behind her ear then hurried to meet up with him.

He already had Keaton by the hand and Katy in his arms when she caught him. On the pretext of straightening his tie, but more because she itched to touch him, she ran her fingertips across the hair in his temple. A little silver had started to mingle with the black there making him more distinguished looking. And hotter than ever. "I'm so proud of you, Kai. Of everything you are."

He leaned down and kissed her, eliciting a giggle from the kids. "Whatever I am, you've made me." He leaned closer and whispered, "And if you need any physical proof of what you've made me, just take your hand..."

She pulled away shaking her head in disgust but gave him a seductive wink. "Later." She smiled at him sweetly. "So, do you think they've finished the gazebo on the grounds yet?"

Kai groaned in response.

Closing the door behind them, she was surprised to see three limousines. She'd only expected two. "Why three limos?"

Kai's chuckle still stirred her to the core. "Because the Praters couldn't get their entire brood into one. With kids and spouses and boyfriends and girlfriends and grandchildren, they've become a force to be reckoned with. Your parents, my family, and Beth and Pryce were picked up at their houses by the way. They're all going to meet us there."

The driver opened the door, and Jade climbed in.

"Hey, Chickie-boom!"

Jade turned to find Gram in the corner seat, brandishing a glass of champagne. She looked beautiful in her navy satin dress, her hair pulled up in a loose twist that left soft tendrils around her face. Surely, she couldn't be eighty-eight.

Jade gave her a hug and slid into the seat beside her as Kai handed in the kids. They squealed when they spied Gram and fought briefly over who would get to sit by her. Keaton gave in finally and let Katy sit there, making Gram promise that the place of honor would be his on the trip home.

"I thought you were going with Mom and Dad." Jade was sure those were the last plans Gram had given her.

"Well, um, I didn't make it to their place last night." Gram shrugged.

Was she blushing? "Gram, have you met a man?" Jade prodded. Actually she hoped it was true. Gram had been terribly lonely since Marvin's death two years ago.

Gram lowered her voice to a whisper that was unnecessary since the kids were singing along with the radio. "I've met two."

"Two?" Jade feigned shock. "What will you do

with two?"

The look Gram gave her made Jade's face get hot. "I mean, I know what you'll *do* with two, but how will you choose between them, uh, if the time comes to choose."

"Well, I'm thinking about starting a journal and setting up a scale to rate them with." Gram's dimple appeared. "Seems to have worked pretty well for you."

Jade wagged her finger. "Ah, but Gram, it took me ten years to perfect mine."

"Well," Gram drawled, "I don't have to deal with all those variables you did. I only have one criterion."

Jade knew she was being set up, but she had to ask. "And what would that be?"

Gram managed to keep her face straight. "If they don't die during sex, they win. And since they've all got one foot in the grave, I'm thinking the appropriate title might be Mr. Cool."

Jade dissolved into laughter, drawing a squint of inquiry from Kai.

"You girls need to pull yourselves together, now." The twinkle in his eye belied the growl in his voice.

Jade made a bow from her seat. "Anything you say, Your Hotness...I mean, Your Highness." She blew a kiss to the man of her dreams.

Without a doubt, His Hotness. In the flesh.

A word about the author...

Maybe growing up in the South didn't have any impact on Pamela Hearon's writing, but she has her own theories and believes otherwise. A lifetime of sultry, Southern nights surely infused her blood with a special heat—the kind that transforms simple love stories into tales of romance and desire. And her most powerful writing happens at some of the oddest times—in the garden ... in a dream ... even in the shower. Unexpected moments of inspiration bring dialogues together, make characters come to life, and fill gaping plot holes.

Her writing process wouldn't work for everybody. It is, after all, a bit out of the ordinary. But Pamela embraces it because nobody wants a book that's ordinary.

Visit Pamela at www.pamelahearon.com

Thank you for purchasing
this Wild Rose Press publication.
For other wonderful stories of romance,
please visit our on-line bookstore at
www.thewildrosepress.com

For questions or more information,
contact us at
info@thewildrosepress.com

The Wild Rose Press
www.TheWildRosePress.com

Other Champagne titles to enjoy:

HOW MUCH YOU WANT TO BET? by Melissa Blue. Neil never thought a game of pool could change the course of her life, but against Gib she may lose both the game and her heart.

CATASTROPHE by Sharon Buchbinder. Cats! Twenty-three! Being evicted! Their handsome neighbor doesn't want to lose their curly-haired, curvaceous owner. So what's the rescue plan?

HIBISCUS BAY by Debby Allen. Picture love on a sun-drenched white sand beach surrounded by hibiscus-covered cliffs, with your yacht anchored in a blue Mediterranean Sea.

TASMANIAN RAINBOW by Pinkie Paranya. A concert violinist grapples with remote ranch life, intrigue and the mystery of a missing diary, the peril of a flood in which all could be lost, and the undeniable attraction of the man who would do anything to protect his son.

THREE'S THE CHARM by Ellen Dye. Rachel vowed never to speak to her ex-husband again. When her beloved horse needs a vet and Heath is the only one within three counties of West Virginia mountains, some vows need to be broken.

SEE MEGAN RUN by Melissa Blue. City-successful Megan returns to the boonies to save her childhood home but finds she must not only agree to stay for her mother's wedding but also deal with the man she left when she hitchhiked out 12 years ago.

A MOTHER'S HEART by Misty Simon. Carrie wants a simple life. Helping Gran with the animal shelter: complication. When the new neighbor with two kids comes in for a dog, life goes out of control.

PIGMALION by Sharon Buchbinder. A dream job is almost within Sam's reach, but only Levisa can teach him to speak so he can win it—perhaps they can each learn something?